Also by Francisco X. Stork

Marcelo in the Real World

The Last Summer of the
Death Warriors

Irises

The Memory of Light

Disappeared

ILLEGAL

FRANCISCO X. STORK

SCHOLASTIC PRESS / NEW YORK

Library of Congress Cataloging-in-Publication Data available

ISBN 978-1-338-31055-9

10 9 8 7 6 5 4 3 2 1   20 21 22 23 24

Printed in the U.S.A.   23
First edition, August 2020

Book design by Christopher Stengel

FOR ROSALYN MAE STORK

CHAPTER 1

SARA

The Fort Stockton Detention Center was an elementary school not too long ago. Some of the sayings meant to encourage the children are still on the walls. I was in a line with twenty women all dressed in blue jumpsuits when I read one of them:

It's nice to be important but it is more important to be nice.

Yes, but I wouldn't mind feeling a little more important to the United States. Even just a tiny acknowledgment from the government that I existed and that I was not lost in a sea of asylum petitions.

I counted the number of women ahead of me. Nineteen. There were so many of us in this school-turned-detention-center that there was always a line for everything. The worst line was for the showers, which we all needed to take at the end of a hot day. There were fourteen showers for two hundred and twenty women. A week ago, the private company that operates the detention center solved the toilet-line problem by installing ten portable toilets behind the gym, but now our outside time stinks.

Another sign. This one on top of a row of yellow lockers. The picture of an angry bull inside a circle covered with a red X. Underneath it, the words:

This is a no-bullying zone.

Tell that to La Treinta Y Cuatro, the guard who made everyone's life harder than it needed to be. Yesterday she asked me if people from Mexico used toilet paper. I felt like reminding her about where her ancestors came from. She sees herself as different from the rest of us. And not only different but better. And as my luck would have it, La Treinta Y Cuatro was up ahead, doling out job assignments. I was hoping to get one of the jobs that was advertised by the pro bono legal firm representing many of the detainees. They had put up a notice for someone who spoke English and Spanish who could help them with the interviews. But with La Treinta Y Cuatro deciding? My chances were slim to none. She didn't like me. She didn't like anybody, that was true. But she seemed to have a special something for me. Did she know what I did before I got here?

Three weeks ago, I was a reporter in Ciudad Juárez, Mexico, writing about the hundreds, thousands, of girls who disappeared from the city's streets. Most were discovered dead weeks or months later, but some were never found. My editor received an e-mail threatening me and my family if I wrote about Linda Fuentes. Linda, my best friend, had disappeared months before. I investigated the source of the e-mail and eventually discovered where Linda and other young women were being held captive. The State Police, with the help of the FBI office in El Paso, located Linda and freed her and the other women.

Before Linda was freed, she sent me the cell phone belonging to Leopoldo Hinojosa, the man responsible for her enslavement. Hinojosa set out to retrieve his phone and to kill me and my family. We left our house a few minutes before it was destroyed by machine-gun bullets. My mother went to live with her sister in the interior of Mexico, and my brother, Emiliano, and I had no choice but to cross illegally into the United States, where I planned to seek asylum while Emiliano went with our father to Chicago.

I kept the cell phone in the hope of finding someone in the U.S. who could open it and use the information to help other women still in captivity. I can only imagine all the connections that phone will reveal between Hinojosa and other corrupt government officials or cartel members. Two of Hinojosa's men attacked us in the desert after we crossed into the United States. One of the men ran away and the other was wounded in a struggle with Emiliano. We couldn't let the man bleed to death, so I went to look for help.

On my way to get help, I ran into Sandy Morgan, a park ranger. She brought me to her father, attorney Wes Morgan, and together we decided that I would plead for asylum at the Fort Stockton Detention Center. Emiliano stayed with the wounded man until help arrived and then set out alone with Hinojosa's cell phone.

The school was transformed into a prison by the simple act of enclosing the buildings and part of the grounds with a twenty-foot chain-link fence with rolls of razor-sharp wire on top. They brought in a trailer with eight commercial-size washers and dryers and they built three cement-block isolation cells with small windows on the top where detainees who misbehaved could be kept. Oh, and they also installed cameras every twenty-four feet. Lucila, my new friend from El Salvador, liked to tell me that as prisons go, this one wasn't so bad. And it was at least safer than what awaited Lucila in San Salvador . . . or me in Juárez. And besides, this was a temporary stay, no? No one knew how temporary, but sooner or later we would be free. That was our hope.

So far, Lucila had been detained three months and I only ten days. Lucila hoped to be reunited with her four-year-old daughter, who was with a foster family in Indiana. She still believed that this country would look upon her suffering with compassion. And I too had faith in the United States and its laws. I remembered what I told my brother, Emiliano, as we were deciding to cross: For all its flaws, the United States justice system was as good as it gets on this here earth. But after ten days here, my faith was beginning to crack.

Now there were only four women ahead of me. Across from where I was standing was the room with the dozen or so telephones available to the detainees. They were operated via a card that you could buy at another classroom that had been converted into a small general store. The dollar a day you could earn at one of the jobs could be used to buy telephone time, or if you got desperate enough, you could spend your day's wage on a cold soda. I had an account where my father had deposited one hundred dollars when he visited me, so I did not need to work. Not for money anyway. I planned to give my dollar a day to Lucila so she could call her daughter. I needed to work for another reason: to keep my mind occupied and to keep away the nagging thought that no one in this country cared whether I lived or died.

I did not know how long a day could last until I came here. There was a round, white clock on the wall of the gym: The longer you stared at its black hands, the slower they moved. One of the classrooms was a TV room where, depending on the guard on duty, we could watch telenovelas from a Mexican channel. Then there was the "arts and crafts" room, where you could color children's books with broken crayons. The day before yesterday, a group of ladies from the Fort Stockton Baptist Church brought yarn for knitting and pieces of cloth and thread for embroidery. When word got around, the line to get into the arts and crafts room was so long that the guards had to set up sign-up sheets and limit the time per person to one half hour.

As I stood by the door of the classroom that had been turned into the visitors' room, I could see the light blue vans that took women to El Paso for their asylum hearings before the judge. Those same vans also took women to the airport, where they boarded planes that would take them to San Salvador or Tegucigalpa or Guatemala City if their pleas were denied. If you were Mexican, then a green-and-white Border Patrol bus dropped you off at the nearest bridge to Mexico. If you happened to be granted asylum, you were on your own to find your way to freedom. Being asked to climb on one of those buses would be the equivalent of being taken to my death. But those light blue vans always made me think about Emiliano for some reason. Maybe they reminded me of Saturday mornings when Brother Patricio would come by our house with a van full of Jiparis on the way to a desert hike. Wes Morgan told me that Emiliano was rescued from near death in the desert by a rancher and that he was there now, waiting for Papá to pick him up. La prisión, as we liked to call the Fort Stockton

Detention Center, was still a safe place. Hinojosa could not get to me here. But I worried about Emiliano, out there with the cell phone. I was the one who decided to bring the cell phone with us, and now he was the one bearing all the risk.

"Number!"

La Treinta Y Cuatro sat behind a table, pen poised over a sheet of paper, glaring at me.

"What?"

"Your number?"

My number was written on a piece of tape attached to my chest. At Fort Stockton, we were called by the number assigned to our bed. "A-125," I said meekly. I knew from experience and from prison wisdom that submission was the best way to respond to La Treinta Y Cuatro. The *A* in my name meant that my bed was in the converted gym. The *125* meant that my bed was in the middle row of bunks where the air from the four corner fans never reached.

"Garbage."

"What?"

"You deaf? You sorda?"

"No. But I was interested in the interpreter's job. I saw the note outside the legal services room."

"Do you want to work or not? Because if you do, garbage is what we got."

I knew about the garbage job because I had seen women go around all areas of the FDC with giant, gray plastic garbage cans on wheels. I decided to try one more time. "There are very few women here who speak English. I could be more useful . . ."

"*I could be more useful . . .*" La Treinta Y Cuatro mimicked me. "Who do you think you are?"

"I don't think . . ."

"Work is a privilege. You want it or not?"

"I want it," I said, resigned.

"Go see Elva in the cafeteria. She'll tell you what to do."

That afternoon, Elva made the garbage rounds with me, and I became acquainted with the incredible amount of waste generated by people who do nothing all day except hope and wait and pray. My job encompassed emptying all waste receptacles in the facility, including kitchen, bathrooms, dormitories, and offices. I took the contents to a dumpster in the back. The strange thing is that as Elva showed me around, I couldn't wait to get started. I understood a little of what my brother must have felt back in Ciudad Juárez when he took off with his bike and trailer to collect cans on weekends. Yes, Treinta Y Cuatro, you were right, work is a privilege.

And work, I hoped, would keep my faith from breaking.

CHAPTER 2

EMILIANO

The horse started trotting and circling around the corral as soon as he saw me. I walked toward him, talking to him as I went. "You'd be free right now if you hadn't stopped for me. Estarías libre."

"That horse no habla Español. Or English. Or horse language for that matter," Gustaf said, coming out of the barn. He was carrying a bucket of oats, the horse's favorite.

"He doesn't like the corral."

"That running around? Nonsense. He's glad to see you." Gustaf hung the bucket over one of the posts. We both moved back to give the horse space to eat. "I ought to sell him for dog food except no dog would have him."

"You went looking for him when he ran away."

"Yeah, hope that wasn't a mistake." Gustaf grinned at me and then spat tobacco juice in the direction of the horse. "So, there's another message from your father. He wants to know when he can pick you up. I'm guessing you still haven't called him."

I turned to look at the Sierra Madre mountains behind me. Out there, when I thought I was going to die, I was ready to go with my father to Chicago if I somehow managed to live. And now? When did the old resentment for my father abandoning us creep in? Why this reluctance to go live with his new family and act as if nothing had happened? Or maybe my doubts came from the peace I found here in Gustaf's ranch. The hard work during the day and the exhaustion at night didn't leave room for thinking or remembering. That kind of hard yet simple life, free of confusion, was just what I needed. I knew I couldn't go back to Mexico, not now. Hinojosa and his men would find me and kill me for sure. But why couldn't I stay with Gustaf? Wouldn't that be better for all concerned, including my father and his new family? I couldn't imagine his new wife was very eager to take in a stranger, an illegal stranger.

"Look," Gustaf said, reading my mind. "You know you're welcome to stay here. I could use your help. Got plenty of room. My Gertrude died last year. My son's happy with his job and family in Austin. You like to work. But . . ."

"I'm illegal. You could get in trouble."

"Shoot! This thing about who can come into this country and who must stay out is all new to me. Gutierrez, the guy who helped me for thirty years, never had any papers. He used to cross the Rio Grande and then go back to see his family every month or so and no one cared. And when we needed more hands here at the ranch, he'd bring his cousins. The border looks different down here than it does up there in Washington. So, papers or no papers, if you want to stay, you can stay. But you need to decide now, and your father needs to know."

Gustaf's stern tone surprised me. But he was right. I could not avoid a decision or talking to my father any longer. He was staying thirty miles from Gustaf's ranch in a motel in Sanderson and he had left three messages since yesterday.

Gustaf continued, his voice softer. "I can't tell you what to do, but I've lived long enough to know that sometimes we find where we belong from the places we don't."

I thought about that for a while. Was Gustaf telling me to give Chicago and my father a try? Maybe I owed it to myself to find out what living with my father was like. The horse was done with the oats and was now moving his head up and down in the direction of the house.

"What's he saying now?" I asked Gustaf.

"About the same thing I told you."

"Yeah."

"Your father's number is on my desk in my office. You might as well use the phone in there."

I started toward the house, wondering what I was going to say to my father, and then I remembered Hinojosa's cell phone. "Can I use your computer? I need to send an e-mail."

"Yeah, sure. You'll need my password. GERTRUDE. All caps."

"Of course."

Why wouldn't Gustaf's password be the name of the one person he loved and missed the most?

It was crazy, but there, sitting at Gustaf's cluttered desk, I actually had the urge to call Perla Rubi. It was crazy to want to call her because I knew that, accidentally or on purpose, she told her father where Sara and I would be crossing into the United States. She was the only person other than Brother Patricio or my mother who knew the location. She knew because I told her. And I told her because I trusted her and because I . . . loved her. It felt very strange to put that word in the past tense.

Gustaf had written down my father's number on a white napkin. I recognized it as my father's cell phone number from the times he called my mother and Sara. He even tried calling me directly a few times, but I just let it ring and then erased whatever message he had left, without listening to it.

"You have to admit that he never totally abandoned you," Sara used to say to me. "He writes you, he tries to call you, he sends you money."

I exhaled. I picked up the receiver, held it against my ear and mouth, and then put it down again. Besides not calling my father, I had also been avoiding contacting Yoya, the hacker in the United States who would help us open Hinojosa's phone. There was something evil and scary about that cell phone and everything connected to it that made me want to stay as far away from it as possible. But I could no longer put off the promise I'd made to Sara. Quickly, I turned on Gustaf's computer. It was an old desktop with an oversize screen. It looked as if the Internet connection was through a cable outlet on the wall beside the desk. I typed in the password and then maneuvered my way to Gmail, where I had an account. I had Yoya's address memorized. I took a deep breath, then panicked. What was Sara's friend's name. The IT colleague at *El Sol* who told her to call Yoya about Hinojosa's phone? Ernesto. But what was Ernesto's last name? I tried to regain some kind of calmness. I didn't need the last name. Ernesto would have told Yoya about Hinojosa's cell phone. *Just keep the message short and to the point*, I told myself.

Hello. I am Emiliano Zapata from Ciudad Juárez. Sara Zapata is my sister. She worked with Ernesto (the Jacquero) at El Sol. Ernesto told us to get in touch with you when we got to the U.S. Ernesto said we should give the phone to you. Can you help us? Can you give me an address where we can send you the phone?

I read the message one more time. I wasn't sure whether it was *can* or *will* you help us? I didn't know whether I should say more about the cell phone, like the kind of information it was likely to contain and also that people had already tried to kill us for it. But those were things I could tell Yoya later, if she had questions. After reading it a few more times, I added the following line:

Can you respond right away if you are there? It's urgent.

Then I hit SEND.

I sat there staring at my list of e-mails. For a moment I was tempted to read the last e-mail I had received from Perla Rubi, but I stopped myself when I saw that I had a new e-mail from my best friend, Paco.

Estela Gómez from the State Police told us not to try to communicate with you, but I'm going to do it just this once. I know you man. I know you're probably going to try to come back from wherever you are. Don't do it! You'll be killed if you do!!! Bad people have been asking everyone around here about you and Sara. There's a black car on your block with some nasty dudes inside just waiting to see if someone shows up. Please listen to me for once. You're a dead vato if you return.

Okay man, this is my last communication. It's better if you don't try to get in touch with anyone here.

Tu carnal,

Paco

I had never read anything from Paco that did not contain a single attempt at his silly humor. I could only imagine how afraid he was to write what he did, and I felt responsible for what I was putting him through. Paco knew me better than anyone other than maybe Sara. He was right that there was a part of me that was still hoping to return to Mexico. When Gustaf talked about knowing where you belonged, it was my run-down house in Juárez that immediately came to mind.

I was daydreaming about my room back home, the posters of Mexican fútbol players on the walls, when the phone rang. I don't know why, but I was certain that the phone call was for me. It was probably my father again. I let it ring one more time. What was my decision? Chicago or no Chicago? Going back home was out of the question. *Give that dream up along with all the other dreams you've had to give up*, I told myself.

"Hello," I said, expecting to hear my father's voice for the first time in five years.

"Emiliano?"

I was momentarily stunned by the sound of a young woman's voice.

"Emiliano!" This time the voice was like a sharp slap, waking me up.

"Yes," I said cautiously.

"This is Yoya. You just e-mailed me."

"How did you get this phone number?"

"That's what I do, and I'm very good at it. Now, you said Ernesto gave you my e-mail address and told you to call me. What's this about?"

"You haven't talked to Ernesto?"

"Not in a long time. But he's a friend, so I'm listening."

"I have the cell phone that belongs to a very bad man in Mexico. His name is Leopoldo Hinojosa. He was involved in kidnapping young women and using them as slaves. Ernesto told my sister to contact you when we were in the United States so that we could give you the phone. That you would know how to open it and use the information in it. It must contain important information. His men almost killed us trying to get the phone back. I'm sure they're still looking for it."

There was silence that lasted so long that I thought Yoya had hung up.

"Hello. Hello."

"I'm still here. I'm thinking."

"If you give me an address, I will send you the phone as soon as I can."

"No, that won't work. I see that you're in Sanderson, Texas, at the home of Gustaf Larsson. Is your sister with you?"

"No. She sought asylum. She's in a detention center at Fort Stockton."

"All right. Emiliano, I need to do some research now. I'll try to find out if there is any chatter on the web about you and your sister. A couple of things. Don't ever e-mail me again. It's dangerous to me and to you. Do you have caller ID on the land-line phone you are using?"

"What?"

"Can you see my telephone number on your phone?"

"Yes."

"Okay, write it down as soon as we hang up and use that number to call me, but only from a burner phone. You know what a burner phone is?"

"Yes. One with prepaid minutes."

"You got it. Buy a cheap one so you can throw it away after a few calls. Are you going to be at this location for a while?"

My mind froze. Was I going to be with Gustaf Larsson for a while?

"Emiliano?"

"I'm not sure."

"If you have the option to go to a metropolitan area, that would be better. We have more resources and can work better with you in a big city."

I had to decide. Now.

"I can go to Chicago with my father."

"That's good. We'll get this done in Chicago. And if people are after you, you'll be safer in a big city like Chicago. Your sister should be safe in that detention center. Call me tonight or tomorrow. Day or night, it doesn't matter. I'll answer. But remember, burner phone only. Bye."

I sat there with the phone against my ear for a few moments. What had just happened? When Yoya asked me if I was staying with Mr. Larsson for a while, what came to my mind was Sara's words out in the desert when I was thinking of going back to Mexico: *You can't let all that I've done be lost*. And then when Yoya said that a big city would be better, it was clear to me that I must go to Chicago. Because all that Sara had done to save the missing girls, all that she had sacrificed, all that she was going through at the detention facility, all that could not be lost.

Brother Patricio claimed that we all had an invisible moral compass inside of us that pointed us in the right direction if we but let it. I had been struggling with whether to go to Chicago for days, but it seemed that, when I finally let it, my invisible compass pointed north. Yoya saying that I would be harder to find and that she could help me better in Chicago confirmed that it was the right thing to do.

I picked up the phone and dialed the number that Gustaf had written on the small piece of paper.

"This is Emiliano," I said, when I heard the voice that, despite the years, I recognized as my father's.

"Oh, thank goodness, son. I've been waiting for you to call."

I had no words. Not one word came to me.

"I'm sorry I couldn't come before." My father spoke quickly, as if trying to fill the awkwardness of my silence. "I had to go all the way to Odessa to borrow money for the bond we thought Sara was going to need and then I had to meet with Mr. Morgan, Sara's lawyer. He's appealing the decision to deny Sara a bond."

There was a pause.

"I'm glad Mr. Larsson found you."

There was warmth and concern in my father's voice. It was the same voice that used to comfort me when nightmares woke me in the middle of the night.

"Okay."

"Okay?"

"You can come pick me up."

"Good, Emiliano. That's good. I will be there in an hour."

"Do you know how to get here?"

"I know how. I got directions from the owner of the motel. Everyone here in Sanderson knows Mr. Larsson. I would have come earlier except Sara insisted I call you first. She thought it was important . . . to give you a chance to . . . decide . . . on your own. So, you want to come to Chicago with me?"

How was I supposed to answer that? Want? Did I want to go to Chicago with my father? Yes and no. I wasn't even sure that *want* was the right word. Then I remembered Yoya's words: *We'll get this done in Chicago. And if people are after you, you'll be safer in a big city like Chicago.*

"Come anytime. I'll be here."

I hung up. I was totally drained. It felt like after one of my soccer matches when every ounce of effort had been given to the game. When that happened, when I knew I had given everything I had, it almost didn't matter if we lost.

But in this game, if I lost, I would be sent back to Mexico, where I would be killed.

CHAPTER 3

EMILIANO

The van, a modern-looking vehicle with an aerodynamic roof, went around the driveway in front of the house and stopped in the direction it had just come from. The driver's door stayed closed and Gustaf walked toward the house. My father was sitting in the driver's seat, talking into a cell phone. When he saw me, he smiled apologetically and stuck his hand out the window, fingers waving.

I stood by the side of the van, reading:

Able Abe
Commercial and Residential Heating and Cooling
Year Round 24/7 Maintenance and Repair

Below that was a website address and a phone number. On the top right-hand corner of the van, there was a portrait of a robust, smiling man in his sixties.

After a few minutes of standing there, I started to walk back to the corral. What phone call could be more important than greeting the son you left behind five years ago?

"Emiliano!"

I stopped and turned, slowly. My father had filled out, but he was still the same handsome man. There were patches of white on his temples, which made him look successful. With the cell phone still in one hand, and before I could react, he embraced me. "God almighty, I'm so glad you're safe." I let myself be hugged, arms limply by my sides. The body pressed against me had the same strength that I remembered, but it was also different, softer somehow.

When he finally let go of me, I muttered, "Hola."

"Hola, hijo!" He held me by the shoulders so he could get a better look. "Dios mío. You grew up on me. You're a man now."

"Un poco," I said, loosening myself from his grip.

"Y yo, más viejo." My father touched the white hair on his temples. I did not return his smile. He went on. "But listen, from now on, only English, okay?"

I stared at him for a few seconds. Was I going to let him tell me what to do? Could he not see that I was no longer twelve years old? I exhaled, softly. "Okay. English, then."

"Perfect. Because the better your English, the better you will do. You know?" My father looked at his cell phone briefly as if realizing that it was still in his hand. He stuck it in his pants' right pocket and then looked away, as if he wanted to ask a question but was afraid of the answer. "So? You ready?"

I turned to the horse, who whinnied and stomped the ground. The horse was telling me not to go; that's how I interpreted his movements.

"I'll go get my backpack," I said without looking at my father.

My father rushed to my side and put his arm around my

shoulders. "I know this is hard for you, but it's going to be all right."

Just then then the muffled sound of "La Bamba" came from my father's cell phone. He made an expression as if to say that it was a call he had to take and dug the phone out of his pocket.

The old, green canvas backpack was the same school backpack Gustaf's son had used all through high school. In it were a pair of pants, a cowboy shirt, a few pieces of underwear that had belonged to Gutierrez, the belt with a bucking-horse buckle that Gustaf insisted I take, a toothbrush, and at the very bottom, the metallic bag with Hinojosa's cell phone. I reached down and felt the phone through the bag. How could something that weighed so little contain so much evil? I had carried heavy backpacks in my desert hikes with the Jiparis, but I suspected that none would be heavier than the one I was about to carry now.

Gustaf came out of the kitchen, holding two brown mugs of coffee. He nodded when he saw the backpack in my hand as if to let me know that it was the right thing to do, hard as it was. We walked out of the house side by side.

"Ahh, Mr. Larsson, so good to finally meet you! I'm Bob, Emiliano's father."

Bob? Yes, when I looked at him again, my father seemed more a Bob than a Roberto. He was stashing his cell phone in the pocket of his neatly pressed blue pants and stretching his free hand all at once. "I want to thank you so much for what you did for Emiliano. You saved his life!"

"Naah, the horse did that."

"What is it with the horse?" My father looked at me quickly and then back at Gustaf.

"It's a long story. Emiliano here can fill you in." Gustaf winked at me.

"Ahh."

A strange look appeared on my father's face. As if he envied the closeness that had developed in the past ten days between Gustaf and me.

"I can put this in one of those plastic cups. I think there's some in the kitchen," Gustaf said, still holding out the brown mug.

"No, no. Don't bother. I'll drink it quick," my father said, reaching for the mug carefully with both hands. "Emiliano, I don't know if you know, but all the roads going north have Border Patrol checkpoints. I needed to come up with a way to get you past them." He sipped from the brown mug and then placed it on the front porch. He opened the back doors of the van and climbed inside. Gustaf and I moved closer and peered. The van was filled with pieces of air conditioners: belts, corrugated filters, propeller-looking blades, rolls of electrical wire, tubes of soft aluminum. My father pushed his way to the front, moved two large, heavy boxes that apparently contained air-conditioner units, and opened the hatch to a big metal box at the front of the van. "This is for tools, but Emiliano can fit in here if he lies sideways and bends his knees a little. There's ventilation. I had one of our boys in the shop ride in it for a couple of blocks to make sure no exhaust went in." He waited for us to respond, but I didn't know what to say and, apparently, neither did Gustaf. Finally, my father said, "Emiliano, you want to try?"

I looked at my father with disbelief. Did he really think that was going to work? For a moment there, I thought maybe he was trying to send me back to Mexico. I wouldn't have minded so much except that now I *had* to get to Chicago and call Yoya, and there was also the small matter of me getting killed if I returned to Mexico.

"Won't the Border Patrol inspect the back of the van?" I asked. "I would. And that toolbox there would be the first place I'd look."

"They have to go through all the stuff." My father pointed at the clutter of air-conditioner parts. "And the two big boxes here will cover the handle to the toolbox."

I didn't know how to respond. If I were a Border Patrol agent, I'd make my way through the van and move the boxes. "A heating and cooling van with Illinois license plates? I don't know. That would make me suspicious." I looked at Gustaf to see if he agreed with me, but he only scratched his chin and smiled. Clearly, he thought my father's scheme would not work. But this was something I had to work out with my father, adult to adult.

My father closed the hatch to the "secret" compartment and bounded out of the van. "I thought of that too!" he said, beaming. He led me and Gustaf to the side of the van and pointed to a spot just below the phone number. "All our other vans have the company's address in Aurora, but I took it off this one."

Gustaf and I moved closer and bent to better examine the place where the address used to be. Sure enough, there was a patch of white where the address had been painted over. Gustaf and I looked at each other and I know we were thinking the same thing. The repainting would be the first thing the Border Patrol would notice.

"As to the plates," my father continued, totally unaware of the look Gustaf and I had given each other, "I can say that the company leased the vehicle, and everyone knows leased vehicles come with license plates from all over." My father waited to make sure Gustaf agreed, but Gustaf's face was as blank as it was when he beat me at poker the night before. Then my father turned to me expectantly.

"It's not going to work," I said, looking steadily into my father's eyes. He had to know that I was not the same little boy he used to comfort when there were nightmares.

My father clenched his jaw. It was a gesture I remembered. He used it when he needed to control rising anger. Still, there was a tone of irritation when he spoke. "I thought about this carefully. If I'm stopped, I'll say that my company is in San Angelo and I came to install some new units at the Desert Air Motel in Sanderson. I paid Mrs. Ortega, the day supervisor at the hotel, twenty dollars to say that was the case. If the Border Patrol doesn't believe me, I'll hand them her phone number and ask them to call her."

I smiled. That sounded a lot more like the father I used to know. The man who thought he could convince anyone to do things for him. And when they didn't, he got quietly angry.

Father walked to the porch for the coffee. He sipped to see if it had cooled down and then drank half of the liquid in one gulp.

Gustaf smiled at me and then approached my father slowly, eyes on the ground, pondering. He looked up and tugged at his ear before speaking. "Speaking as an impartial observer, I have to say that there's something fishy about a repair vehicle full of disorganized equipment. And, no offense, but you seem like the kind of guy who would try to sneak a Mexican in the back of his van."

There was a moment of silence. My father's face turned red. Then I laughed.

Gustaf seemed relieved that his observation had been well received, at least by one. My father still seemed too flustered to respond, so Gustaf pointed in the direction of the barn. "Follow me," he said. "I got an idea."

My father took his cell phone out to check on the time. The old watch with the worn-out leather band had been replaced by the cell phone. "We really should be going," he called after Gustaf. "I'd like to make it to St. Louis, Missouri, tonight. Then get home tomorrow morning."

Gustaf did not hear or chose not to. He walked to the side of the gray barn and stopped in front of a rusty aluminum trailer. The back of the trailer was a ramp. Gustaf lowered it, lifted the bar that went across the entrance, and walked in. In front of the trailer was another bar. Gustaf lifted that as well. Just beyond the last bar, the trailer had a built-in container for hay. Gustaf reached in there and lifted out a dusty blanket. He turned to my father. "Emiliano can crouch in here. I'll sprinkle some hay on top of him and put the horse in the trailer."

"Thank you. He'll go in the van."

Gustaf ignored him, looked at me, waited for me to decide.

"I'm grateful for all the planning you did." This was true. It was obvious that my father had put in a lot of thought on my behalf and part of me was touched. But it was not up to him anymore to make decisions regarding risks that affected my life. I went on, looking straight into my father's eyes. "But this is my life and it is my decision. I'll go in the trailer."

My father shook his head, more sad than angry, it seemed. He said to Gustaf, "Do you know the risk you are taking? Why would you want to take that risk?" Then, looking at me, "Do you want him to take that risk?"

For a moment there, it felt as if I had to choose between two fathers. But it wasn't about picking sides. "It's about me not getting caught. I can't afford to get caught." *There's something I have to do in Chicago.* "It is much less likely that I will be caught in the horse trailer. Much less. Look at him." I pointed at Gustaf. "They will never suspect him. He's Gustaf Larsson. He's the kind of person they want in this country."

Gustaf coughed and laughed and choked all at the same time. When he recovered, he said to my father, "You asked me why I would want to take the risk. First, I'm with Emiliano. I don't see the Border Patrol searching me. I've gone through that checkpoint on 285 must be fifty times by now and they just wave me by. So I don't see much risk. And . . ." Gustaf looked at his feet, stammered, and turned slightly red. "If Emiliano wants to go to Chicago, then he must have good reasons for wanting to, and I'm willing to help him."

There was silence. The only thing I could say was thank you. Finally, my father spoke. He sounded slightly defeated. "All right."

Gustaf spoke up before my father could say anything else. "There's a fork in the road where 285 meets Farm Road 2400. That's about twenty miles after the checkpoint. I'll go first and wait for you there. I'll get the halter." Gustaf disappeared inside the barn.

The horse in the corral stopped and pricked up his ears, as if aware that he was being talked about.

"You really prefer to ride with that smelly animal?" my father asked when Gustaf was far enough not to hear.

"That smelly animal never abandoned me," I answered.

Then I went to get the horse.

The horse skittered and pulled and kicked a few times, but he finally let me lead him into the trailer.

"This isn't a good idea," my father said from outside the trailer. "The box Emiliano's going in has no cover. Anyone who peeks in the trailer will see him."

"I'll throw some hay on top of him," Gustaf said, moving my father aside and climbing in. "All right. Assume the position," he said to me with a grin.

I took a deep breath and crouched into the hay trough. I could lie on my back with my head resting on a dusty blanket and my arms crossed on my chest.

"You look like you're in a coffin," Gustaf said, trying not to laugh. "Now close your eyes." Gustaf began to sprinkle hay on top of me. "I'm thinking that maybe I'll just drive on to San Angelo and sell you to the dog food people."

It took me a few moments to realize that Gustaf was talking to the horse.

I sneezed. Sneezing, that was something we had not anticipated. If I sneezed when we reached the checkpoint, then what? Getting caught by the Border Patrol would be the end of Sara and me. I'd get sent to a detention center. Hinojosa's phone would be taken away from me. Hinojosa's men would find Sara before Yoya and I could stop them.

"I'm going to tap the brakes three times when I see the Border Patrol. You'll feel the trailer lurch. After that, no sneezing or any other noises that don't sound like horse. All right?"

I sneezed again.

"Practice squeezing your nose and holding your breath before we get there. The whole thing won't take but thirty seconds. You won't die if you don't breathe for thirty seconds. Either that or practice making your sneezes sound like a snort."

"I hope he's okay in there," I heard my father say.

"Ahh, he'll be fine."

Then a door closed and the engine roared. I smelled exhaust, and we were off. I removed some of the hay from my face and placed it by my chest where I could reach for it and cover myself when the time came. The horse breathed on my face.

"Stop it," I told him. "You stink."

The horse shook his head and neighed in what sounded an awful lot like mischievous laughter.

It would be a half hour or so before we reached a Border Patrol checkpoint. I put my hand over my abdomen to still the nervous cramps that I was getting. Small pieces of straw somehow found their way into my armpits. Drops of perspiration rolled from the top of my head down my forehead and into my eyes. I knew it wasn't the heat that was causing the perspiration. *You are afraid, that's what you are.* Speaking to myself was another sign of fear. I couldn't stop thinking of all that would be lost if I got caught. Not just my life, although the fear of losing that was considerable. It was Sara's sacrifice and my mother's. My poor mother choosing to be without her son and daughter so that we could live, so that I could be the person God wanted me to be. But I did not believe in God, did I? Something happened to me out there in the desert when I thought I was going to die that made me . . . what? Believe? Yes, it was a kind of new belief. I started to believe, if not in God, then in the need to do something good with my life.

"Why not?" I asked the horse. "Don't you think I'm capable of doing something good with my life? I know that my recent past was . . . well, I made some mistakes. But you probably have too. Don't look at me like that. I'm not just saying all this because I'm scared. And anyway, you'd be scared too if the roles were reversed. If I get caught, I could die. My sister could die. There are girls who are suffering right now, being forced into different kinds of slavery, who will never get any help unless we get the names hiding in the cell phone. So you have to act normal when we get to the Border Patrol. Don't prick up your ears like you do when you see me coming."

The horse only nibbled at the hay on my hair.

Then I felt the trailer slow down and lurch three times. It was Gustaf letting me know that we were approaching the checkpoint. I reached down to the sides and threw as much hay as I could over my legs. The horse sensed that something dangerous was about to take place because he neighed and then I heard the sound of his hoofs on the trailer. I had this incredible urge to pray. I thought of my mother and Sara saying the Rosary together and now I wished I had not made fun of them so often. Suddenly, I realized that we had stopped and the words "Help me" came out of my lips. I buried my head deeper in the blanket, grabbed a few more strands of hay, and placed them over the top of the blanket. The horse's big head hovered over me. There was a thumping coming from somewhere and then I felt that it was my heart. I inhaled and held my breath. After a silence that lasted longer than I could hold my breath, I heard a strange deep, gruff voice:

"Good morning, sir. Can you get out of the car and open the trailer for me?"

CHAPTER 4
SARA

We sat at two school desks facing each other. We laughed when we discovered that we could still fit in them. It was Sunday, one of the two days when women detainees could receive visitors. The dozen tables that crammed the classroom that was now a visitors' area were all occupied.

"I want to thank you . . ." I started to say as soon as Sandy sat down, but she stopped me by putting her hand over mine.

"We only have thirty minutes, so let's use them wisely."

I nodded. *No tears.* That's what I told myself while I waited in line to see Sandy.

"Let me go ahead and say it," Sandy said, removing her hand from mine and balling it into a fist. "This is ridiculous! This is . . . I don't even know what to call it. This is . . . unbelievable!"

It was unbelievable to me too at first. But it was beginning to sink in that I could be here for a long, long time.

I turned my attention back to Sandy. She was shaking her head as she spoke. "There's no reason for the ICE officer assigned to this facility to deny you bond. You had a sponsor. You were no flight risk. My dad has been a lawyer in Alpine for forty-two years. I'm a park ranger, for God's sake. I am so incredibly angry . . ." Sandy stopped herself when she saw my eyes fill up with tears. "I'm sorry, my ranting is not going to do you any good."

"It's doing more good than you know," I said.

"You're not angry?"

"I'm afraid to let myself be angry. Anger is not very helpful in here. It doesn't have any place to go, you know."

"My father is appealing the decision to deny you bond with an immigration judge. He's coming over this afternoon so you can sign some papers."

"Maybe the whole image I had of the asylum process was wrong, naive somehow."

"How so?"

"I imagined that all I had to do was show the authorities the evidence of actual persecution, of actual threats, as in people machine-gunning our house in Juárez. I had all that hard evidence I had collected in that flash drive I gave to your father. They would see my articles in *El Sol* about the Desaparecidas, the e-mails threatening my life, the work I did to rescue my friend Linda and the other girls being held by Hinojosa. I imagined I could bring lots of witnesses to testify on my behalf—Special Agent Durand, the FBI agent who helped me, the neighbors who witnessed the shooting of my house. I saw my case as fitting within the legal reasons for asylum under the law of the United States. Was I wrong about the United States?" *Be positive*, I reminded myself again. *You're not being positive.* But I also needed to voice my doubts to someone. Maybe Sandy could help me shore up my ebbing faith.

Sandy shook her head for a few moments and then leaned

forward, all business. "Okay, I guess it's time for me to remind you of the Sara that I found walking quickly, almost running, in Big Bend National Park. Remember how she was determined to get medical help for the wounded man she left a mile or two behind, the same man who had just tried to kidnap her, rape her, and probably kill her. That Sara believed in something. That's the Sara who needs to be here right now, every day, until she gets out."

I exhaled deeply. Sandy was giving me what I most needed. "Yes, you're right," I said.

"Good. Are you okay? Are you being treated well? That's a stupid question, I know."

"It could be worse. That's what we all say in here. It's true, you know."

Sandy sighed. Then, changing the subject, "My dad tells me that Gustaf Larsson has grown quite fond of Emiliano. Apparently, he's a big help to him around the ranch. I know your father was going to pick him up this morning and . . ."

I raised my hand to my mouth and glanced up at the camera in the corner of the room, leaned, and whispered, "It's very important that no one know where he is or where he is going. No one should know that he is still here in the United States."

"The people who attacked you in Big Bend?"

"Yes. They could still be after the phone."

"Do you know for sure?"

"Not for sure. But these are not the kind of people who give up easily."

"But are *you* safe here?"

"Yes. I am. If they found out I was here, they would know

that I don't have the phone with me. Everything I had was taken from me when I was admitted. It's Emiliano I'm worried about. Not just from the people who want the phone but . . . if he gets caught by ICE and deported. He'll be killed if he is sent back to Mexico. I wish I could talk to him . . . before he leaves with Father."

"Why don't you call him? I'd let you use my cell, but they confiscated it when I came in. Can't you call him from the public phones they have here?"

I sighed. "The women here all swear that phone calls are monitored. ICE listens in to find out where undocumented relatives live. I don't want to take a chance. I can't sleep, thinking about Emiliano getting caught. How he's going to make it across the Border Patrol checkpoints."

"He'll figure something out. Did you have a message for him? I could call him as soon as I leave here."

I thought for a moment. What could I tell Emiliano that would not worry him? "No . . . I think it will be all right."

"Tell me." Sandy reached over and tapped my hand.

"Last night I was remembering something that Father said while he was here. I told him about how we were attacked in the desert and he got really nervous. He started talking about his wife and his father-in-law and how afraid they were to be harboring an illegal immigrant. I didn't tell Father the reason we were attacked. I didn't say anything about Hinojosa's phone and I'm glad I didn't, because that would have made his family even more hesitant to take in Emiliano. Anyway, I wanted to warn Emiliano not to tell Father that he is carrying Hinojosa's phone."

"Do you want me to call him and tell him?"

I didn't know what to say. I wanted to protect Emiliano but I also didn't want to influence his relationship with Father's family. "No." I finally decided that Emiliano had good instincts. He'd know whether to tell Father about the phone or not. He had to feel his way through that. How much could he trust Father? That was something he had to determine on his own.

"Your father is quite the go-getter," Sandy said, smiling. "He tried to install an air-conditioner system in my dad's law offices while we waited to hear about the bond. My dad tactfully declined, but your father gave him his business card and told him he'd come over and install it anytime."

"That sounds like my father, all right." I remembered the fancy business card he had shown me. "He likes being Bob Gropper."

We laughed.

Sandy said, "I'm sorry . . . all of this is so hard."

I stared out the window and shook my head. Then I said slowly: "What's so hard is that it doesn't make sense. The whole process of who gets asylum and who gets detained, who gets a bond and who gets released, who gets a visa and who gets deported. I mean, it's not as rational as I imagined it would be."

"I don't think acting rationally is a top priority for the politicians running this country." There was a touch of anger in Sandy's voice for the first time. When she spoke again, her voice was soft, but also firm. "But you need to believe that somewhere along the line, people will do the right thing. My father will make sure that they do."

I was grateful for her confidence just then. Her faith was

stronger than mine. "Is it bad for me to doubt and to be afraid? For me, for my brother?"

"I think that it is very normal for someone who has gone through what you have gone through, both in Mexico and after you crossed over, to be afraid and to not trust."

"Wrap it up, folks! Start saying your good-byes! Five minutes!" a guard shouted into the room.

"Hang in there, Sara." Sandy leaned over, grabbed my shoulders, and shook me, as if to awaken me. "Keep the faith. And don't be afraid to be angry. Anger can help you be the Sara I picked up on that dusty road, the one who believes in doing good no matter the cost." We stood at the same time and faced each other. Sandy took a step toward the door and then turned toward me. "Remember when I offered to introduce you to my father and said that he could help you with your asylum petition?"

"Yes."

"Remember when you asked me why I was helping you?"

I nodded.

"I didn't answer you then. But the answer is because I don't know if I have ever met anyone who believes in doing good regardless of the personal cost as much as you do. That's who you are. I know it is easy to forget who you are in a place like this. But I'll be here to remind you. Don't lose your faith in this country. We want people like you here."

"Yes. Yes. I will keep the faith."

CHAPTER 5

EMILIANO

I heard a clanking. It was the doors of the trailer opening. How many seconds did I have before I was found? How many hours or days before I was sent to Mexico? How long after that before I was found by Hinojosa's men? How long did I have left to live? The seconds after the doors opened were happening so very slow. They were crawling up the Sierra Madre mountains, it seemed. I tried to swallow but there was no saliva. Then there was Gustaf's voice.

"You're one of Antonio Lopez's boys, aren't you?"

"Yes, sir. Raúl Lopez."

"I thought I recognized you from your high school days. You played football with my son. Jimmy Larsson."

"Sure, Jimmy L."

"You were the best defensive end the Eagles ever had."

"Thank you, sir."

"Careful. Don't stand right in back of him. He's ornery. I better take him out if you want to go in and look."

"No, that's all right. You go on ahead. Have a good day, Mr. Larsson. Sorry for the stop. We have orders to stop everyone today."

Then there was movement again. Was that it? I imagined

the Border Patrol officer remembering Jimmy Larsson, waving Gustaf on. I made it! I escaped detection. I laughed to myself. Three weeks before, you could not have dragged me into the United States and now here I was, rejoicing to have made it in. We traveled on for another twenty minutes and then another stop. I heard the back ramp open and Gustaf's voice: "You can come out."

I rose out of the hay and placed my hand on the horse's forehead.

"Gracias."

I lingered a moment in that touch and then moved away.

Gustaf was standing outside, putting a plug of chewing tobacco in his mouth and staring at the road we had just come from. "That was close," I said. "If it hadn't been for you . . ."

"Naah." Gustaf waved me off. "I remembered that boy. Jimmy brought him to the ranch once. He was afraid of horses. He was just looking for a reason not to go in that trailer."

I wiped the sweat from my forehead with my arm. "Where's my father?"

"He's coming. The Border Patrol pulled him to the side to search the van. I saw it in the rearview mirror." We exchanged knowing glances. Gustaf didn't want to say *I told you so*, but I knew what he was thinking.

I was glad I had resisted my father's plan. I coughed and dug a strand of hay from under my collar. I looked around. Nothing but nothingness. A tumbleweed rolled across the road. This was it, then. Now it hit me that I would be living with my father for . . . who knows how long. I wondered if he and his new wife had plans about what I would do in Chicago.

"Things aren't always as bad as they look," Gustaf said, still watching the road. "Work with whatever life throws at you, good or bad."

I saw the van, a white dot in the distance. "That's your advice?"

"It's worked for me, more or less." Then he took two twenty-dollar bills out of his pocket. "Take this. I owe you much more for all your help around the ranch. This is just so you'll have a little money in case of an emergency."

"Thank you," I said, taking the money. I knew Gustaf well enough by then not to argue with him. And I needed money to buy a burner phone as soon as possible.

When my father's van pulled off the pavement onto the gravel side road, I said, "You should name the horse. He should have a name."

"Name him. Go ahead."

"Amigo." It was the first and only word that came to mind.

"Amigo it is."

My father got out of the van slowly. His shoulders were hunched. He had considerably less energy and bouncy optimism than when I first saw him earlier that morning. "I can't believe they stopped me and searched the van. First place they searched was the tool compartment where Emiliano was going to hide. I guess you were right." He looked at Gustaf. "I do look like someone who would sneak in a Mexican."

"Don't take it personally," Gustaf said.

"Hard not to," my father responded.

Gustaf winked at me. Apparently, he decided not to tell my

father that they were stopping everyone that day. And I was all right with that.

"Ready?" my father asked.

I nodded. I turned to Gustaf, shook his hand, and looked into his eyes for the briefest of moments. Then I went to the passenger side of the truck to get my backpack.

"I don't know how to thank you for all you've done for us," I heard my father say to Gustaf. "I'd like to pay you."

How could my father say something like that? Gustaf saved my life. He took care of me and made me feel like a member of his family. He showed me a way to live I had never known before, and just a few moments ago, he smuggled me into the United States at great risk to himself. How could you ever offer someone money for that?

"No," I heard Gustaf say after a long silence.

"Here. Take my business card at least. If you ever need an air conditioner or anything."

I came back with my backpack and saw Gustaf take the card without looking at it. Then he was opening the truck and getting in. He was moving uncharacteristically fast, like he was trying to keep me from rushing at him and asking him to take me back to the ranch with him—which is exactly what I wanted to do. And what I knew he'd welcome.

My father and I watched the truck and trailer move away in the same direction we were going. Gustaf was going to drive up to the next state road and then turn back to Sanderson a different way.

A knot inside me began to come loose.

We drove in silence. I was thinking about the close call I'd just had and how unexpectedly afraid I had felt when I thought I'd be found. Was it always going to be like that? That fear of being found out only a heartbeat away?

I looked out the window. What was the difference between the desert landscape I was seeing out the window and the landscape I saw on the drive to the border with Sara and Brother Patricio? The land was similar, but it felt different. It was like I was watching a movie instead of driving through the land. The windows of the van were closed, and the air conditioner blasted cold air into my face. In Brother Patricio's beat-up Toyota, the hot air from the open windows was more real. There were smells back then: roadkill, burning brush, the magical odor of eucalyptus appearing out of nowhere. The only smell inside the van was my father's cologne, a mixture of alcohol and something flowery that was making me nauseous. How is it that a person cannot smell himself? The height of the van, the cold air, the smell, these were not the only differences. Outside, the land was all fenced. There was no inch of territory that was not closed in by some kind of wire. Thin, green aluminum poles held the strands of wire, barbed and not barbed, in place. Somewhere back in that desolation, there must be a ranch with a few cows that are let out to graze; otherwise why the need for a fence? A few places had fences that were ten feet high and I couldn't understand why until I saw the sheep and then I knew that the fence was not so much to keep the sheep in but to prevent someone from stopping by the road and putting one of the animals in their truck.

My father seemed preoccupied, upset about something.

Now and then he would shake his head and whisper a word that sounded like "ship." I smiled when I finally understood that he was swearing softly about being searched by the Border Patrol. Was he upset that his plan nearly got me sent back to Mexico or that he got treated differently than Gustaf? I wondered how my father saw himself. Did he see himself as fully American? Sara told me once that he had obtained a permanent resident visa through his new wife and had applied for citizenship. Was that enough to make you feel offended when the Border Patrol stopped you?

"Your English is pretty good," my father said. "The five words I heard you say." There was a slight, sarcastic grin on his face.

"You don't talk much either."

"I apologize." He gripped the steering wheel tightly with both hands. "Those phone calls I got when I got to the ranch were from Abe."

"Abe?"

"The owner of the company. My boss. You know Able Abe? On the side of the van." A pause, then, "He's also my father-in-law."

It took me a few seconds to realize what *father-in-law* meant.

"Your suegro?"

"Yup. Mi suegro. Abe Gropper is Nancy's father. Nancy, that's my wife. Nancy Gropper. Gropper is spelled with two *p*'s."

"Gropper," I muttered. Nancy Gropper was his wife. Good for him. At least he didn't say she was my stepmother.

"It's also my name now," my father said, interrupting my

thoughts. The van swerved briefly onto the opposite lane as my father dug in his back pocket and pulled out a thick wallet. He held the wallet with the hand holding the steering wheel while he pulled out a business card. He passed me the card and I read.

Able Abe
Commercial and Residential Heating and Cooling
Robert "Bob" Gropper
Director of Sales and Marketing

There was a telephone number and an e-mail address below that.

"Bob Gropper? This is you?"

"The same."

I could not restrain a chuckle.

"I changed my name after I met Nancy. I didn't have a permanent visa then. It just made things easier for everyone."

"Okay." I handed the card back to my father. Bob Gropper. I tried out the name silently. It was hard to believe. Why would anyone in their right mind exchange Roberto Zapata for Bob Gropper?

"Keep it," my father said. "It has my cell phone number."

I dropped the card into my backpack. My father reached up to adjust the rearview mirror and I noticed his disfigured pinky finger. I was ten years old when I saw a cement block fall on my father's hand. It was a Saturday and my father had taken me to the construction site where he worked. After the block smashed his finger, my father had a coworker pull the finger as close to its former shape as possible and then went back to work. That crooked finger now belonged to someone named Bob Gropper.

"A penny for your thoughts."

"What's the name of your son?"

"Which one? One of them is named Emiliano." I remembered my father's old charm. Only it wasn't working on me right then.

"The other one."

"Trevor," my father said. "He's been asking a lot of questions about you. You're going to like him. He's super smart."

There was something odd about my father's words, but I had no time to find out what because I was suddenly filled with an emptiness as barren and desolate as the view outside my window.

"I told Abe I'd be there tomorrow at noon. Nancy's been filling in at the office while I'm away, but she's got her own job at the firm. She does all the books. And, of course, there is Trevor." My father began to tap the screen of his phone. He was glancing at a GPS map, making mental calculations. "Springfield, Missouri, is about twelve hours. We can get there around eleven tonight. Get up at four a.m. We could be in Aurora by noon tomorrow."

"I can drive," I suggested, not eagerly.

"Yeah? When did you learn?"

"Brother Patricio showed me." I hadn't meant it to come out the way it did, as in *since you weren't around*.

"Maybe." Then he added, "But if you have an accident,

Abe will kill me. Our insurance only covers employees of the company."

My father took out a phone charger from the console between the seats. He tried to connect the charger to the phone and the van swerved again. I took the charger and the phone and finished the task. I wasn't quite ready to give up on my miserable life.

"We should talk about what you're going to do," he said, fiddling with the radio.

"In Chicago?" Of course, in Chicago, where else?

"Actually, like I said, we're going to Aurora. Our house and the company are located there. It's next to Chicago, a suburb, but a separate city. Aurorians don't like to be lumped in together with Chicago." He spoke like a proud Aurorian.

"Aurora. Sounds Mexican."

"The first immigrants in Aurora were Irish, but there's lots of Mexicans living there now, all right. About a third of the people who live there are Hispanic. Mostly of Mexican descent but more and more from Central America. Guatemala, El Salvador. Honduras." My father didn't sound all that happy about these last migrations. "Part of my job at the company is getting the Latino business."

"Fixing air conditioners."

My father coughed into his hand. "When I started with the company five years ago, I fixed air conditioners and furnaces. Now I'm an officer in the company. The equivalent of a vice president, only we don't have titles like that."

"Vice president," I repeated, impressed. Not bad for a man who had been building brick houses back in Juárez. There was no doubt that I got my love for work and hustle, my wheeling and dealing, from him.

"We have a fleet of eighteen vans. Sixty-two employees. Abe wants to retire next year, so he's giving me more and more responsibility. I pretty much run the place now. When he retires . . ." He stopped himself. The van slowed down abruptly. Ahead of us, in the middle of the road, stood a jackrabbit with ears as big as a mule's. My father honked, and the rabbit scampered out of the van's path in the nick of time.

"Jesus," my father said. "That's one big rabbit."

Brother Patricio called those rabbits black-tails and said they were the golden eagle's favorite snack. The eagle glides five thousand feet and then silently swoops down on the unsuspecting jackrabbit. The image made me grab my backpack with Hinojosa's cell phone and put it on my lap.

My father was speaking again. "Unfortunately, I'm not sure we can get you into school this year. Nancy made some calls while I've been here. It's going to take us a while to get the necessary paperwork. Vaccinations, transcripts from Colegio México. You don't have to be . . . documented . . . with a visa . . . to go to school in Aurora, but . . . maybe it would be better to wait until next fall."

It came to me that I had not given any thought to what I would do all day in Chicago. How would I spend the hours, minutes, and seconds of each day? The only thing I knew was that I would call Yoya as soon as I got there and get the phone to people who could help us. But then?

My father continued. "I wanted you to work at Able Abe's. Go out with the guys on their daily rounds, learn how to install

45

cooling systems. It's just that the laws against employers hiring undocumented workers are . . . they're cracking down. ICE is coming down hard on businesses. With raids and everything."

"I don't have to work in your company," I said, trying not to sound hurt. "I can work in other places. I will find work."

"Nancy and I thought that you might want to take care of Trevor in the afternoons, after he comes home from . . . kindergarten."

My first instinct was to say no. Actually, I wanted to *shout* no. Babysitting was not in the cards. Then it hit me. "How old is Trevor?"

My father hesitated. Then spoke softly, the way one speaks when the question you've been dreading is finally asked.

"Six."

He kept on speaking, but I had stopped listening. I was doing the math in my head. My father left for the United States five years before. Trevor was six. "Trevor is not your son?"

My father slowed the van to sixty. "My adopted son. Nancy was married for a brief time and then divorced. She got divorced before Trevor was born."

I crossed my arms, tucked my hands in my armpits to keep them from shaking. Why should it make a difference that my father chose to adopt a son rather than come back to the one he already had? Why all the old anger rising up again?

"You all right? You look kind of pale. Want me to stop?"

"Did Mami know? Sara?"

"Know what?"

"That you married a woman who had a son?"

"Not at first. I told your mother later, after I married Nancy. I told you about Trevor . . . in my letters."

The letters that I threw unopened into a shoebox in my closet.

When my father spoke again, the tone of his voice was serious. "When I first came to the States, I used to stand outside a lumberyard, waiting for carpentry jobs, or any kind of jobs. Abe Gropper came by and said he needed someone to put a new roof on his daughter's house. That's how I met Nancy. Trevor was eight months. We . . . fell in love."

"I don't need to hear this."

But my father was determined to finish the story. He spoke faster now. "We moved in together. Abe wasn't happy. He hated me. Blamed himself for hiring me to fix the roof. But then, finally, when the divorce with your mother came through and I married Nancy and adopted Trevor, after I changed my name and everything, he gave me a job at Able Abe's. I got my plumber's license in three months, went to community college to learn English. He saw how hard I worked, how much I cared for Nancy and Trevor. Then . . ."

"What's it like, the detention center where Sara is being held?" I interrupted. I could not take any more of my father's newfound happiness.

"Detention center is just a fancy name for prison," my father said, a twinge of anger in his voice. "I only saw the place once. Imagine a one-story brick school with a gym in the back, a big playground and a soccer field all enclosed by a tall fence with spotlights and cameras all around. The place is in the middle of nothing but cactus and tumbleweeds." My father pointed to the barren landscape outside the window. "There was no need for her to turn herself in. She could have filed her asylum application from Aurora." My father opened a small compartment between the seats, took out a pair of aviator sunglasses and put them on. "The lawyer should have never let her turn herself in."

"I don't think Sara had a choice," I said. "She went out looking for help to save a man's life. Sandy, the park ranger, rescued her." Then, after a moment, "And what would your plan have been for getting both of us across the Border Patrol checkpoint?" I regretted the angry tone in my voice. It was a long ride to Chicago. I needed it to be as peaceful as possible.

"I know," my father said in a softer tone. "I know you guys had a rough time out there. Sara told me about how you two were attacked. I still don't understand how the people who were after Sara found out where you were crossing."

So my father did not know it was my fault. I wondered if he knew about the cell phone inside my backpack.

"And why were they after you anyway?"

He did not know about the cell phone, now I was sure. But I decided to test my assumption anyway. "Revenge," I said. "Hinojosa wanted to kill Sara for exposing him and all his corruption."

My father shook his head.

"At least she's safe now," I said quietly, mostly to myself.

"Yes, at least you are both safe."

That was a lie. I wasn't safe. I was in this country illegally. There could be more checkpoints up ahead. It was also a lie to say that the only motive for the attack was revenge. The cell phone I had with me was the motive. It occurred to me that my father and his happy family in Aurora were not safe as long as that cell phone was with me. I was tempted to tell him the truth: that Sara and I were attacked because of my actions, that danger followed Sara and me into the United States. But I didn't say anything. I looked at my father, at this man who called himself Bob Gropper, and I was not sure I could trust him. I was no longer absolutely certain that he would put Sara's and my welfare and safety above everything else. Where were Sara and I in the hierarchy of Bob Gropper's heart? It seemed to me that we were below Nancy and Trevor and Abe and his position as director of sales and marketing at Able Abe's. And when you think about it, that's pretty far down. I felt guilty for lying to my father about the cell phone, but I could not deny what I felt. I realized that the main thing that had been lost when my father decided not to come back to Mexico was trust—the trust I once had in him. Maybe that trust would come back someday, I didn't know. I was willing to give it a chance and hope that it would. But at that moment, all I could feel was its gaping absence.

My father fiddled with the air-conditioner knob. "It was just hard to see Sara dressed in a blue jumpsuit like a criminal. Anyway, it won't be for too long. Mr. Morgan is appealing the denial of bond to an immigration judge."

"And if she is let out with the bond?"

"Sara has decided to stay with Sandy Morgan and her father in Alpine until her asylum hearing. If the hearing is in El Paso, she can bring witnesses from Juárez who will testify to the persecution she went through and will go through if she returns. I checked with Nancy and Abe and they both think that's the right decision."

My father checked with Nancy and Abe about Sara's decision? Why? What's it to them what Sara does? I was glad I hadn't said anything about the cell phone. It also made me wonder if the only reason I was going to Chicago was because Nancy and Abe had approved my coming. I tried to open the window, but the switch did not respond. Where were the mountains? There were no mountains anywhere. When Sara and I walked across Big Bend National Park, the Sierra Madre mountains were always visible. Here the world was flat. I leaned my head against the windows and shut my eyes. I hugged the backpack closer to me.

Out there, in the desert, I forgave my father. I had to remember what that was like. It felt right and good and peaceful. Maybe I was already in another reality when that happened, a reality where forgiveness was easy.

In this world, forgiveness is hard, I said to myself.

CHAPTER 6

SARA

The gym where children played basketball and volleyball and climbed to the rafters using thick ropes now held ninety bunk beds. The beds were so close together that from my top bunk I could reach over and touch the head of Lucila on the adjoining bunk. It took about two hours after the lights went out for the room to get quiet enough for sleep. First there was conversation, then whispers, and then later the muted sounds of women sobbing. But at 2:00 a.m., all you could hear was the sound of your own thoughts.

Sandy had left a message for me to call, and when I did, she told me that her father came by in the afternoon but was not allowed to see me. Wes Morgan was so outraged that he was driving to El Paso first thing tomorrow morning to file a complaint with the commissioner of ICE in charge of detention facilities. That was the bad news. But the good news was that Emiliano had made it past the Border Patrol checkpoint and was now on his way to Chicago. Gustaf Larsson snuck him across the checkpoint in the back of a horse trailer. I laughed when Sandy told me that, and then I was filled with love and gratitude for my brother. I knew he was doing something that he did not want to do and that he was doing it, in part, for me.

I was sure that Emiliano had Hinojosa's cell phone with him. I only hoped that he was able to call Yoya while he was with Mr. Larsson and that he made arrangements to give her the phone. In the daytime, it is easier to believe that bringing that cell phone was the right decision. But at 2:00 a.m., fear outweighed my initial act of courage. I had to reach out in the dark and borrow Linda's courage, the courage that prompted her to steal the phone from Hinojosa and send it to me. I had to remember Linda's suffering. It was up to me and now up to my brother to make sure that what she went through was not in vain. I had to remember that people were willing to kill for that phone for a reason. There were more girls out there in captivity and the phone could mean their freedom.

Lucila next to me was crying in her sleep. I reached over and placed my hand on her shoulder. I didn't want to wake her up, but I also wanted her to know that she was not alone. I touched her very gently until the crying stopped. I turned around and saw the woman on the other side of me smiling. She was an older woman from Guatemala named Colel. She spoke a mixture of Spanish and a Mayan dialect. No one understood what she said. She came with her son and her two grandsons. The son was sent to the men's detention center in Sierra Blanca. She doesn't know where the grandsons went. She had a picture of the two boys that she showed to everyone.

"Dónde están?"

That was the question she asked every person she met.

Then this evening, La Treinta Y Cuatro took the picture from her. It was too much to bear. I had to speak out.

"How does it hurt anyone to let her have that picture?" I'd demanded to know from La Treinta Y Cuatro, full of anger.

La Treinta Y Cuatro turned and smirked. It was as if she had been waiting for me to lose my cool.

"What business is this of yours?" La Treinta Y Cuatro took two steps forward. I felt drops of her saliva on my face.

I cocked my arm and was ready to strike her.

"No, no." Colel was crying and grabbing my arm. "Sólo una foto. Ma' importa. Ma' importa."

"There is no need for your meaness" is all I ended up saying. Colel was right. Violence was what La Treinta Y Cuatro wanted. I let Colel pull me away.

"You think you're special?" La Treinta Y Cuatro shouted after me.

"No," I answered.

"No? You're right. You're not special. You're nothing."

I went over the meaning of those words over and over again, for hours it seemed. *You are not special. You are nothing.* I realized there was a part of me that thought I was more deserving of asylum than women like Colel or Lucila. I spoke English. I could write articles for newspapers. As a reporter, I was persecuted because of membership in a particular social group, one of the specific categories for asylum under United States law. La Treinta Y Cuatro was right. I thought I was special.

Colel's missing-tooth smile on the bunk next to me brought tears to my eyes. What made her travel so many thousands of incredibly difficult miles to the United States? When I asked her about her son and grandsons, she made a waving gesture with her hand as if to say that they simply flew away. How could she smile at me with so much love even after so much loss and so much yet to lose?

Mami used to say that every day brings a new message from God if we but listen. Every day is a new lesson.

What were the lessons to be learned from Colel and from Lucila and from all the world's poor?

That I was not special was one lesson, I was sure.

But the other one was that we all were.

CHAPTER 7

EMILIANO

At 11:00 p.m., my father, or Bob, as I decided to call him somewhere in the middle of Oklahoma, pulled into a motel outside Springfield, Missouri.

The room had two beds larger than I had ever seen before. Bob sat on the orange bedspread of one of them and dug his cell phone out of his pocket. "Do you want to take a shower first?" It was his way of asking me for some privacy.

Inside the bathroom, I heard isolated words from Bob: *unexpected delay, Border Patrol, trouble.* Words like that. Then there was a long pause and Bob's tone became softer. I turned on the shower after the word *sweetie.* I let the warm water hit my back and closed my eyes.

When it was Bob's turn to take a shower, I opened my backpack and took out the disposable phone I'd bought at a gas station with the money that Gustaf gave me. I could have told my father that I needed my own phone to call Sara or Mami, but instead, I listened to the lack of trust I felt inside me and bought it while he was in the restroom. Now I took the phone out of its plastic package and then took out the slip of paper where I had written Yoya's phone number. I remembered Yoya's words to call day or night and I was about to punch in her number, when I heard the water in the shower stop.

I placed the plastic wrapping and the burner phone at the very bottom of my backpack, under all my clothes. It was then that I noticed the envelope for the first time. The envelope was from a tractor company and was addressed to Gustaf. It was open and had a green rubber band around it. I removed the rubber band and opened the envelope just enough to see what was in there. It was a Greyhound Bus gift card for two hundred dollars and a yellow sticky note with Gustaf's scribbling. I unpeeled the note from the card and read the shaky writing:

Gustaf Larsson's phone: 432-555-1699
In case you get lost.

I smiled. *In case you get lost.* Gustaf wasn't talking about geography. I folded the note and stuck it and the gift card in my wallet. I reached over to the lamp next to the bed and clicked it off. I turned on my side with my back to Bob's bed. He came out and I heard him searching in his suitcase. The smell of the now familiar cologne filled the room.

"Emiliano, you asleep?"

I didn't move.

"I'm really glad you're coming with me. I know you don't think I'm a good father. But it doesn't matter to me. I want what's best for you now. I talked to Nancy while you were taking a shower. She's looking forward to meeting you and to having Trevor get to know you."

"I am not going to Chicago to babysit your son." I was polite, but firm.

There was a long pause. "Let's cross that bridge when we get to it, as they say in America. It's going to be all right, you'll see."

I heard Bob pull the bedspread back and get in bed. The last light in the room went off.

"You're going to like our house," Bob's voice came from the dark. "We fixed a bed in the basement for you. Trevor plays down there, but he goes to bed early. You'll have your own TV. Your own bathroom. We want you to feel at home. Be part of the family. But no one is rushing you. You take all the time you need." A pause. "I apologize for any mistakes I made. I'm sorry. What more can I tell you?"

I waited a long time before speaking.

"There's no need to say anything else. Let's move on."

"Agreed. Let's just move on. Good night, Emiliano."

Good night, Bob Gropper, I said to myself.

I opened my eyes, startled. The digital clock next to the bed read 3:00 a.m. What woke me up was a dream of Sara crying. She was in a ship, trying to pull up women and children who were drowning, but the current was too strong, and she could not hold on to them and there were just too many women and children. I sat up gasping for air and then I lay down again, grabbed the edges of the pillow, and pushed them against my ears as if to keep out the sound of Sara's sobs.

After a few minutes I knew that sleep would not return. I

sat up and looked at the room's air-conditioner unit. It was silent. I bent over the unit and pushed buttons until I heard a rattling. The air coming out was warm, but it was air. I touched the perspiration on the back of my head. I stretched out on the bed again and listened to Bob's snores. Now and then he whimpered, as if he was running from someone, Able Abe probably, I joked to myself. Only it wasn't funny.

I put on my pants, grabbed my backpack, and stepped outside. There was a metal chair outside our room. I sat there under a yellow light bulb and dug out the burner phone. *Day or night*, I repeated Yoya's words.

Yoya answered on the second ring.

"It's me. Emiliano. Is it too late to call?"

"No," Yoya said calmly. There was no annoyance in her voice. She sounded fully awake. "You got a burner phone. Good."

"Any news?"

"Some. Hold on one second. I took some notes." There was a sound of someone tapping words on a laptop. "Okay. So. Your sister's name came up in a criminal incident report from the sheriff's office in Alpine. According to the report filed by one Sandy Morgan, your sister was attacked by two men at Big Bend National Park. One of the men, Lester Mannix, was flown by helicopter to Medical Center Hospital in Odessa. That's where he was arrested pursuant to a complaint filed by Sandy Morgan. Sara Zapata is listed as the victim of the attack. The report states that the victim is in the custody of Immigration and Customs Enforcement at the Fort Stockton Detention Center, where she is waiting resolution of her asylum petition."

"What does that mean?" I asked, concerned.

"Well, there's nothing in the incident report about you. So that's good."

"But what does it mean for Sara? If you could find out where she is, then so could Hinojosa's men."

"That's the other thing I found out since we last talked. This is from our Jacquero friends in Mexico. Hinojosa was killed soon after he was arrested—probably by someone in his organization who was afraid he would talk. It's not Hinojosa or his men who are after you and your sister."

Yoya paused. It was one of those pauses that implied that the worst was yet to come.

"Then who . . ."

"Hinojosa was on the Mexican side of a human trafficking scheme between Mexico and the United States. Some of the women were kept in Mexico to be abused by people like Hinojosa, but others were sent to the United States. We have our share of pigs here as well. If anyone is going to come after the cell phone, it would be these U.S. pigs. Their identities are probably in that phone you are carrying. That's what I think, and it corresponds with the chatter on the Internet that my Jaquero friends have picked up. I'll start looking into this as well tomorrow."

I was silent. I had hoped that maybe I could get away from Hinojosa. Every day, I was farther away from Ciudad Juárez and his reach. But where could I or Sara hide if the evil was American?

"Is Sara safe?" I was afraid of the answer, but I had to ask.

"Honestly, I don't know the answer to that right now. I'm going to try to hack into the detention center tomorrow . . . I mean later today. I'll know more next time you call. But these criminal incident reports from the sheriff's office are easy to obtain. So it is possible that the pigs know where Sara is being held."

I felt my heart sink into quicksand deep and dark.

Yoya continued quickly, as if sensing where I had gone. "On the other hand, if the pigs know where Sara is being detained, then they will most likely also know that Sara does not have the cell phone with her. All personal items are confiscated at admittance to a detention center, and it is very easy for someone to find out what personal property is being held for a particular prisoner."

"Then they will only be after me."

It was a relief to know that I would be the target and not Sara.

"You don't seem to be on anyone's radar so far. But the other man who attacked you probably told whoever is calling the shots that you were there. They are probably looking for you. No one knows that you were staying with Gustaf Larsson, right?"

I thought about it. "My father. There was a nurse who treated me when Mr. Larsson found me. My sister's attorney, Mr. Morgan. Sandy Morgan."

"Who knows that your father lives in Chicago?"

"Tons of people back in Juárez. But my father doesn't exactly live in Chicago. He lives in a place called Aurora. No one knows that. And he changed his name from Roberto Zapata to Bob Gropper. That is also a new development that no one back home, other than my mother or Sara, knows about."

I heard a small laugh on the other line. I laughed too. How

could anyone not laugh a very soft laugh when they heard that Roberto Zapata had become Bob Gropper?

"Well, that helps," Yoya said. "Let's hope your father is very discreet."

The image that immediately came to mind was the aerodynamic van with the big ABLE ABE lettering on the side. Also, my father handing out business cards to everyone he met. How many people in Sanderson had his director of sales and marketing cards?

"Call me tomorrow," Yoya was saying. "I have some ideas about how we can narrow down the identity of the U.S. pigs. Oh, and, Emiliano. I would not call your sister or even write to her right now. Don't take any chances that someone may be listening to her calls and I know for sure that detainees' mail gets read. You want to be invisible and stay invisible. Okay?"

"Okay."

"Talk soon."

I stayed outside that motel room thinking. It came to me that my only alternative was to fight. Sara had decided to fight evil despite the risk to her life. Yoya and the Jacqueros were out there fighting as well. Couldn't I try to do the same? I saw a light go on in the room and went inside. Bob was already getting dressed.

"It's 4:00 a.m.," he said. "Are you ready?"

"Yes. I'm ready."

I was ready.

CHAPTER 8

EMILIANO

A chaotic sea of concrete. As many cars as there are stars. The infinity of man-made things as we approached Aurora reminded me in a strange way of the nights in the desert under millions of stars and galaxies and unknown planets. It was the same feeling of being puny and lost and insignificant, but without the serenity of the desert.

Bob picked up his cell phone and read the time just as we passed the sign announcing Aurora's city limits. "Eleven fifty-six! We got here before noon just like I said."

We were off Highway 88 now, stopped at a red light. I was surprised to see open spaces, trees with the tender green of spring on their branches. Back in Oklahoma, I had seen the oil pumps pierce the red, hot earth. Here the ground was soft and brown. I opened the window and stuck my hand out. The temperature was cold, uncomfortable.

"I'm going to drop you off at home and then head to the office," Bob announced. "Make yourself a sandwich, take a nap, watch TV. Nancy will be home with Trevor around three. Okay?"

The thought of seeing Nancy Gropper and Trevor made my stomach churn. I had played soccer in front of ten thousand people, been nearly killed a few times, and had not felt one single flutter of an intestinal butterfly. Now there I was, wishing Bob would not leave me alone in a strange house to meet strange people.

"Relax," Bob said, "Nancy doesn't bite. Trevor, I'm not sure."

Bob laughed. In the nineteen hours that we had traveled together, I discovered a new humorous side to my father. Humorous as in he liked to joke and laugh at his own jokes. I turned to look out the window. It took me a few moments to discover that I was looking at a golf course. Jorge Esmeralda, Perla Rubi's father, wanted to teach me how to play golf. Perla Rubi had told me. It was her way of telling me how much I had impressed her father when I met him. If I had stayed in Juárez, if all that had happened to Sara had not happened, I'd be playing golf with Mr. Esmeralda. Not that I liked golf. Acres and acres of land dedicated to men riding for hours in little carts, occasionally hitting a tiny ball with a stick. It all seemed like such an extravagance of space and time, a vain luxury, a waste. So much of what I saw in the United States went beyond what was needed for the sake of convenience or speed. Two highways, four lanes each, going in opposite directions when maybe one two-lane highway would have been sufficient. But then Bob would not have made it to Aurora before noon.

"This was all wheat fields not too long ago," Bob said. "We live on the west side, which is less populated."

"Where do the Mexicans live?"

"All over," Bob said, ignoring my bitter tone. Then, as if deciding to tell the truth, "Mostly on the east side. We turned off the highway before we crossed the Fox River, but once you cross the river, you're on the east side."

The way Bob said it, I got the impression that crossing the Fox River was not a good idea. Bob slowed and pulled to the side to let an ambulance with flashing red lights go by. "Around 1970, the railroad, the big industry in the city, left, and all the workers employed by it started leaving. Latinos from Chicago moved in to take advantage of the cheaper housing. Then some of the gangs came with them. The city had a big problem. Things are much better now, but there's still a few people who don't like Mexicans."

"There's many people in this country who don't like us." I pointed with my chin to the Trump sticker on the bumper of the truck in front of us.

"That's just politics," Bob said as he turned the van into a smaller street. "I sell lots of air conditioners and furnaces to people who are in favor of the wall. It's all about the person-to-person connection, you know?"

What would it be like to do business with people who don't like you as a human being? Could I pretend to be friendly with people who resent my presence in their country, for the sake of the dollars? I was going to ask Bob how his "person-to-person connection" was with people who did not want Mexicans coming into the U.S. but decided that my brain could not take anything serious at the moment. Instead, the mention of the wall made me think of the place on the Rio Grande where Sara and I had crossed into the United States. After we crossed the shallow Rio Grande, we climbed a rocky ledge and stood for a moment to look at the scattered adobe houses that made up the town of Boquillas. There was a dirt road that crossed through the center of the town and ended at the edge of the river. That's where I last saw Brother Patricio. He was waving good-bye, or a blessing, or both.

"To tell you the truth," Bob continued, "one of the reasons Able Abe has done so well is because of the connections I have made with the Latino community. One of the first things I did when I started working with Abe was join the Aurora Hispanic Chamber of Commerce. I just started going to every event they had and soon I was getting orders from restaurant owners, insurance companies, schools. All business consists of personal connections."

"Yeah," I said. I thought of the kids back home who made piñatas so I could sell them downtown. They were my friends and we made money together. It pained me to admit that Bob and I had things in common.

"We're almost there."

The houses that lined the street all had the same basic design. Two-story houses with a garage, a driveway, front yard and backyard. There was space between the houses, not like in my neighborhood back home, where I could stick my hand out the kitchen window and get a warm tortilla from Mrs. Lozano next door. The major difference between the houses here, besides their size and good condition, was their subdued colors, as if people were afraid to call attention to themselves. The way Bob had described his success at Able Abe's, I had imagined something flashy, along the lines of Perla Rubi's house. But Bob's neighborhood was still impressive, especially if you compared it to the place where Mami, Sara, and I lived.

Bob pulled into the driveway of a pale blue house. It was a two-story house like all the other ones on the street, only there was something cleaner, more streamlined about the house.

"Aluminum siding," Bob said when he saw the questioning look on my face. "The paint on wood houses peels and flakes during the winters here. But not aluminum. I got out the pressure washer the Saturday before I left for Texas and gave the house a nice cleaning. Looks like new, doesn't it?"

I had to admit that the house looked better kept than all the other ones on the block and there was a flash of pride inside me for my Mexican father. Then it crossed my mind that under different circumstances, I might have been able to make some money by cleaning houses with Bob's pressure washer. But I hadn't come to Chicago to make money.

Bob stood in front of his house, one hand on his broad hip and the other pointing at the windows. "Those are state-of-the-art storm windows, the best you can buy. They lowered our heating bill this winter by six hundred dollars. I used to go to a house and install a new gas or oil furnace. But I'd see old drafty windows. So I saw an opportunity. This is a good example of what I was telling you about connections. I know this guy who owns a hardware store. His name is Pepe Romero. So we connected, you know? I get a commission from Pepe every time I get a house to install storm windows, and that's how it goes." Bob walked to the front door, dug keys out of his pocket, and opened the door. "By the way, don't tell Abe about the commission I get from the storm windows. That's a little private side deal I got going."

I couldn't help smiling when Bob winked. Bob was a more

polished, refined, efficient version of the Roberto Zapata I used to know. His old talents and skills had found a place to shine.

Bob took me to the kitchen, opened the refrigerator, and pointed to the compartment where the ham and cheese were stored. The loaf of bread was on the top shelf of the refrigerator as well. *In Mexico we can buy fresh bread every day at the corner bakery*, I said to myself.

"We keep the sodas out here in the garage." Bob opened and closed a door at the end of the kitchen. "Come, I'll show you your room."

Bob rushed down the wooden stairs. "There's a guest bedroom upstairs that you can also use, but Nancy and I thought you'd be more comfortable down here."

I did not anticipate the sadness that came over me as I walked down the steps to the basement. I should have been glad for the privacy, but all I could feel was . . . unwanted. There were three rooms, including a small bathroom with a shower. The large room had a brown leather sofa facing a flat-screen TV on the wall. Wires dangled down messily from the TV to the cable box on the floor. There was a card table where someone—Trevor, I assumed—was working on a Lego spaceship. Next to it was a box filled with the remaining pieces.

"Trevor's an extremely bright little boy," Bob said. "Nancy and I worry about him. He spends too much time inside his head. It'll be good for him to have a . . . friend."

My first impulse was to remind Bob that I was not there to be either babysitter or friend to his new son, but I was too overwhelmed by a dark emotion I had never felt before.

"And this is your room," Bob said, trying to dissipate the

tension created by my silence. There was a washing machine, a dryer, a small tool bench, and a table with clothes neatly folded. Next to it was the hot water heater and a furnace connected with iron pipes to the ceiling. There was a stationary bicycle and a rowing machine and behind these was a single bed with one of those goose-feathers quilts that Sara and I had once thought of buying for Mami but couldn't because they were so expensive. The only light in the room came from a small window on top of the dryer.

"We can move the exercise equipment out of here if it seems too crowded."

"No, it's okay." If the anger I was beginning to feel continued to grow, the equipment would come in handy.

"It's cozy in here." Bob pointed at the furnace. "The heat will keep you warm and it is the coolest room in the house in the summer. I can bring you a fan if it gets too hot."

I made my way past the exercise equipment to the bed, sat on it, and immediately felt the exhaustion in my limbs. All I wanted now was to be alone. "It's okay. Thank you."

"I'll let you rest now."

"Okay."

Bob was still standing by the doorway. Was he waiting for a more enthusiastic response from me? "I'm all right. I'll be fine." It was all the enthusiasm I could muster.

"This is your home now, Emiliano. I'm glad you're here."

Bob waited a few moments before leaving. I heard his feet climbing up the stairs, heard the front door close. I did not hear the van start. I stretched out on the soft quilt and listened for other sounds but there were none. I always liked silence. I enjoyed the desert hikes primarily because of the quiet. But the silence I heard now was different. It was the silence of being forgotten.

I closed my eyes and repeated: *This is your home now, Emiliano. Home. Home. Home.* As if repeating a word could make it true.

CHAPTER 9
SARA

There was so much empty time. My job as garbage collector consisted of going around the facility, collecting garbage three times a day: early morning, midday, and at 6:00 p.m. If I went slowly, which I liked to do, each round could take as much as an hour. That still left an awful lot of hours in the day, considering that we got up at 6:00 a.m. and the lights were turned off at 10:00 p.m. As much as I tried to keep busy helping the women with their forms or doing jigsaw puzzles, time ticked on painfully slow. I never realized the passage of time could hurt so much, but it did. Time was the big topic of conversation. How many weeks before the credible fear interview? Four weeks for a decision after that. A month or two after that before the hearing with the judge. And even those dates were uncertain. None of us had any idea when our next hearing date was or when some decision would be made on our petition. In my rounds as garbage collector, I had seen official documents in the garbage I picked up from the containers in the administration rooms. For all we knew, our asylum petitions would meet the same fate.

We got to go outside for two hours every day. One hour at 11:00 a.m. and one hour at 4:00 p.m. Often, there were dust storms so strong that outside time was canceled. Outside was a concrete slab about the size of a basketball court. The only shade was from the wall of the building where we came out. Lucila taught me to stand near the door around 10:50 and 3:50 so we could rush out and get a spot in the shade.

We were sitting against the wall with our eyes closed during the afternoon's outside time when Lucila suddenly said, "La Treinta Y Cuatro was right. You are special. You are smart. You went to high school. You were a reporter. You have your very own lawyer. You have a place to go in the United States if they let you out. You have a real chance at getting asylum. Your story is different. Most of us here have the same old story. Gangs were after us back home. Bad men wanted us to pleasure them or work for them. Those animals didn't care about my baby. If I wanted to feed my baby, I had to do what the men wanted."

"But all of that is true."

"It is true of all poor women in all poor countries of the world. Can the United States take us all in?"

I didn't know what to say. A few moments before, I had told Lucila about how I stayed up all night feeling guilty for thinking that I deserved asylum more than the other women in the center.

"We all believe that we are special," Lucila said, putting her hand on top of mine. "Even me. When I was traveling with two hundred other people from El Salvador, I felt that me and my Iliana would be one of the few allowed to stay. It is only human to feel that we are better than the rest of the group. There's no need to feel bad about something that is so human."

"Maybe it's only human to feel that, as you say, but we don't have to believe it is the truth."

"Now you are thinking too much."

I remembered suddenly the way Lucila slurped her spaghetti noodles. The memory made me grab her hand and give it a loving squeeze. "You *are* special! You're pretty smart, wise even, you know that?"

"I was the best student in the third grade and then I had to sell candies on the streets to help Mami. I think I could have been an airline pilot if I had stayed in school."

We laughed and then abruptly stopped. In front of us was a pair of black shoes and khaki pants. My heart stopped when I looked up and saw La Treinta Y Cuatro staring down at me.

"The assistant field office director wants to see you," she said. Her tone was as friendly as I had ever heard from La Treinta Y Cuatro.

"Why?" I said, not getting up.

Lucila poked me in the leg, warning me not to make trouble.

"Protocol," La Treinta Y Cuatro answered. "Your lawyer filed a complaint this morning because he wasn't allowed to see you yesterday, and Director Mello is following up on the complaint."

I stood and looked at Lucila as if to say *Wish me luck*. La Treinta Y Cuatro led the way to the front of the detention center, where Assistant Field Office Director Mello had his office. All the other guards at the detention center made the detainees walk in front of them. La Treinta Y Cuatro walked a few steps ahead as if to let me know that I was a nothing, no one she needed to worry about for one second.

On the way to the office, I thought of Sandy's advice to me: *Don't be afraid of anger. Anger can be helpful.* Not that I necessarily planned to express anger in front of Director Mello. But anger kept in check could help me to not be intimidated and to not be scared like I was at that moment.

La Treinta Y Cuatro opened the glass door to Director Mello's office and motioned me to go in. I expected her to close the door and leave me alone with Director Mello, but she came in after me and closed the door. Then she pushed me gently onto a white plastic chair and sat down on the chair beside me. Director Mello's face was hidden behind a brown file. He put the file down and left it open on his desk. Then he picked up a single piece of paper and read out loud: "A-974864778." It was the Alien Registration Number that I was given when I entered the detention center.

Assistant Field Office Director Mello reported to the field office director in El Paso, but it was clear to all that he alone ran the Fort Stockton Detention Center. He was the kind of middle-aged man who had been an athlete as a young man and was still trying to look slim and fit but not all that successfully. Although he was an ICE officer, he did not wear any kind of uniform. His short-sleeve white shirt and dark blue tie made him look more like a shoe store manager. The only other time I had spoken to him was when he informed Wes Morgan and me that my bond request was denied.

"Is that your number?"

"Yes. 778," I said. The last three numbers were all that we needed to memorize.

"You were a reporter in Juárez."

I wasn't sure whether that was a statement or a question, but the way he said it could only mean that he thought having a reporter in his detention center was a problem.

I hesitated answering. How did Mello know that? Wes Morgan had told me that the initial application for asylum was a simple form that did not require any detail. All of that was to come in a more extensive application that we planned to submit to an immigration judge.

"Were you a reporter in Juárez?" he asked this time.

"Yes," I said. Whatever fear I felt inside, I was determined not to let them see it.

"Are you writing an article about the detention center?"

I stared at him with a big mysterious grin on my face. I was stalling while I decided how to answer. A couple of times I had thought about writing an article about the women I met at the detention center. I wouldn't have been much of a reporter if the thought had not crossed my mind a few times. But behind Mello's question I saw a flicker of fear and I decided to use that to my advantage.

"No." I let that sink in and then, "I'm writing a book."

I saw Mello and La Treinta Y Cuatro exchange glances. *I told you she was dangerous*, La Treinta Y Cuatro seemed to be silently saying.

I realized at that moment that these people were not playing games. They had the power to stop me from writing a book by the simple act of killing me and then shredding all the paperwork that spoke of my existence. I felt powerless. All I could do was pretend to be brave. Try to threaten them with something . . . but with what?

Mello folded his hands together as if he was about to pray. He cleared his throat and smiled. He had the whitest, straightest teeth I had ever seen. I looked to the side and focused on the pictures of the children on the credenza next to his desk. *How bad can the father of those beautiful children be?* I thought.

"Your attorney filed a complaint with Field Office Director Harris in El Paso." He picked up the same piece of paper from which he had read my registration number and put it down again. "Wes Morgan. That's your lawyer?"

"Yes."

"The same man who shouted at me about your bond?"

"He was just doing his job. There was no reason not to let me out on bond."

La Treinta Y Cuatro shifted in her chair. I glanced sideways and caught her hateful stare. She was clearly not in favor of detainees arguing with authority.

Mello cleared his throat a few times before speaking again. "Please tell your attorney that we apologize for not letting him see you. We thought a detainee was missing and we had to secure the facility."

I wanted to say that other attorneys were allowed to see their clients while this detainee had gone missing, but Mello handed me a piece of paper. "Please, if you could just sign this."

"What is it?"

"Just a form we need. That you were informed of the reasons why your attorney was not allowed to see you."

"But those reasons are not the truth."

Mello grinned, the way someone who is very experienced in the ways of the world grins at someone who is very naive. I had seen that grin on countless government officials in Juárez when inquiring about a missing girl and they told me she had probably run away with her boyfriend. "Please," Mello said. "It's just a formality. All it means is that you were given a reason for your attorney being denied access, and our apology."

"No, thank you," I said very politely. It was a stupid form and it probably didn't mean anything, but I did not want to be complicit in a lie.

Mello nodded as if he understood and shrugged. He closed my file and leaned back in his chair, his hands crossed on top of his stomach. "I'm curious. How did you enter into this country?"

I was stunned. Mello saw the shock on my face and smiled. His question had had the desired effect. Wes Morgan and I had been very careful in leaving Emiliano completely out of everything we said and wrote on paper. As far as everyone was concerned, I came across the Rio Grande by myself and turned myself over to Park Ranger Sandy Morgan when I ran into her at Big Bend National Park. I even insisted that we leave out of any part of my asylum petition the fact that I was attacked in the desert.

"I came to you petitioning asylum. You didn't catch me trying to enter the country illegally. It doesn't really matter how I entered."

"But why Fort Stockton? Out here in the middle of nowhere? Why not El Paso? All you had to do was cross the International Bridge and say to a Border Patrol officer: 'I want asylum.'"

"There were people in Juárez who were trying to kill me. I was running away from them and where I crossed was the safest place."

"Ahh!" Mello said with mock admiration. Then, looking at La Treinta Y Cuatro: "She has all the right answers, doesn't she?"

"She's special, all right," La Treinta Y Cuatro said sarcastically.

"Okay," Mello said, "why don't we continue with this some other time." He started to get up and so did I. "Oh, one more question," Mello said when he was up. "Was there anyone with you when you crossed?"

"No," I said quickly. "Just me."

"No family member?"

"No." I looked straight into Mello's eyes because I had learned as a reporter that people who are lying look away from the person they are lying to. Of all the questions that Mello asked, this one scared me the most. Emiliano had to remain invisible.

But the smirk on Mello's face told me that he did not believe me.

La Treinta Y Cuatro took me out of the administration side of the center and let me walk back to the gym by myself. Just before she left, she grabbed me by the arm and said, "This isn't over yet."

I couldn't shake off the dreadful feeling that there was something threatening and ominous about Mello's questioning. Today he had just probed to see if I had any weak spots. But what was he after? Why so much interest in how I got into this country and whether a family member had been with me?

I did not want to let myself think the worst—that he was out to find Emiliano so he could deport him. And what did La Treinta Y Cuatro mean when she said that *this* wasn't over? I felt so alone and so afraid. So weak and powerless.

When I got to the gym, I saw Lucila sitting with a group of women who were saying the Rosary. Lucila moved to the side of the metal chair so I could sit beside her. She grabbed my hands to keep them from trembling and then she hugged me when the sobs came.

I wasn't crying just for me. I was crying for Emiliano. I was crying for all of us.

CHAPTER 10

EMILIANO

I woke up not sure whether I had slept for three minutes or three days. Only the light coming from the small window told me that the day had not moved fast enough. I had not meant to fall asleep. All I wanted to do was close my eyes for a few minutes before I called Yoya. I needed to know whether anyone was after Sara. If I was going to fight these animals (I didn't want to call them pigs anymore—Gustaf had two pigs and I liked them), then I needed to know what they were thinking. I needed to put myself in their place and ask myself what I would do to find me and the phone I was carrying if I were them. And what I came up with is that if I were them, I would try to find where I was by threatening Sara.

I sat on the edge of the bed and rubbed my face. I had to get ahold of myself. I was in Aurora now and I had come to Aurora in part because Yoya said that she had more resources to help me in a big city. I grabbed my backpack and dug out the burner phone. The phone had cost me $24.99 plus ten dollars for a SIM card with thirty minutes of talk, text, or web. The card could be used for international calls, so I could even call my mother. I could have bought more minutes for it, but I remembered Yoya's advice to use it only for a few calls. The phone reminded me of the old-fashioned flip phone that Mami used. Sara and I once bought her a newer model for Mother's Day and she was happy and grateful and then the next day she made us return it and get our money back.

I found Yoya's number in the phone and hit REDIAL. Yoya answered on the third ring.

"Hello, Emiliano. Where are you?"

"I'm in Aurora. Am I calling you too much?"

"No. But after this call, I want you to hold off calling me. I'll call you, okay?"

"Okay."

"It's safer for you and for me that way."

"I understand."

I actually didn't understand. Was Yoya under some kind of surveillance? I knew that a lot of what she did, hacking into the government's computers, for example, was illegal.

"I found some information," she said.

"Yes?"

"It's not good."

I took a deep breath. I think I knew what she was going to say before she said it.

"Tell me."

"I was able to get into the e-mails of one Walter Mello. He's in charge of the Fort Stockton Detention Center. Last night at around seven, he received an e-mail from the sheriff in Alpine. The e-mail had an attachment containing that incident report that we talked about already and a copy of Lester's confession."

"Confession."

"Yes. He's pleading guilty to first-degree assault. He spells out how he attacked you and Sara."

"He mentions me?"

"He says good things about you. Says you saved his life."

I was trying to understand the implications of people at the detention center knowing about me. They still did not know where I was.

"I don't get why that's bad news."

"The heading of the e-mail from the sheriff in Alpine said: 'Per your request.' Why would Mello be interested in the incident report and in the confession?"

"He wants to catch me and deport me."

"Mmm. I hate to break it to you, but I don't think Mello is interested in the Lester file so he could find you and deport you. ICE has bigger fish to catch."

"Then . . ."

"There must be something else behind his request. That's the bad news. That's what me and my team are going to figure out. Why is Mello interested in the incident report and Lester's confession? Mello's pretty good about deleting his e-mails and emptying his trash file at the end of the day. That in itself is also suspicious behavior. We're going to dig a little further into him. Don't worry. I'll call you as soon as I have something."

"If Mello is a bad guy, then he could hurt Sara to get to me."

"Don't get ahead of yourself. Stick to the facts."

"Why can't I call you? Is something wrong?"

There was a pause, then, "Not sure. Just a precaution. Your burner phone is safe but only up to a point. Someone with sophisticated tracking expertise could pinpoint the general area where you're calling from. We'll need to keep our conversations short. I have to go now, Emiliano. Hold tight for a few days. I'll call you soon."

I heard footsteps upstairs, so I hurriedly grabbed the metallic bag with Hinojosa's phone and looked around for a place to hide it. I looked and looked and finally slid the metallic bag under the dryer and pushed it in the length of my hand. It was a temporary hiding place.

I went back to the bed, my head full of questions. Who was this Mello and why was he interested in Lester's confession? I had a bad feeling. Something was not right. But then I remembered Yoya's words: *That's what me and my team are going to figure out.* There was a team of dedicated fighters out there watching out for Sara, and that gave me comfort. I had to stay calm and not imagine the worst. Stick to the facts.

I began to put on the same hiking boots that I had brought from Mexico. My boots and my Swiss Army knife were my two constant sources of comfort. The boots were lightweight and strong and expensive—a gift from my fellow Jiparis for my seventeenth birthday, although I knew the funds for the boots had come from Brother Patricio. The Swiss Army knife was from Linda, who had a knack for perfect gifts. I put the opening of the boot over my face and inhaled. I had tried to kill the smell by dumping in the athlete's-foot powder that I found in Gustaf's bathroom, but it was clear I hadn't succeeded. I remembered how Mami and Sara would wrinkle their noses and say "puchi" whenever I took off my boots in front of them.

The smile that came to me from that memory disappeared when I noticed the boy standing quietly just outside the open door. He was studying me carefully, as if he were looking for a resemblance to Bob Gropper. I studied him back. Trevor looked like a miniature adult, with his round glasses and his blond hair neatly combed and parted on the right side. He stood very still, arms by his sides, and I got the impression he could stay that way for a couple of hours. It was going to be up to me to make the first move if a move was to be made.

"Hey there," I said.

No answer.

"What does your shirt say?" I said, pointing.

Trevor looked at his chest and then at me. "E equals MC squared."

"Energy equals matter times the speed of light squared." I had forgotten most of what I learned in my physics class, but somehow that formula stuck.

"Actually, it means energy equals *mass* times the speed of light squared." The voice was a child's, but the tone was of an old man.

"Isn't mass and matter the same thing?"

Trevor's eyebrows furrowed in deep thought. Then, "Actually, mass is a quality of matter. It is matter after it's been weighed."

I began to feel lightheaded. I stood slowly and held on to one of the aluminum bedposts. I had yet to see a smile on Trevor's face and yet the boy's look was not unfriendly. "That makes sense," I said, although it didn't.

"I wanted to call you Emi, but Mommy said I should ask you first."

"I prefer Emiliano." I was not about to start down the Bob

Gropper route. No one had ever thought of calling me Emi before. Even when I was a child, everyone went ahead and said my full name. "Can you pronounce it? E-mee-lee-a-no."

Trevor repeated, "E-mee-lee-a-no."

"My last name is Za-pa-ta."

There was a look of momentary confusion on Trevor's face. Something didn't add up, but he didn't know exactly what it was. I waited for the confusion on his face to clear up. When it didn't, I asked, "What do people call you?"

"Trevor. It's hard to make a nickname from that because it is already a short name." Then, after a pause, "Sometimes at school, people call me gopher, but I don't like that."

A gopher was an animal of some kind. A rodent. I tried but couldn't come up with the Spanish name for it. Was there something rodent-like about Trevor's face? His thick glasses made his eyes appear small and bright; was that it?

Then Trevor explained, "It's because they think gopher sounds like Gropper."

"Ahh!"

"I prefer Trevor."

"Okay. I prefer Emiliano."

I turned my head toward the footsteps upstairs. "Your mother?"

"She told me not to wake you if you were sleeping."

I let go of the bedpost and took a few steps forward. I stopped by the rowing machine. "Who exercises?"

"My daddy . . . sometimes."

My daddy. The words a sharp prick in my chest.

"Hardly ever," Trevor added. And there for the first time his lips stretched into a thin line that could have been a smile.

We walked up the stairs together, Trevor taking two steps at a time. There was a small tuft of hair sticking out vulnerably from the back of Trevor's head. I followed him into the kitchen and stopped when I saw the back of a woman who was opening the refrigerator door.

The first thought that popped in my mind when Nancy Gropper turned around was: *You left us for this?* She was so different from the image I had created up to then. I had imagined a woman not necessarily beautiful but at least attractive. Nancy Gropper had a tired-looking face with blondish hair in a disheveled braid that came halfway down her back.

"Ahh," she said, putting down a carton of milk on the counter. She tightened the belt on a green bathrobe and walked slowly toward me with hand extended. "I hope Trevor didn't wake you. I told him not to."

"I didn't, Mommy! He was wide awake."

"Good. I am Nancy, Bob's wife."

"Emiliano." The thought of saying "Bob's son" came to me, but I did not act on it.

Her handshake was quick and soft—the opposite of welcoming.

"Well," she said—and paused as if looking for words—"are you hungry? Trevor was going to have two cookies, weren't you, Trevor?" She opened the cabinet next to the refrigerator and took out a package of cookies.

"I'll have a cookie," I said, trying to get a smile out of

Nancy. But she didn't hear me. Her eyes were moving all over the kitchen, looking for something.

"Looking for this, Mommy?" Trevor handed her a glass of water.

"Yes, thank you." She took the glass and then, still not looking at me, said, "Excuse me, I have a very bad migraine. I have to close my eyes for a moment." Then she walked out of the kitchen.

I watched her shuffle to the stairs in her green robe and flapping slippers and didn't know what to think. Maybe she was in pain. Or maybe she just plain was not happy that I was in her house.

I turned to Trevor. He looked less tense with his mother out of the room. Trevor took out glasses and plates from a cabinet and then reached for the package and took out two cookies. He looked at me, and I understood that I was being asked to sit down.

We ate side by side in silence. Now and then I thought of a question to ask but decided against it. I grabbed another cookie and Trevor did as well. There were four stools on either side of the island where we sat. This must be the place where the family ate all their meals. The wooden table by the room's only window was covered with folders and notepads, an open laptop. Next to the table was a round wicker basket filled with torn envelopes and discarded pieces of paper. That section of the kitchen was the only disorder I had seen in the house. The rest of the kitchen was so clean and bright, it looked almost unused. There were no smells anywhere. I looked at the cookie in my hand and noticed for the first time that it tasted like coconut. Trevor was examining the milk carton.

"You know how to read," I remarked.

Trevor raised his eyes and blinked as if to say, *Of course, why wouldn't I?* Or maybe he was trying to determine if there had been a question mark at the end of my words. Then, as if he had suddenly remembered the rules of polite conversation, Trevor asked, "Do *you* like to read?"

I thought about this for a few moments. There was no need to pretend in front of this six-year-old. Besides, he seemed like the kind of kid that liked straight talk. "No. I had to read a lot in school, but I can't say I liked it."

"Most kids in my school don't like to read. Probably because they don't know how."

"How did you learn?"

There was a look of terror on Trevor's face, as if this was precisely the type of question he feared the most. "I don't know," Trevor said with a high, whiny voice that finally made him seem like a child. "I started reading when I was little."

"When you were little?"

"More little."

There. Finally. A full smile. The kid had a sense of humor. You had to dig for it, but it was there. Trevor reminded me of Javier—a boy in Juárez who made the most beautiful piñatas. Javier was a former drug addict who at twelve was wise beyond his years.

"If you don't like to read, then what do you like to do?" Trevor asked, wiping milk from his upper lip with the back of his hand.

"I like to play fútbol. You call it soccer here in the United States. I like to hike. Back in Mexico, I belonged to a club called the Jiparis that went on long hikes in the desert. Sometimes we spent nights out there." I also liked Perla Rubi and I liked making money, but there was no need to tell the boy everything.

Trevor raised a thumb to his mouth and then quickly put it down. "I'm not very good at sports."

The way he said it reminded me of the loneliness I felt in that basement room after Bob left. I turned sideways and saw a room where there was a sofa, an armchair, and another flat-screen TV. Over the sofa, there was a picture of two blue lines and two orange lines on a background of pink. There was a hum that came from the refrigerator and the ticking of a clock somewhere, but otherwise the house was silent. It was hard to believe that the father I had grown up with lived in this house.

"We play kickball and other sports in my school. I go to regular kinder in the morning and then to Kinder-Plus until two p.m. In Kinder-Plus we don't have to play sports."

"What do you do? When you come home from Kinder-Plus and your mother takes a nap."

"I make myself a snack. Sometimes I play Legos. I'm building the First Order Star Destroyer. Do you know what that is?"

"No."

"It's one of the spaceships from *Star Wars*."

"I know *Star Wars*."

Trevor's eyes lit up. "The First Order Star Destroyer has one thousand four hundred and six pieces. It's the third time I've put it together."

Trevor carefully slid down the stool. He took his empty glass and plate to the sink and then he returned the milk and cookies to where he had found them. I drank the remaining milk in my glass with one long swallow. I was about to take it to the sink but stopped when I saw Trevor's serious face.

"I don't actually need anyone to take care of me."

"Okay."

Trevor looked as if he were trying to hold back tears. "Mommy said you didn't want to take care of me."

I stood, took my glass to the sink. I suddenly felt a strong dislike for Nancy Gropper. I turned to face Trevor. What was there to say? It was the truth. I did not want to babysit him. But he was just a kid with a tuft of hair sticking out. I spoke as gently as I could manage and said the first thing that came to my head. "I need to get a job. I need to make some money."

"I can take care of myself, but Daddy and Mommy say there has to be an older person in the house with me." Trevor kept his eyes fixed on his feet. Then he looked up, remembering something. "I have money. I have four hundred and fifty dollars. Popsy gave me the money."

"Who's Popsy?"

"My grandfather. He didn't give me the money all at once but little by little. I was supposed to buy toys with it, but I don't play with toys . . . hardly."

I heard a toilet flush upstairs. I moved away from the island and looked out the window. On the sidewalk in front of the house, a mailman was talking to an old woman with a sausage-like dog on a leash. The dog had a green sweater with jingle bells. Where was I? I could have been on a different planet for how strange and alien it all seemed. I turned quickly to Trevor, who was standing behind me, watching me.

I needed something normal. "Is there a park with trees

around here?" I realized immediately how stupid the question sounded. Don't all parks have trees?

"Yes. Five and a half blocks from here."

"Can you take me there? You want to ask your mother?"

"That's not necessary." Trevor walked to the laptop on the table and tapped the keys with one finger. "All set. I texted her." He went to the hall closet and pulled out a bright blue windbreaker. I followed him out the front door.

"Wait here. I forgot something." I went back in and ran to the basement for the burner phone. I knew Yoya said it would be a few days before she called, but what if she found something about Mello and decided to call me?

Trevor and I walked three blocks in silence before we came to a stoplight. What I thought about the most during those three blocks was that it was possible that I had brought danger to Bob and Nancy and Trevor, and I was sorry about that, but it could not be avoided.

When the light turned green and we began to cross, Trevor instinctively raised his hand for me to hold.

I looked at the small, fragile hand for a long moment before taking it.

CHAPTER 11
EMILIANO

That first night when we sat down to a supper of Chinese food, I searched Bob's face for some kind of love toward Nancy.

"Is your migraine any better?" Bob asked when we sat down.

"No." Nancy shoveled white rice onto Trevor's plate with a single chopstick.

"Maybe you should go see Dr. Arnold and get an injection."

I stared at the chopsticks. Bob saw my look, dug in the bag, and handed me a plastic fork.

"It's only the second day," Nancy said. "I like to wait three full days before the injection." Turning to me: "I get migraines when I'm stressed. I'm supposed to inject the Sumatriptan at the onset of the headache, but I only use it as a last resort. The injection can be auto-administered, but I prefer to do it in the doctor's office."

"In case there's a reaction," Bob added.

"And because I'm afraid to inject the medicine into a vein or a muscle. I have a CPA, not an RN or an MD."

It occurred to me that I was the "stress" that brought the migraine. Her eyes bored into me when she said the word.

We were sitting around the kitchen island. Trevor, next to

me, was watching a YouTube video of someone building a Lego city. Nancy reached across and grabbed the iPad. She turned it off and put it next to her. "You know the rules," she said when Trevor pouted.

"Abe was sure happy to see me," Bob said. He offered me a container. "Colonel Chow's chicken. It's good."

"*General* Chow," Nancy corrected him.

"I always get the ranks mixed up." Bob laughed, but only Trevor found his mistake funny. I thought about the time Sara and I took Mami to the Palacio Peking for her birthday. My mother laughed when she read the fortune in her cookie. *La felicidad te espera.* Happiness awaits you.

Nancy raised her hand to her forehead and breathed deeply.

"Honey, why don't you go lie down in bed? I can bring you a plate later."

Nancy shook her head. She looked at me. "I'm sorry, I didn't get a chance to chat with you this afternoon. Trevor said you went to the park?"

The way she asked. Did I do something wrong? "Yes. I needed air."

Nancy looked at me. I knew it sounded like a complaint, but it wasn't.

"You should ask Emiliano to teach you how to play soccer," Bob said to Trevor as he speared a piece of chicken with a chopstick. I remembered how when I was Trevor's age, my father would set Coke bottles in the street and he would show me how to dribble around them.

"You mean fútbol." Trevor pronounced it *foote-bole.*

There followed a period of silence when I knew that Nancy

and Bob were thinking about my refusal to take care of Trevor in the afternoons. I sipped water from the glass in front of me and cleared my throat. "I can stay with Trevor. Until I find a full-time job." It was the first time the idea of finding a full-time job had occurred to me. But what else could I say? Until Yoya and I start looking for the men who want the cell phone?

"Really? That would be great if you could do that!" Bob gave me a two-thumbs-up and a wink. "Trevor, looks like you got yourself a fútbol coach."

"I don't really like fútbol." Trevor was trying to pick up a single grain of rice with his chopsticks.

Nancy Gropper looked at me with misgiving. Like she was trying to see the real motive behind my sudden kindness. Or was she trying to determine whether Trevor was safe with me? Bob reached across the table and gently touched the back of Nancy's head. Was that an expression of love on my father's part? I remembered how he touched my mother's head the same caring way.

Nancy smiled at Bob, squeezed his hand, and stood up slowly. "I'm sorry. I'm feeling sick. I'm going upstairs to lie down in the dark."

Bob stood as well. He reached out for Nancy's arm, but she shook his hand gently away. "You stay with the boys. Save the leftovers. We can have them for lunch tomorrow."

"Do you really think you'll be able to go to work tomorrow?"

"Oh, yes. One way or another. Popsy is even more nervous than usual about all the work that accumulated while you were gone." Then to me: "There are some instructions about Trevor's allergies and some emergency numbers that you should know about if you're going to watch Trevor in the afternoon. I will write the allergy precautions and emergency numbers and leave them at the table. The main thing is: No peanuts! Nothing with peanuts! We don't have anything in the house with peanuts or peanut derivatives, so you don't have to worry about allergy reactions in here. But *out there* is a very different story. I would prefer it if you didn't take him out of the house until we got you a phone."

"I'll get you a phone tomorrow," Bob said.

"Emiliano already has a phone," Trevor said. "He had it when he took me to the park. So there's no need to worry, Mommy."

"I bought a cheap phone on the way here to call Sara and Mami," I said quickly.

"You could always use mine," Bob said. He sounded suspicious or hurt, I couldn't tell which.

Nancy continued, businesslike: "I pick Trevor up at school at two p.m. and we're home by two thirty. I'll drop him off and then go back to work. Please be here between two and two thirty since you have agreed to watch him."

The way she said *since you have agreed to watch him.* The woman did not like me, did not want me in her house. She was trying, I gave her that. She tried all during dinner to be nice, but in the end, she couldn't hide her dislike.

Nancy turned to Trevor. "Don't forget that tonight is a bath night." Then she walked away.

We ate in silence. As soon as we heard a door shut upstairs,

Bob put his chopsticks down and pulled out another plastic fork from the bag. "Eating's easier when you don't have to work at it," he said to me.

"I can show you how to do it, Daddy," Trevor said. "It's easy."

"That's okay. Eat your broccoli. It's good for you."

"If I take a vitamin, it will have the same effect."

Bob shook his head. "Kids these days. They know too much."

I looked at my plate. I stuck my fork in a piece of chicken, colonel or general, who gives a crap? I could tell that Bob was embarrassed by his wife's . . . rudeness. Maybe it wasn't rudeness exactly. Then what? Some deficiency in basic human warmth. An inability to courteously hide the stress caused by my presence? How long was I going to be in that house? Whatever amount of time was too long. I wasn't going to make it. There was a pressure in the middle of my chest, a bubble of longing and sadness and anger about to pop.

"The migraines are hard on Nancy. She's not herself," Bob explained. "Thank you for staying with Trevor. That's a big help."

The big help was that Nancy would be less annoyed with my presence.

"Sure," I said, with zero enthusiasm.

"Would you like to call your mother?" Bob asked, perhaps sensing what I was feeling.

I thought for a moment, then, "Not today." If she heard my voice, she'd know immediately how miserable I felt. When I talked to her, I wanted to sound strong and content. Strong and content enough for her not to worry, for her to believe that her sacrifice was worthwhile. "Tomorrow."

"It gets better. Believe it or not."

I nodded the way someone nods when a comment is not worth a response.

"Daddy, is Emiliano my brother?"

There was a pleading look in Bob's eyes. As if he wanted my permission to answer yes. I looked out the window.

"Yes," Bob finally said.

"Then why does he have a different last name?"

"He's your half brother."

I could see that there was still a question on the boy's lips. He was about to ask it, but Bob cut him off. "Not now, Trevor. Eat your broccoli. Please!"

That's when I first felt something very much like pity for Bob Gropper.

We were all silent for a few moments and then I said, "You used to eat some of the broccoli on my plate when Mamá wasn't looking. Remember?"

"But now I have been given another chance to fix my mistakes," Bob said with a grin.

And for a moment there, Bob Gropper was my father again.

CHAPTER 12

SARA

All night long I went over the ways Mello could find out where Emiliano had gone. The only people who knew that Emiliano had gone to Chicago with Father were Wes and Sandy Morgan and Gustaf Larsson. They were not going to tell Mello about Emiliano. Then, around dawn, it came to me in a wave of panic that Father had visited me and that all visitors had to sign a visitors' log and state their relationship to the detainee and their home address. It was probably illegal to ask for people's home address, but then again, detaining a person who is seeking asylum must also be a violation of some international law. If Mello found my father's entry in that visitors' log, they would be able to find Emiliano that way. It was hard to imagine that Mello would go to all that trouble to apprehend one single undocumented Mexican, but it was impossible to ignore the implication behind his questions . . . or his smirk.

Visitors entering the building had to turn in all their personal property to a guard as they came in. Their cell phones, wallets, purses, keys, everything was put into a paper bag with their name on it. Then they passed through a metal detector. Past the metal detector was a table with the visitors' log. I had seen those visitors' logs when I made my garbage rounds through the administration offices of the center. They were kept in three-ring binders in a small office next to the entrance. Each binder had that week's list of visitors. Father visited me on a Monday the week before, so all I had to do was find the sheet for that day and rip it out.

That was easier said than done. There was always a guard in the office. In fact, I was not allowed to enter an administration office unless there was a guard or another staff member present. My instructions for conducting the garbage rounds had been very clear: I should knock on an administration door, say "garbage," and wait for someone to give me the okay to enter. If no one was there, I skipped that office. It was going to be impossible to open a binder, find the right page, and rip it out with a guard present. But what I thought I could do was "accidentally" dump last week's binder in the "whale," which is what I called the big, gray plastic container that I wheeled around. I decided that the best time to carry out my plan was during my early morning round when the guard on duty was a friendly young man named Mario.

At 7:00 a.m., Lucila, Colel, and me sat at a stainless-steel table in the cafeteria, eating our usual bowls of oatmeal. It was a special morning because the oatmeal came with raisins and tiny pieces of dried apple—a rare treat. Colel picked up one of the pieces of apple, studied it, and then shrugged before tossing it in her mouth. Colel never failed to make Lucila and me laugh. How someone carrying so much grief inside could be so light in spirit was beyond me.

"You're not hungry?" Lucila asked, looking at my untouched bowl.

"No, I don't feel well this morning." It was not a lie. My stomach was in knots. If I got caught stealing the logbook, Mello would figure out what I was trying to do—I would point him right to Emiliano's location and would make things so much worse for Emiliano.

Lucila leaned closer to me and said with sadness in her voice, "There are rumors that decisions for the women who have been here the longest will come this week. The women say that maybe day after tomorrow and then the buses to take us to the airport will come the day after," Lucila said, stirring the oatmeal with a plastic spoon. Colel was having trouble opening the tiny milk carton. I took it from her and pried it open.

"But how do the women know about these things? It is just talk. People talk to pass the time. And what makes you think it won't be good news?"

Lucila smiled at me. "You'll see," she said quietly. "Maybe this is my last week here."

"What does your lawyer say? Even if the decision is a no, you can appeal." Lucila was represented by a young pro bono lawyer.

She shook her head sadly. "I put in your bag the phone and address of Iliana. When you get out, will you . . ."

"Lucila, you must not think that way."

"She sounds happy. But if I knew that you would check to see how she is."

"I'm not going to listen to this. Snap out of it."

"Okay, I snap out." Lucila sat up and made a determined face. The look of a warrior.

"There, that's better."

I stopped by my bunk after breakfast and, sure enough, in the plastic bag where I kept my underwear and toiletries, there was the piece of paper with the phone and address of Iliana's foster home. I made a face similar to the one Lucila had made and then I went out to get the whale.

It felt good to be doing something that would help protect Emiliano, and underneath my fear I could also feel excitement. I got the whale from the back of the cafeteria and proceeded to empty into it the garbage from the kitchen and from the cafeteria. The whale was almost full, but I decided to go to the administration offices instead of taking the whale to the dumpster like I usually did. I figured that it would be easier to hide the logbook inside the whale if it was full of kitchen and cafeteria garbage. It was 8:00 a.m. and some of the center's staff were just arriving for their shift. I hesitated a moment before crossing in front of Mello's office. His door was open, and I could hear his voice coming from inside. Everything had to look normal. I had to look bored. I took a moment to collect myself and then I rolled the whale past his door. I knocked on his door and saw Mello on his telephone. His head was down, so I waited until he raised his eyes and saw me. He looked surprised or embarrassed, I couldn't tell which. I pointed at the plastic container by his desk and he immediately shook no with his finger. I nodded and moved past his door. I don't think he heard the big sigh that came out of me when I was down the hall.

Mario was putting paper into the printer when he saw me come in. He smiled and said, "Oh, man, you really stink today."

"I think some of the meat got spoiled," I said, trying not to look at the logbooks on the ledge behind his desk.

"At least they're not feeding it to you," Mario said.

He had told me on a previous visit how happy the people in Fort Stockton were when the U.S. government accepted their bid to turn the old school into a detention center. The revenue from the lease payments would keep the town afloat. But the best part was the thirty or so jobs for the residents of the town.

"It was going to be the army for me until this came along," he'd confided.

"You have an air conditioner?" I said, pretending I had never noticed it before.

"I know. It gets hot in that gym at night, doesn't it?"

"May I?" I put my arms in front of me and raised my hands as if to better receive the flow of cool air.

Mario looked around briefly and then said, "Sure, be my guest."

"How cold can you make it?" I said, standing in front of it. I moved the whale to my side. The binder for last week was the last one in the row of binders. It was about six feet to the right of the air conditioner.

"It can go pretty cold." Mario left the printer and leaned over the controls of the air conditioner. I stepped back to make room for him and with my left hand toppled the paper cup with hot coffee that was on the edge of the desk.

"Oh, I'm sorry," I said. "I'm so sorry."

"Just a little coffee. No big deal. I'll get some paper towels."

There was a bathroom with a toilet and a sink at the other end of the room. As soon as Mario went in, I grabbed the visitors' logbook for last week and stashed it under a mountain of potato peels.

"Let me do it," I said, taking the paper towels from Mario's hands.

But Mario insisted on cleaning the spilled coffee himself.

"You're a good man," I said to him when I left.

"Not all that good," he responded sadly, and I had a feeling that he was referring to his work at the detention center.

I rolled the whale quickly down the corridor past Mello's office. I didn't look in his direction, but I heard his voice still on the phone. My heart was racing a hundred miles an hour. It was going to take a while for the adrenaline to wear itself out, but I didn't care. Out by the dumpster I would tear out the page with my father's name and address and then tomorrow I'd return the binder to its place. I had taken away the only means that Mello had for finding Emiliano. I had done something for my brother.

Emiliano was safe and that made me happy.

CHAPTER 13

EMILIANO

Next morning, I stayed in bed until the footsteps above me stopped. Then when I was getting dressed, I heard the buzz-buzz of my phone. It took me a few moments to remember that the phone was under my pillow. I knew it was Yoya, because who else knew my number? She started talking as soon as I said hello.

"We're getting someplace," she said. "Remember I told you about the e-mail to Mello from the sheriff in Alpine with Lester's confession? Remember the sheriff's e-mail was titled 'per your request'?"

"Yes."

"Well, now I know that Mello specifically requested the report and we know why he requested it. I found an older e-mail in Mello's computer. It was an e-mail from someone calling himself furryfox. When I opened the e-mail, I knew I had struck gold. The message said:

"*Lester sang. Get the papers from sheriff in Alpine. The girl's brother has the phone. The incident report could help us find him.*

"So, bingo, right?"

Yoya was going so fast, I had the impression that she had been up for hours eating doughnuts and drinking Cokes.

"I don't follow. Who is furryfox?"

"Here's where it gets interesting. I remembered that in Lester's confession, he said he was following the orders of a certain Marko Lisica. That rang a big bell in my little brain because, guess what."

"What?" I wished Yoya would stop asking me to guess and just spell out the bad news for me. I had the uneasy feeling that the more she discovered, the worse it was for Sara.

"Lisica is the Croatian word for 'fox.' So the furryfox of the e-mail has got to be Marko Lisica. Marko Lisica orders Lester and another man to attack you and Sara in the desert. Then he orders Mello to get the incident report hoping that the report will lead them to you and the phone."

"Mello is . . ."

"Mello is working for Lisica either through bribes or threats. I did some digging on Lisica. He owns the Odessa Agricultural Cooperative. He's served time in prison for raping his own wife. He's a nasty guy, but he's not the kind of major player that would be interested in protecting the names in that phone. The person who wants that phone so desperately is someone with a lot more status and influence and connections. Someone who has much more to lose than a relatively small crook in Odessa. Lisica is taking orders from someone and that's the person we need to find. Big Shot."

All the pieces were beginning to fall into place, and it did not look good. The bad guys had found out where Sara was. They knew the phone could not be with her. That left me. But there was no way they could find out where I was from Lester's confession. They could only get at me through Sara.

That thought froze me and filled me with fearful energy all at once. "If Mello is working with Lisica, then Sara's in danger. We have to do something."

"They want you, not her. The people who run these human trafficking rings, which I think is what we are dealing with here, are very wary of any kind of attention. They will carry out criminal acts, but they will do so very discreetly. I guess that's the right word. Your sister has visitors, right?"

"Wes Morgan, her attorney. Sandy Morgan."

"Mello will be careful, then. He knows people would miss her and ask about her if anything happened to her. I don't think you need to worry about her. They may ask her about you, but I don't think they will torture her to get at you."

The word *torture* made me laugh. It was crazy to even think of that possibility. This was the United States. "I want to call her lawyer and tell him he has to move Sara out of that facility."

"I don't advise it, Emiliano. They may have tapped his phone, waiting for you to call."

"So what good is the burner phone?" I said, irritated.

"I understand your frustration. The best way to help Sara and you is to find out who is behind all this, who is Lisica's boss? There must be something in Lisica's e-mails that will lead us to him."

"What about Hinojosa's cell phone? Do you have someone here in Chicago who can open it?"

"That's more complicated. We need to make sure that what's in that phone can be used by law enforcement people. Let me work on that a little more. We're making good progress, Emiliano. I'll get back to you soon."

And just like that, Yoya was gone.

I wanted so much to talk to Sara. But the only way to talk to someone in the facility was to call, leave a message, and wait for them to call you back. Now, after what Yoya told me, calling her was impossible. But I decided that I would call Wes Morgan despite Yoya's advice not to. He had to know that Sara was in danger. He had to be seen visiting her. If possible, he needed to get her into another detention center, away from Mello. I found my father's business card at the bottom of my knapsack.

"It's me," I said when he answered.

"Emiliano?"

"I need the telephone number for Sara's lawyer."

"Hold on. I'm driving now. I'm pulling into a parking lot." There was silence for a few moments. Then, "Why do you need his number? Is something happening with Sara?"

"No. I don't know. I need to check on her, but I don't want to call her directly. I don't want them coming after me."

"I have Wes Morgan's number in my contacts."

"Wait a second." I ran upstairs and found a pencil on the kitchen table where Nancy Gropper did all her work. "Okay."

"Here we go: 432-555-3304. Wesley F. Morgan, Attorney at Law."

"Thank you."

"So, what are you going to do this morning?"

I didn't say anything. What could I say? *I'm going to be worrying and thinking about Sara.*

"Emiliano? You still there?"

"Yes."

"You'll be there when Trevor comes home, right?"

"Yes."

"Around two?"

"Yes."

"I'll call Sara from the office."

I thought of Mello waiting for a call for Sara that would lead them to me. "Maybe you should hold off on calling her from your phone or your office. ICE might be listening and then they'll come after me."

"Oh. I never thought about that."

"You need to get a phone like mine—with prepaid minutes. It will be safer to call Sara that way. Good-bye."

I didn't mean to be rude, but I had to save the minutes on the burner phone for talking to Yoya.

I went downstairs, got dressed, and called Wes Morgan. Five rings and then voice mail. I left a long message for him, telling him that Sara was in danger from the people who attacked us in the desert. He had to get her out of that detention center or at least visit her often so that people would see she was protected. Then I went upstairs again and looked at the clock in the microwave. It was 8:30 a.m. I found the cereal and the milk and sat down to eat. What was I going to do? I looked around and knew that I could not stay inside all day long. When Trevor came home, we'd go to the park. But until then? I had to find some kind of occupation, some activity that would keep me from going crazy. When I finished the cereal, I cleaned the bowl and spoon and then grabbed the key to the house that Nancy had left for me, and I went out the kitchen door.

During my walk with Trevor to the park, I had noticed that

many houses had paint that was peeling. I thought they must have been damaged in the snow and rain and cold weather. Now, as I walked, I wondered if maybe there was a way to keep myself busy while waiting for Yoya to call. I needed to move because only by moving could I keep the dark thoughts away. Getting tired by doing something useful had saved me in Mexico, so why not in the U.S. as well? Work had always filled my days with a kind of simple joy. And I liked making money. Like Bob Gropper. Maybe the apple did not fall far from the tree.

I decided to start with the house next door. A man in a gray suit, a very well-pressed blue shirt, and a yellow tie was getting into a brown car.

"Good morning," I shouted from the sidewalk. The one thing I knew about business is that you need to be bold. You need to just put yourself out there and state clearly what you want and what you can offer in return.

The man in the suit froze, his hand on the car's door handle. He looked like a man about to be robbed or killed. I suddenly remembered I was wearing the same cowboy shirt, jeans, and hiking boots I had worn for the past three days. I had not counted on people being afraid of me.

"Yes?" the man said tentatively.

"I saw the wood trim on your house. The paint is coming off. I can paint it for you."

"Where did you come from?" The man's eyes went down the street and then up the other way. He gave me the impression that he was looking for the rest of the gang to come out of hiding and jump him.

How was that question to be answered? I could say I came from Mexico, crossed the Rio Grande undocumented and quite illegally twelve days ago. I decided to answer more narrowly. I pointed at Bob's house.

"Bob and Nancy? You're staying with them?"

"Yes."

The man grinned. "No."

"No?"

"No, I don't want you to paint my house."

The man opened the car door and slid in. He drove away without looking at me.

The next two houses did not open the door for me even though I could hear the television inside. I was about to try one block over when I heard the wail of a police siren coming closer and closer. I ran back to Bob's house and, from the kitchen window, saw the police cruiser drive by slowly. I felt a little of what Sara must have felt in that detention center. She was behind barbed wire and I was behind an invisible fence. I knew it was risky to step outside that fence, but it was either that or be eaten alive by worrisome thoughts.

That afternoon, when Nancy had gone upstairs to nurse her headache, I had a conversation with Trevor.

"I need your help."

What is it about asking a child for help that makes them instantly pay attention to you?

"I need to get a job. It will take time to find a real good one that pays lots of money. I can't stay inside the house all day. I will go, how you say, honkers."

"You mean bonkers?"

"Yes. Bonkers. I will explode. Bonk!"

Trevor imitated the movement of my hands pulling away from the top of my head, fingers opening. "Bonk." He laughed.

"In the meantime, so I don't go bonk, I can paint some of the houses around here. I can paint in the mornings until you get home and then we can do stuff."

"I want to get the Death Star 75159. It has four thousand pieces. It costs four hundred and ninety-nine dollars and ninety-nine cents. I currently have four hundred and fifty."

"The thing is worth four hundred and ninety-nine dollars?"

"And ninety-nine cents."

"Four hundred and ninety-nine dollars! In Mexico, a family can live on that for a year."

Trevor didn't know what to say.

"Okay, okay. If you help me, I'll give you the rest of what you need." Assuming I first found a paying job.

I made Trevor put on a jacket because it was cold and then we went out to knock on doors.

"Do you know anyone around here?" I asked Trevor.

"No."

"How about kids from your school? Any of them live around here?"

"I don't think so. I've never seen any."

"Older kids that babysit for you?"

"My mommy calls an agency and they send someone. Usually, an old lady."

There was a dog barking in the backyard of one of the houses. I saw through the gate in the fence that it was the same dog with the green sweater I saw when I first arrived. "Let's try this house," I said. "Someone who worries about their dog getting cold can't be all bad."

"What?"

"Hold my hand and try to look like a little kid."

"I *am* a little kid."

"Just let me do the talking."

The lady who opened the door was in her seventies or eighties. She had on a blue dress that reminded me of the one my mother wore to church every Sunday. Her initial frown turned into a smile when she saw Trevor. My plan was working.

"Good afternoon! I noticed that the trim of your house had paint that was flaking. I could paint it for you, if you wish."

"And is this your little helper?" She looked at Trevor, who had put on an angelic smile. He was about to say something, but I squeezed his hand.

"Ouchy."

"Be quiet, Dagwood!" the lady said to the dog, who was going crazy barking.

"I'm not going to help him paint," Trevor said in a loud voice. "I'm only here to help him get the job."

I knew I couldn't trust the boy to keep his mouth shut. But the old lady found Trevor's statement very funny. She laughed and started to cough so hard I thought she was going to choke.

Trevor waited until she had pulled herself together and then said, "We live down the street. My name is Trevor Gropper."

"Gropper? Ahh. I know your grandfather." Then, at me: "How much do you charge?"

I should have been prepared for that question, but I wasn't. I stepped back. It was a two-story brick house with yellow wooden trim that had not been painted in a good ten years. I figured it would take me about three days to paint. Three sounded like a good number. "Three hundred dollars?" I didn't mean it to sound like a question.

The old lady raised her eyebrows in surprise. Did she think my price was too low or too high? But then she said, "Three hundred dollars but that includes all the trim and all the windows and the back porch."

I looked up and saw the three windows on the top floor facing the street. They had wooden frames, and the glass panes were separated with thin strips of woods. This was detailed, careful work that would take hours. But then, what else did I have to do?

"All right," I said.

"Good." The old lady grinned. "I have a ladder. I'll buy the brushes and the paint. Come by tomorrow morning."

"He can only work until two p.m. and then he has to come home to be with me. I don't need anyone to take care of me, but my mommy and daddy don't want me to be alone."

"Is that right?" the woman asked.

I nodded.

"Fine." She closed the door and then opened it. "Your name?"

"Emiliano Zapata."

"What?"

"Emee-lee-ano," Trevor told her.

"Okay, Emiliano. My name is Irene Costelo, but people call me Mrs. C. See you tomorrow."

On my way out, I glanced at the side of the house and saw eight windows and in the backyard I could see a large wooden porch. I had a feeling that the sweet-looking Irene Costelo, or Mrs. C, as people called her, had just outsmarted me.

I was awake the following morning when I heard noises in the kitchen. I knew it was Bob getting ready to go to work. I walked upstairs and saw him at the kitchen table. The digital clock under the microwave told me it was 5:00 a.m.

"Emiliano, what are you doing up so early?"

I didn't tell him that I had stayed up all night calling Wes Morgan every hour. I didn't tell my father about the certainty I had that something bad was going to happen to Sara.

"Did you get the burner phone so that you could call Sara?" I demanded to know.

"Oh, God. I totally forgot. Did you call her lawyer?"

"Yes, but he hasn't returned my call."

"If there was bad news, I'm sure he would have called you. Look, from what I understand, asylum petitions can drag on for weeks, months even. We need to be patient." Bob stuck the ham and cheese sandwich he had just made into a small plastic bag. He looked stressed, but I didn't think it was about Sara.

"Can you buy a phone and call her this morning?"

"Why don't you call her? You have a phone." He sounded annoyed. Then, quickly, in a softer voice, "I'm sorry. I'm . . . It's been so busy at work. Catching up on the week I was away. Then the hot days we had last week reminded people that summer was coming and the orders for cooling systems have started to come in. I'm working on a bid for a couple of city buildings which, if we get, we'll probably need to hire ten more technicians. Abe is going crazy with all that needs to get done. Today,

I have a meeting with the regional manager for Safeway. If we get their maintenance account, it will be big. It could—"

"I can't call her," I said, interrupting. "I don't want people in the facility to know that Sara has a brother who is in this country illegally. It could hurt her case. Or immigration could come looking for me."

Bob placed his sandwich into a square, black briefcase that looked as if it were made out of cardboard. "That's true. I hadn't thought about that."

"Sara has to be a priority for you. What happens to her has to be important to you."

"It is. You don't think it is?"

"No."

"Look," Bob said, serious. "When your mother called . . . I didn't care how much work I had or how worried Nancy was about the cartels or about bringing you and Sara to live with us. We thought it was going to be the two of you. Abe thought I was breaking all kinds of laws. I didn't care. I left everything and went to get you and Sara."

"You finally decided to act like a father."

Bob closed the mayonnaise jar with an angry twist. He went to the sink and rinsed the knife he was using. I recognized the tightening of the jaws, the biting of the lips. It was what he did when he tried to control the anger. Finally, he said, looking at me, "Give me a break, okay? Just give me a break."

At first, I thought he was asking for a freno, a brake that would keep him from sliding into an explosion of anger. But if anger was coming, then let it come. An angry Bob would be more real than the strange person he'd become.

Bob sat and pointed to the stool across the island, but I remained standing. He exhaled and looked at me with sad eyes. He was searching for words but couldn't find any. He finally said, "Whatever you have to say to me, just say it. Get it out of your system. About me not being a father or being a bad father. Whatever. Just go ahead and say it."

I felt a rush of raw energy through my body. It was an energy like hatred and it was also like love and it was all I could do to keep my fists from striking his face.

"You need to keep calling Sara," I shouted before walking out.

I got dressed and set off for the park. I sat on a swing and saw kids on the way to school. I tried Yoya again. When she did not answer, I did not bother leaving a message. I stood and made a motion as if to throw the damn burner phone as far as I could. Then I remembered Mrs. C. I regretted taking on that job. But then, maybe moving a paint brush up and down would keep me from totally losing it. I put the phone in my pocket and headed to Mrs. C's house. There was a note on the door. It was written with a shaky hand.

This is an old house. Paint it with love.

CHAPTER 14
SARA

The following morning when I knocked on Mello's door and asked if I could come in to empty his wastebasket, he motioned me in.

"Sit down, Sara," he said, using my name for the first time.

When I was seated across from him, he closed the brown folder on his desk and looked straight into my eyes.

"Your brother. He crossed with you into the United States, didn't he? Where did he go?"

I felt the blood drain to my feet. My mind was blank. I had no words.

Mello pushed himself up from his chair and moved the whale out of the way so he could close the door. He came back to his desk and sat down. His tone was conversational, like two friends chatting over a cup of coffee.

"You and your brother were attacked in Big Bend National Park. Your brother and one of the attackers struggled. Well, you know the rest of the story. So the question is, Where is your brother now? Emiliano. That's his name, isn't it?"

"Why?" I said.

"Why what?" Mello crossed his hands over his belly and leaned back in his chair. He was getting comfortable.

"Why do you want to know where he is?" I was slowly recovering my senses. *Stay calm, Sara. Don't let him intimidate you. He's just another puchi guy.*

"I want to enforce the laws of this country. I'm doing my duty as a citizen."

"And with all that you have to do as a citizen with a busy job, with all the people coming into the U.S. every day, you are worried about my brother?"

Mello shrugged. "That's correct."

But I did not believe him. Everything in my body told me that Mello was corrupt. There was a chill that went through my body when I realized that Hinojosa's power had reached even here. It was strange, but just then I felt some of my strength return.

"Where is your brother?" Mello asked again.

You can't give up now. Fight. Fight for Emiliano.

"My brother went back to Mexico." I was looking at Mello when I said this, and my words were full of anger.

Mello's eyes narrowed as if he were trying to see inside my head.

"He went back to Mexico?"

"Yes. He never wanted to come to the United States in the first place. It was me who was being persecuted in Mexico."

"Sure." Mello did not believe me.

I don't care what happens to me or what they do to me. That is all I will say. I will not give up Emiliano.

"What was your plan? What were you planning to do before you were attacked? Where were you and your brother headed?"

I sat straight in my chair and faced Mello again. I found

that there was enough courage still left in me. "I would like to talk to my attorney. I am not going to answer any questions without him."

"I have to ask you these questions," Mello said. He sounded as if he regretted having to do it. "Asking them is my duty."

I tried to swallow, but there was no saliva in my mouth. I could feel my racing pulse in my throat and in my temples.

Do not cry! Do not let these people see any tears. Think of Mami. The strength she had in letting me and Emiliano come. How she held back her tears when we said good-bye to her so that we would not see her sorrow.

"I am not going to tell you where you can find Emiliano. You can keep asking all you want. It is not going to happen."

"That's too bad."

"Did you really think I was going to tell you?"

"I was hoping," he said, smiling. He picked up his phone and pushed a button. "We're ready."

A few moments later, La Treinta Y Cuatro entered Mello's office.

"I think we need to put Ms. Zapata in isolation for her own protection."

La Treinta Y Cuatro grabbed my arm and began to lift me out of my chair. She led me out the front door and to the side of the gym where three new cement block units had been constructed. These were the solitary confinement rooms where detainees were taken for their own security or for violation of a detention center rule. La Treinta Y Cuatro punched a code into a panel next to one of the doors.

"I have a right to tell my lawyer that you are putting me in here," I said with as much conviction as I could muster.

La Treinta Y Cuatro shook her head. "You don't get it, do you? You don't have any rights. You are worse than a criminal. They have more rights than you do. We can keep you here as long as we want."

"Don't do this," I pleaded. "My attorney filed a complaint when you didn't let him see me. What do you think he'll do when he finds out you put me here for no reason?"

"But we do have a reason," she said, a satisfied smirk on her face. "We are putting you here for your own safety. We received information that two Guatemalan women want to hurt you. I guess they resent you for being so special. *You* are asking us to put you in here so you won't get hurt."

"But that's not true."

"We have women in the pods who tell us what is going on. They've signed affidavits spelling out that they have heard threats against you. So"—La Treinta Y Cuatro waved at the empty room—"your stay here is per ICE regulations. Perfectly legal. For as long as it's needed. Know what I mean?"

Before I could say anything, she put her hand on my back and pushed me into the room.

Then I heard the door close behind me.

There was a combination sink and toilet and a cement platform with a blue foam mat for a bed and a green blanket for a pillow. The door had a vertical-looking glass window and there were four narrow windows near the ceiling. They were so high up that they could be opened or closed only with some kind of pole. A fluorescent light flickered on the ceiling. There was no sound. No sound. I fell to my knees. I would find a way to be strong again somehow. I would start thinking and fighting and hoping again, somehow.

But just then I had to let myself fall.

CHAPTER 15

EMILIANO

"Emiliano." Mrs. C was calling my name through a window below me. "Remember to put a plastic tarp on the ground when you're scraping. Otherwise the paint drops will kill my plants."

"Yes. I'm sorry. I have one down there now, but I forgot to move it." It was my third day painting Mrs. C's house and so far, not a single drop of paint had fallen on her plants.

"I know it. That's why I'm reminding you. Will you be done today?"

"Yes. I have only this window left."

"Make sure you pick up any flakes on the ground and then call me so I can pay you."

"Yes, Mrs. C."

I finished with the trim on the window and started down the ladder. People in the United States worried about so many things that no one in Mexico cared about. Like the insurance regulations that made Bob risk falling asleep at the wheel rather than let me drive. Nancy's list of products containing peanuts was three pages long. The list did not include just food but all manner of things. Who knew that laxatives or shaving cream could have deadly peanut oil? I now knew not to mess with Trevor's bowel movements or his shaving routine.

When I was halfway down the ladder, I felt a buzz in my pocket. It took me a few moments to realize that the burner phone was vibrating. It was a call. Finally. I hurried down the ladder and flipped the phone open without looking at the number of the caller. It could have been only one of two people: Yoya or Wes Morgan, and I was desperate to speak to either one of them.

"Emiliano?" It was the voice of a man. It wasn't Gustaf's voice and the voice sounded too young to be that of Wes Morgan. My first impulse was to hang up. What if Big Shot found me?

"Yes. This is Emiliano," I stammered. "Who's this?"

"You don't know me. My name . . . You can call me Louie. I . . . work with Yoya. She asked me to call you."

"Where's Yoya?"

"Yoya had to go underground for a while."

"Underground?"

"She's hiding. We're not letting her talk to anyone right now. She escaped a few moments before her apartment was raided."

"Who?"

"We don't know, exactly. Homeland Security, NSA."

I remembered Yoya telling me that she thought she was being watched.

"Was it in connection to what she was working on with me?" I asked, afraid of the answer I would get.

"We were doing so many investigations, it's hard to know.

We must have triggered some warning system or other. But I need to be quick now and tell you what Yoya wanted me to tell you."

I walked to the back of Mrs. C's house and sat on the porch steps. "Go ahead."

"Yoya intercepted an e-mail from Lisica to Mello. I'll read it to you. It said: 'We got the father's business card from the lawyer (attached). Talk to the girl, see if you can make it go down easy. We'll handle it on the Chicago end.'"

"The business card? My father's business card? Wes Morgan gave it to Lisica?"

"Ahh, I don't think Wes Morgan gave it to him, exactly. Yoya checked the sheriff's crime report in Alpine—Wes Morgan was killed during a burglary of his home."

"Ay! No! That was Sara's . . . Sara has no protection now." I said the first thing that came to mind. "It was Lisica who killed Wes Morgan. The police have to know. And Sara needs help."

"Whoever did it covered their tracks. They made it look like a burglary gone bad. Morgan's antique guns were taken. No fingerprints. No witnesses. But listen, Yoya thinks that the rest of the message means that they're going to try to get Sara to convince you to return the cell phone you are carrying."

"Return it?"

"Yoya thinks that's your best bet right now. Just give them back the phone when your sister asks you for it. To save yourself and your sister. These people are smooth and sophisticated. Our guess is they'll try to do everything aboveboard, at first anyway, but keep in mind that they kill when they need to.

Give them back the phone. Yoya thinks that they are just waiting for you to charge it and turn it on so they can track you down. They are that good. Okay, that's all I have to say. Be careful."

"Wait! Please. Yoya . . . she was going to help us find the women who are slaves. The phone is the only way."

"As soon as the heat dies down, we'll continue investigating Lisica. We know he works for someone else."

"Big Shot."

"Yeah. This Big Shot is the puppeteer. He coordinates with Mexico for the women, distributes them to . . . influential men here in the U.S. He protects these men. That's why they want things done quietly, legally if possible. That's what we've come up with so far. When things cool down, we'll continue monitoring Lisica. He'll lead us to Big Shot. In the meantime—it would be better if you returned the phone."

"And if I don't?"

"I don't know. Find someone in law enforcement you can trust."

"Find someone in law enforcement I can trust," I repeated, incredulous. "Where . . ."

There was a click and then the signal that the call had ended. And what I felt inside me was similar to that flatline signal. It was as if something had died inside me.

"Sounds like you're in some kind of trouble," I heard Mrs. C say behind me. She was sitting in a wicker rocking chair on the porch. She had heard my whole conversation. "Sorry. It sounded important. I didn't want to intrude but I knew that if I moved, it would disturb you. You want to talk about it?"

I shook my head. What would talking accomplish? I had just lost the reason why I came to Chicago. Yoya had been my hope. I felt alone. I tried to remember the exact words in the e-mail message that Louie had read. *See if you can make it go down easy.* I did not understand them. They could have been spoken in a foreign language. They *were* spoken in a foreign language: English.

"Thank you," I said. "I'll finish the last window."

I stood and was about to go to the front of the house when Mrs. C spoke. "I am a good judge of character, Emiliano, and I can tell you're a good person. I don't know what kind of trouble you're in, but I know it's not because you are a bad person. Am I right?"

I nodded. It felt reassuring to have Mrs. C recognize that I was a good person.

"Well, then. I want to tell you something. When I was very young, before I met Alfred, I dated a young man. We were very serious, but then he went to Vietnam and things were . . . different when he came back. We didn't see each other anymore. I married Alfred and, after a while, this young man got himself together and found a lovely woman to marry. He joined the Chicago Police Department. I know all this because I ran into him once at the courthouse. I don't know where he lives, but if you go to St. Hyacinth Basilica in Chicago and ask anyone for Stanislaw Kaluza, they'll tell you. He's retired by now, I'm sure. I don't think he died because I read the obituaries religiously and his name hasn't popped up. He's a bit rough around the edges, but he's got a good heart. Just tell him Irene Costelo sent you. I bet he'll help you. You can trust him."

I climbed the steps again and helped Mrs. C out of the rocking chair. She held on to my hand as I led her into the house. "Stay here," she said. A few minutes later, she came back with four one-hundred-dollar bills. On top of them was a sticky note with the words:

Stan Kaluza—St. Hyacinth Basilica

"This is more than three hundred," I said.

She waved me away. "It's still less than what's fair for all you did. Now excuse me, I have to go nap. All this thinking has exhausted me. Put the paint and brushes in the shed after you finish." Mrs. C closed the screen door behind me when I left, and then opened it again. "Oh, Emiliano. I forgot to tell you. Don't talk to Abe Gropper about the things we talked about. I know he's your family, but he's . . . well, he's a dishonest man. He installed the gas furnace in this house and a week later it exploded. Alfred had to sue him to get it fixed. A word to the wise."

Then she closed the screen door and disappeared into her house. I put the money and Mrs. C's note in my wallet and then went to finish painting the last window.

The last window.

Just when I thought everything was closed, a small window had opened.

CHAPTER 16
SARA

I was lying down on the floor with my eyes closed, when I felt her presence. Even before she said a word, I knew that La Treinta Y Cuatro was standing over me just watching. I felt her boot on my shoulder, shaking me.

"Let's go. You got a phone call."

I opened my eyes with expectation. Wes Morgan? But one look at La Treinta Y Cuatro's smirk and I knew my hope was unfounded.

"It's your credible fear interview," La Treinta Y Cuatro told me as we walked out of the isolation room—my home for I don't know how many days and nights.

"But . . ."

"Got to follow protocol," La Treinta Y Cuatro said with a smile.

"But I need my lawyer."

La Treinta Y Cuatro stopped. "Want me to take you back?"

I shook my head. Maybe there was a way to get help from whomever was interviewing me. We walked to the other side of the processing center, where the interview rooms were held. One of the hallways had a large window and through it I could see a line of women getting into a light blue van. I stopped. In the middle of the line was Lucila. She was wearing blue jeans and a gray polo shirt, and she was carrying a cheap-looking red backpack. All the women were carrying an identical backpack. La Treinta Y Cuatro had kept on walking but came back to where I was and looked out with me.

"The van is headed to the airport in El Paso. From there they go to Miami and then on to wherever they came from." There was no malice in La Treinta Y Cuatro's voice. She was simply stating the facts.

"Lucila's daughter . . ."

"She's lucky. She gets to stay."

Just then, something made Lucila turn around, and our eyes met. I saw her smile when she saw me. The kind of smile you make when you see someone you thought was dead. I pointed my hand at my heart and then waved. Then La Treinta Y Cuatro pulled me away from the window.

We entered a small room with a chair, a metal table, and a telephone. The door to the room had a window but when I looked around the room, I saw that there were no cameras. La Treinta Y Cuatro pushed me into a corner of the room where we could not be seen by people walking by outside. Without saying a single word, she punched me in my abdomen. I bent over with pain, gasping for air. Then she pulled me up by my hair and said, "Watch what you say! I'll be right here listening."

I shook myself loose from her grip and took two steps so I was now in front of the open door. La Treinta Y Cuatro smiled when she saw what I was doing. She put her arm around my shoulders. "Oh, you okay? Poor baby. Having cramps? Let's go sit down." She sat me down, closed the door, and went to stand in the corner.

I was still gasping when the telephone in front of me rang. I picked up the receiver and noticed that my hand was trembling. *Sara, you are strong. You can do this. You've been through worse before. Think of Mami.*

"Hello."

"Sara Zapata?"

"Yes. This is Sara Zapata."

"You speak English?"

"Yes, I speak."

"You can have an interpreter."

"I speak English. I don't need an interpreter." I heard La Treinta Y Cuatro cough behind me.

"Let's do it in English, then. It will be easier. My name is Norma Galindez. I am the asylum officer assigned to you. You are requesting asylum from the United States, correct?"

"Yes."

"I work for the United States Citizenship and Immigration Services. The USCIS. I'm with the Asylum Division of the USCIS. USCIS is a division of the Department of Homeland Security or DHS."

"DHS," I repeated. Did I make a mistake in choosing to speak to this woman in English? I was already feeling lost. She was speaking fast as if she were reading from a printed card in front of her. And the punch by La Treinta Y Cuatro didn't help my ability to comprehend. The pain in my abdomen was coming from my lower right-hand side, from where people tell you the appendix is located. I saw that the phone had a speaker function. I pressed it and put the receiver on the table. That allowed me to press down with two hands on the area where the pain was pulsating. Norma Galindez continued to speak rapidly. I shut my eyes and forced myself to listen. Behind me I could hear La Treinta Y Cuatro breathing.

"The purpose of this interview is to determine whether the asylum seeker, that is you, has a credible fear of persecution or torture on account of his or her race, religion, nationality, membership in a particular social group, or political opinion if returned to his or her home country. Currently, you are being detained by DHS and are subject to an expedited removal process. United States law allows you to apply for asylum in the United States as a defense against expedited removal. Do you wish to apply for asylum and avail yourself of this defense?"

"Yes."

"When you entered the West Texas Detention Facility, you were given a number. Do you remember that number?"

I had that number memorized. It was in my head someplace but the pain in my side and however many days I spent in isolation prevented me from remembering it.

"Hello?"

"I . . . don't remember right now. I wasn't expecting this call."

"All right. I'm going to read that number to you and you tell me if it's right."

"Okay."

"A-974864778."

I remembered the two sevens and the eight at the end. "Yes. That sounds right."

"Perfect. Let's get started." I heard a click on the other end. "This conversation is for the determination of credible fear for Sara Zapata, A-974864778."

"Excuse me."

"Yes?" Norma Galindez sounded annoyed.

"I am represented by an attorney. His name is Wes Morgan . . . Shouldn't he be here or on the call?"

"You don't need an attorney for this interview."

"But I can . . ." I hit the speaker button and spoke into the receiver. If I could speak softer maybe my stomach or whatever organ La Treinta Y Cuatro hit wouldn't hurt as much. "But I can . . . I have a right to have an attorney with me, even . . . if you don't think I need one."

There was a long silence at the other end. Norma Galindez was not used to detainees talking to her about their rights. When she spoke again, her tone was different, like she had finally noticed I was on the line.

"If you want to set up another call with your attorney, it will be . . ."—I heard pages turning—"two months from now."

"Two months?"

"That is correct. Look. This is simply to determine whether you have a credible fear of persecution. When you go before the immigration judge and make your case for asylum, your attorney will be present."

"But . . ."

"Even if your attorney was with you now, all I would do is

listen to your story. Nothing he said would have a bearing on my decision. It's what you say that counts right now. Is the fear you have credible? Do I believe you when you tell me you are afraid to go back to Guatemala?"

"Mexico. I'm from Ciudad Juárez, Mexico."

"Yes. Mexico."

I realized then that Norma Galindez was just doing her boring job. It was good to know that she was not part of the evil people who were after me and Emiliano. I was just the next file on her desk. A file in an enormous stack. Somehow my file moved into this week's pile instead of next week's or the one for the week after. How that happened, I don't know. There were women back in the pod who had arrived at the detention facility weeks before me and they had not had their interview.

The one thing you quickly learn in detention is that you accept gratefully whatever bit of good fortune comes your way. So I decided to go ahead and talk to Norma Galindez as if talking to her might make a difference. If it was fear she wanted to hear, I could give her that. In a way, I had La Treinta Y Cuatro to thank for bringing that fear to the surface. My voice quivered as I related to Norma Galindez my story of persecution. I started with the threatening e-mail received by *El Sol* and continued step by step until I got to the part where Hinojosa's men destroyed our home with machine-gun bullets minutes after Mami, Emiliano, and I escaped thanks to Ernesto's warning. I didn't tell her about crossing into the United States or being attacked in the desert.

"Is there anything else?"

"Only that . . . my brother, Emiliano, got me across and then he went back to Mexico."

I heard a short laugh behind me. The kind of laugh you make when you don't believe someone.

I heard a click on the other end and then the tapping of keys on a computer. When the clicking and tapping ended, Norma Galindez said, "Okay, Sara. This concludes the credible fear interview."

"But . . . what is your decision? On the credible fear?"

There was a knock on the door. I turned to see Mello motioning for La Treinta Y Cuatro to step out. As soon as she was out and the door was closed, I said to Norma Galindez, speaking as quickly as possible, "Norma, I know that deep down you're a good human being, so I'm going to ask you a favor, one human being to another. One woman to another."

"Excuse me."

"Shh! Listen, please listen. I only have seconds here. My life is in danger in this place. I can't explain. You need to call Wes Morgan, my attorney in Alpine. Tell him *Hinojosa found me*. He'll know."

"What?"

"Wes Morgan. Alpine, Texas."

"I don't . . ."

When the door opened again, I said, "Thank you," and hung up.

I wiped my eyes with the back of my hand. I took a deep breath and tried to think of something joyful. The image of Emiliano's bicycle came to me. I called the bike Rocinante because it was ugly and falling apart like Don Quixote's horse.

I don't know why that image came to mind just then, but I was glad it came a minute before the door to the room opened. There was no way I was going to let La Treinta Y Cuatro see my tears.

But it was not La Treinta Y Cuatro who came into the room, it was Mello. He waited a few minutes for me to compose myself.

"You want to talk for a minute? Have you had time to think about things?"

"How to make isolation cells more humane?" I asked with a grin.

I pushed the chair from the desk and tried to stand, but the pain stopped me. Mello came over and helped me up. "I'm sorry," he said. "Sometimes we do what we have to do even if we don't like it."

When we got to his office, I sat in front of his desk. He went out and came back with a glass of water. I drank it. Mello waited, watching me. The pain in my stomach came in waves. Every thirty seconds, there was a sharp pain.

"Speak to me. The sooner you speak to me, the sooner things get back to normal."

The word *normal* made me smile. Then, "I know what you want." I gasped. "You want the cell phone that belonged to Hinojosa. My brother doesn't have it. He went back to Mexico. I hid it in the desert. I know where it is. I can take you there."

Mello smiled and then went to his desk. He opened a drawer and took out a sheet of paper with a printed image of a business card.

It was my father's. All the information needed to find him was there.

Who did my father give his business card to? A better question would be: Who didn't he give his business card to? Father was so proud of his position at Able Abe, he probably handed out his card to everyone he met.

"Where did you get that?" I asked.

"It doesn't matter." He reached over and pushed the phone on his desk toward me. "Call him and tell him you want to talk to your brother."

I shook my head.

"We know where your father lives. We know your brother is with him. We can get the phone the easy way or the hard way. It's up to you. The easy way is for your brother to give us what we need. Call him and tell him that someone will contact him soon. When they do, he should hand over the phone. It's as simple as that. The hard way is for someone to take the phone away from him. The hard way involves . . . you already know, I'm sure, a lot of people will get hurt, not just your brother and not just you. It's up to you."

I played out in my mind all the hurt that could fall on Emiliano, on me, on my father and his family. And he gave me the time to sit there and think about how we were doomed. Finally, I nodded to Mello and took the phone. I didn't need to look at the sheet of paper that Mello held in front of me. I had my father's number memorized from all the times we called him from Mexico.

"Sara, are you all right?" my father said, surprised to hear from me.

"Yes. But I can't talk to you right now. I need to talk to Emiliano."

"He'll be home at two. In fifteen minutes. I'll give you Nancy's number."

I wrote down Nancy's phone number on a piece of paper that Mello handed me.

"Everything is good. I had my credible fear interview. Things look good. Bye."

Mello came and sat in the chair next to me.

"You're doing the right thing, Sara."

"No," I said. "I'm not doing the right thing. I'm doing the only thing left for me to do. But it is not right."

CHAPTER 17

EMILIANO

Nancy Gropper's white Camry was parked in the driveway when I got home after finishing with Mrs. C. I remembered that it was Saturday and Trevor didn't go to school. Did watching Trevor include Saturday afternoons? I hoped not. I wanted to lock myself in my room and think about the phone call from Yoya's colleague. Now that Yoya was out of the picture, I needed a new plan of action.

If Nancy Gropper was home, she was probably working on her laptop in the kitchen, so I decided to go in the front door, where I had a clear, unobserved descent to the basement. Unfortunately, the front door was locked, and I'd forgotten my key.

The kitchen door was locked as well. I could see Nancy Gropper in her usual spot at the cluttered kitchen table. She was tearing papers and throwing them into a paper bag by her side. There was no way around not knocking and there was no way around not facing Nancy Gropper. I considered tapping on one of the four small basement windows and getting Trevor to come up and open the door for me. But that was ridiculous. What was I afraid of?

I rapped on the kitchen window. Once. Twice. Louder the

third time. Nancy jerked her head, startled, and then frowned when she saw me. Then she got up with monumental effort and headed for the front door.

"Sorry," I said.

"No problem," she said, smiling. I was about to walk past her when she said, "If you have a moment, I would like to talk to you."

My heart immediately sank. Whatever was to come would not be pleasant.

"Sure," I said. Reluctantly, I followed Nancy to the kitchen. She was wearing a flowery dress and instead of her usual purple slippers, she had on pink shoes with a small, flat heel. *I almost died in the desert*, I told myself. A reminder that was supposed to make Nancy Gropper and what she was about to say less annoying. Nancy sat in the chair she had been using. I climbed onto one of the island stools.

"Why don't you sit there"—Nancy pointed at a chair— "that way I don't have to crane my neck looking up at you."

I pulled out the chair and sat. I rested my hands on the table to give her the impression that I was relaxed. Whatever she threw at me, I was ready. What was the worst she could say? *You can't stay here anymore. You have to go back to Mexico.* That wouldn't be so bad, except I had still to accomplish what I had set out to do.

"A couple of things. First, Mrs. Costelo called a few minutes ago to ask if you could come by on Monday. She said she wanted you to paint the tool shed."

"Okay."

"She said she meant to ask you when you were there but forgot."

"All right."

It was a simple message. Why was Nancy speaking and acting as if its delivery was causing her some kind of torture?

"So . . ." Nancy hesitated. She never hesitated. She always charged forward with whatever was in her mind. "Mrs. Costelo appears to like you."

"She likes the work I do." And there was no "appearing" about that.

"And you plan to keep on working for her?"

I nodded. I had finished painting Mrs. C's house, but I didn't want to tell Nancy that. I needed an excuse to be out of the house in case I came up with a new plan for the phone.

"I see." Nancy stuck the plastic straw from the plastic water bottle between her lips and sucked on it. There was a gurgling, slurping sound that would have been funny if it had been made by anyone other than Nancy Gropper. She put the bottle down and fixed her eyes on me. "You realize that Mrs. Costelo has the onset of dementia."

Nancy Gropper liked that word. *Onset.* She had used it before. What did it mean? *Dementia* I understood, but *onset*? In any case, Mrs. C's brain was working fine. I knew that for a fact.

"You don't know what dementia is?"

"I know dementia. I don't know that word, *onset*." *Stay calm. Don't let her get to you.*

"Ahh! I suspected you didn't. It means that the dementia is starting. It is there already, and it is getting worse."

So what? Why was she telling me this? What did that have to do with anything?

"She thinks she remembers things that never happened."

I could see Nancy's discomfort underneath her arrogance. But discomfort about what?

"Did she mention anything about my father?"

Ah! Nancy was worried about her father's reputation. "Only that she knew him."

Nancy's pupils widened. She was definitely scared about me knowing something. Just then, her laptop announced an incoming e-mail. "Anything specific?" Nancy asked, glancing at her laptop's screen.

"Not really."

We looked at each other for a few moments without blinking. Then she pushed the laptop away and said, "Like I said. She's demented and whatever she said should not be believed."

"Okay." I started to rise.

"I said there were three things. I haven't finished with the first."

I sat back down and waited.

Nancy straightened her back. "I don't think it's a good idea for you to work for Mrs. Costelo or for anyone."

"Why?"

I was calm. I asked the way I heard Trevor ask when he was told he couldn't eat strawberry jam.

"Because you don't have the legal right to work in the United States. It is against the law for people to hire you. You are putting the employer at risk."

Nancy's cheeks turned pink, and then red blotches appeared on her neck. I could almost see the migraine inching its way to her head. She shut her mouth tight as if trying to keep the words on her tongue from jumping out. I was about to argue that if Mrs. C was okay with the risk, then what was the problem, but Nancy Gropper could not contain herself.

"And not just your employers; you're putting us all at risk just by being here. I think it's just incredibly irresponsible of you to do that!" She touched the keys on her laptop and then turned the screen toward me. "Read it!"

I kept my eyes calmly and steadily on Nancy's face. There was a thumping in my chest—a sign that anger was not far behind. I had to stay calm. No anger. She was waiting for my anger and I wasn't going to give it to her.

"Okay, then I'll read it for you."

She turned the laptop toward herself and leaned forward. She read slowly as if she were reading to someone who was Trevor's age and not as intelligent.

"Title 8 U.S.C. 1324 parenthesis lowercase a. Offenses. Harboring. Subsection 1324 parenthesis lowercase a, parenthesis 1 parenthesis capital A, parenthesis lowercase i, makes it an offense for any person who knowingly or in reckless disregard of the fact that an alien has come to, entered, or remains in the United States in violation of law, conceals, harbors, or shields from detection, or attempts to conceal, harbor, or shield from detection, such alien in any place." Nancy looked up to make sure I was listening before continuing. "You understand?"

"Yes." *I'm not stupid*, I felt like saying.

"Listen to this: Penalties. The basic statutory term of imprisonment is five years unless the offense was committed for commercial advantage or private financial gain, in which case the maximum term is ten years." Nancy closed the laptop. She grabbed the bottle of water and brought the straw halfway to her mouth before she put it down again. "So, we basically can end up in jail for five years. That's why you can't go around letting people know you're here illegally. That's why you can't work for Mrs. Costelo. She's liable to get ten years, by the way, because she's using you for a commercial advantage. Not to mention the fact that she is also violating the law by hiring you and by not reporting any wages she pays you to the IRS."

"IRS?"

"The Internal Revenue Service. The federal agency that collects taxes. Mrs. Costelo was obligated to file a 1099 with the IRS. You think she did that?"

I was silent. Nancy's outburst had reached its peak. There was nowhere for her anger to go except to maybe kick me out of the house. With Mrs. C's money, I had enough money for a hotel someplace for a little while. But I was glad I had contained my own anger. I did not explode. Nancy Gropper's true feelings about me had come out and there was something peaceful and satisfying about that.

I spoke slowly and calmly: "You don't want me here. I don't want to be here. What do you want me to do?"

"It is not that I don't *want* you here," Nancy protested. "Having you here is a risk. And you being here is wrong. It violates the law. This is a sovereign nation of laws."

I wanted to tell her that Bob was also an illegal alien, a violator of the laws, when she married him. Instead, I said, "But it is not just that I violate the law. I don't think you like me being here. Even if I were legal, you wouldn't want me here. It's okay to admit it. I don't want to be here either."

Nancy sighed. "No, you are wrong." She tugged her braid. "I'm sorry if that's the impression you got. The truth is I like you. I know I haven't shown it and I'm sorry about that. Trevor adores you. How can I not like you?" She did her best to smile. "I'm afraid and when I'm afraid I turn into a real grump. I don't know. I guess I try to protect myself from feeling vulnerable." Nancy's eyes filled with water and I almost reached out to touch her arm.

"Nancy, I . . ."

"Let me finish. I'm afraid for Trevor, for me, for Bob, for my father, for the business we have worked so hard to build. Bob told me about your sister and what happened in Juárez. About the people who tried to kill her in Juárez and even afterward, when you crossed into the United States. Can you tell me one hundred percent that I should not worry that those people won't come looking for her here? They don't know she's in a detention facility. They probably think she's with her father. And how hard will it be to find out where he lives? Don't you think I have cause to be afraid? To not want you here because of the risk you bring?"

Hinojosa's cell phone was under her washing machine. There was no way I could tell Nancy that her fears were unfounded. I looked into her eyes to detect dishonesty, but all I saw was a woman who was very scared. She was right. I was putting Trevor and all of them at risk just by being there. I had to move out of that house as soon as possible. I opened my hands and said, "What can I do?"

"I'm just asking you to minimize the risks."

"I need to work. I don't think I can be here all day . . . without working."

There was a knowing smile on Nancy's face. "Like father like son."

"Yeah." It came to me just then that Bob's need to work, to get ahead in the world, was probably the reason Nancy had married him or maybe even fallen in love with him. "I'll talk to Mrs. C on Monday. I'll tell her I can't paint her shed."

"Thank you."

"You said there were two things. Two things you wanted to talk to me about."

"Your father called. He said your sister wanted to talk to you. Bob told her you'd be here at two and gave her my cell phone number."

I turned to read the digital clock in the microwave. It read 1:57. "In three minutes? Really?" My heart started to race. Sara was going to call me, just like Yoya had predicted. Nancy Gropper entered a password and handed her cell phone to me.

"Go. Go downstairs and talk to your sister."

I never thought I would feel the urge to give Nancy Gropper a hug, but I did just then.

I stood quickly and flew down the stairs to the basement and past Trevor absorbed in reading Lego instructions. The phone began to ring just as I reached my room. I let it ring a couple of times while I tried to calm myself. *Mello is probably listening*, I thought. *Be careful with what you say*, I told myself.

"Sara?"

"Emiliano."

Her voice was cold, distant. It didn't have Sara's warmth.

"What is it? Are you okay? You sound . . . ill."

"Nothing. I am all right. You don't have to worry about me."

"How's your asylum petition going?"

Come on, Emiliano, you can do better than that.

"Good. It's proceeding. I only have a minute, so listen carefully, okay?"

"Yes."

"Do you still have Hinojosa's phone?"

"Yes . . . but I haven't done anything with it. I haven't even taken it out of that metallic bag." Why was Sara asking about Hinojosa's phone? She had to be in danger. She was being forced to call me. "I don't have it with me. I have it hidden."

"Someone is going to contact you soon and ask you for the phone. When they do, I want you to give it back to them."

"Who's going to contact me? How . . . ?" *How do they know where I am?* is what I was going to ask but didn't. It didn't matter how, they knew.

"Someone, you'll know who it is when they ask you for it. The only thing that matters is that you give it to them. Do you understand?"

I understood, all right, but I thought it would be good to pretend I didn't. "I don't understand; who is asking you to do this? Did Hinojosa's people get to you?"

"That's not important. You need to give the phone to the person who asks for it. It's over. You have no choice. It's like when you went to the Tarahumara mountains with Brother Patricio. You had to do what Brother Patricio told you to do. You had to walk where he told you to walk, you had to step where he told you to step. You had to follow his instructions exactly, otherwise you would die. It's the same now. The consequences are exactly the same if you don't do what I am telling you."

"But . . ."

"Just do what I am asking you to do. The phone was given to me. I decided to bring it to the U.S.! It's my decision what to do with it!"

I had never heard Sara speak to me that way. All I could think of was that she was telling me in her own way that she was not free to talk.

"Okay," I said. "Before you go, there's a reporter from El Paso who called Father. He wants to interview you."

"What? Please, Emiliano. I beg you. I have to go now. Do what I'm asking you. Do it for Linda."

I held Nancy's phone against my ear for a few minutes, then I walked out of my room. I sat next to Trevor, who was assembling pieces of Legos into separate piles. I sat there because it was the nearest chair and I was having trouble standing and because, right then, I needed to be next to someone like Trevor. I would think and go over Sara's words all night long and for days after that if needed, but right then I needed to be close to a child, someone still in touch with goodness.

"Liano, look!" Trevor was holding up a huge box. "It's the Death Star. Mommy got it for me this morning when we went to the mall." On the box, there was the picture of a giant, gray sphere with hundreds of separate inner compartments. It reminded me of a beehive for robotic bees. There were green rays shooting out of one of the sphere's sides. The recommended child's age was fourteen, which meant nothing to Trevor. "But you still owe me fifty dollars."

I took the box from Trevor's hands. It was empty. Trevor had already taken out what looked like hundreds of small plastic bags and laid them on the floor in an order that only Trevor understood. There was something about the Death Star, the Empire's maximum weapon, that reminded me of the evil powers that wanted Sara and me destroyed. There was no corner of the universe beyond the Death Star's deadly reach.

"The Death Star is bad. It can destroy planets. Why do you want to build something like that?"

Trevor thought for a moment, then: "Oh, Liano. It doesn't have to be bad. It can be whatever we want. We can make it good. We can make it a Life Star. From now on we'll call it 'Life Star.'"

We can make it a Life Star, I repeated to myself, shaking my head.

If only the real world worked that way.

CHAPTER 18

EMILIANO

Trevor took the cell phone upstairs to his mother and asked for permission to go to the park with me. The park was my idea. I had to get out of the house and think about Sara's words. If I didn't move, I would explode. Sara sounded like she was in pain and her tone and words were not her own. Someone was forcing her to say what she did. But what was the real message that she wanted to convey to me?

When we got to the park, I said to Trevor, "I need to spend some time alone now. I have to think very hard about something. I'm going to go sit on that bench. Look, you see that little girl on the slide. She's playing all by herself. Why don't you introduce yourself and make friends with her?"

Trevor nodded. Then, looking in the direction of the girl on the slide, "What if she doesn't want to talk to me?"

"Just say, 'Hello, my name is Trevor and I'm building a Life Star.' She'll ask you what that is. You explain it nice and slow, and then if she wants to talk to you, she will ask you something else and so on and so forth."

"I don't want to."

"I'll buy you an Icee. A blue one. The kind your mother doesn't want you to have."

Trevor's eyes widened for a second. Then he surprised me by turning slowly around and walking to the bottom of the slide, where he waited for the little girl. I couldn't hear what he said or what she said back to him, but when they walked to the swings together, he turned and gave me a look that seemed to say *It worked.*

I sat on a green wooden bench replaying the conversation with Sara. I thought that whatever it was she really wanted to tell me was hidden in her reference to my trip to the Tarahumara mountains with Brother Patricio. Her actual words in the telephone conversation did not match what happened in the trip. I repeated her words in my mind.

It's like when you went to the Tarahumara mountains with Brother Patricio. You had to do what Brother Patricio told you to do. You had to walk where he told you to walk, step where he told you step. You had to follow his instructions exactly, otherwise you would die.

But Sara knew that during that trip, Brother Patricio did not give me any instructions. He never once told me where to walk or where to step or what to do with my life. He let the mountains teach me whatever lessons I needed to learn.

The trip happened two years after Mami received Bob's petition for a voluntary divorce and two weeks after I was caught stealing an expensive camera. It was all Mami's idea, not the stealing of the camera, the trip. Mami was desperate. She must have looked for signs of repentance in my heart and not seen a single drop. What she saw in there was a stinking mixture of bile, anger, and hatred. Hatred for school, for church, for our life of poverty, and, most of all, for my father.

It was a four-day trip, but two of those days were spent on buses and trains getting there and getting back. I expected constant preaching from Brother Patricio but there was none. There wasn't much of any talking, in fact. All we did was live with the Rarámuri for two days and two nights. We slept in a dirt-floored room and ate tortillas and beans. We climbed in and out of their copper-filled canyons and watched the Rarámuri run barefoot on the dusty mountain trails. There was no single moment when I decided to abandon the path of delinquency I'd been on. Brother Patricio told me that when we got back to Juárez, he was going to start a group of desert explorers who would hike and camp out in the Chihuahua desert on weekends and he wanted me to help him. What was Sara trying to tell me? I was clueless. All I knew was that holding on to the phone could cost Sara's life and that seemed like a very high price to pay.

Then I was plagued with doubts about whether I had made things worse for Sara by making up that stuff about the reporter from El Paso. I thought that if whoever was listening knew that she was being sought for an interview, they would not want to call attention to themselves by harming her, but what if my remarks had the opposite effect? How does one figure out the right things to say and do? I was lost.

On the way back from the store where I bought Trevor the promised Icee, I thought that maybe it wouldn't be so bad living here. If one day I stopped feeling that someone was going to grab me and send me back to Mexico, this place wouldn't be so bad. The grass in the front yards was a tender green and there were trees with small red buds coming out. Apple trees maybe? The oaks, like the one in Mrs. C's backyard, must be the last to bloom. All the yards could use a good raking to get rid of the dead grass and leaves left over from fall. I could make a fortune here. I could train Trevor to help me. The two of us could work together in the afternoons after I finished painting. Why not? When I was Trevor's age, Paco and I would go to the garbage dumps, looking for aluminum. If I turned Hinojosa's phone over to whoever contacted me, I could stay here, make some money, be a big brother to Trevor. And if I returned the phone, Sara would be safe. Returning the phone was the safe path. Maybe it was the only option. The one that would keep Sara and me and others safe.

"Liano?"

I stopped. There were still traces of blue on Trevor's lips and we were only a block away from the house. "Let's walk around the block again so that your blue lips turn normal before your mother sees you. Why doesn't your mother let you have Icees? They're not made with peanuts."

Trevor shrugged. "Maybe because of the chemicals used to make the colors." He stuck out his blue tongue. "She thinks they're bad."

I felt guilty about the influence I was having on Trevor. He wasn't so sure about all of his mother's rules anymore. Either that or more willing to disobey some of them. Well, honestly, I didn't feel all that guilty. If Trevor became more of a kid and less a little adult because of me, was that so terrible? Not to mention it was kind of nice to irritate Nancy.

"Your mother is right. Your tongue looks sick. It might fall off. Then you wouldn't be able to talk." I tried speaking without moving my tongue. "Eoo uuu aaa eeek."

Trevor screeched and tried to do the same. "Aaa nnnn eeeee!"

"Okay, okay." I looked around. The front yards were all empty. It was a gray Saturday afternoon, but the sun was out there somewhere. Trevor had a gray sweater that Nancy made him wear but he didn't really need. A car pulled into a driveway ahead of us and a woman and a man came out and took department store bags from the back seat.

"Liano?" Trevor said, tugging my arm.

"Yes?"

"Do you like the clothes that Mommy got you?"

"What clothes?"

"Mommy put the box in your room. It came this morning in a big, brown truck and Mommy put it next to your bed in your room."

"I didn't see it." All of me had been lost in the call from Sara.

"I was with Mommy when she ordered them online. I gave her some ideas."

"Why? Clothes for what?" When the few clothes I had got were dirty, I walked three steps from my bed to the washer and cleaned them. The washer reminded me of the dryer and the dryer of the cell phone beneath it. Every time I thought of the cell phone, I felt a burning sensation in my chest. I burped.

Trevor tried to burp as well. The art of burping at will was one of the things we had been practicing during our time together. "Do it again. This time real loud," Trevor pleaded.

"No. It will scare the people inside the house. They'll think a lion was loose on the streets."

"Maybe they'll think it was Chewbacca." Trevor found his own cleverness hilarious. I waited for him to stop laughing, grabbed the edge of his sweater, and tried to rub out the remaining traces of blue on his lips. "Maybe they'll think it's Chewbacca and Yoda walking outside," I said, patting his head.

"I don't look like Yoda!"

I pulled both his ears. "Now you do."

"Ouch!"

I stopped in the middle of a driveway. Trevor was pulling his own ears and half closing his eyes like a would-be Yoda. A man watched us through the front window of the house. He did not look like someone who would hire us.

"You have too much hair to be Yoda," I said.

"Popsy could be Yoda. He's bald."

But the picture of Able Abe on the company's van had hair. False advertising. "Is Popsy wise like Yoda?"

"Mmm. Popsy yells at Mommy and Daddy sometimes. Yoda never yells at anyone."

One good thing about Trevor was that he could make me think about things I never thought about before. Like just then. Wise people don't need to yell at other people. Trevor could also make me laugh. He had a funny side that he never showed his parents. Right now, his humor was keeping me from exploding with worry.

"What kind of clothes?" I asked quickly, pushing a painful thought out of the way.

"Black sneakers. I picked those. Mommy thinks your boots are smelly."

I couldn't totally disagree with "Mommy." But the smell was only noticeable when I took them off, wasn't it? Besides, those boots were special. Nancy Gropper was going to have to put up with their smell.

Trevor continued. "Pants and shirts, underwear, socks. I didn't pick those. You can wear the black sneakers tomorrow. They look like regular shoes."

"Tomorrow? What's tomorrow?"

"Tomorrow is Sunday. First we go to church and then we go to Popsy's."

Abe Gropper. What did Mrs. C call him? A jerk? "I'm not going to Popsy's tomorrow. I have some things I need to do."

How would I be contacted about Hinojosa's phone? I looked around to see if there were any unusual-looking cars on the street. They could have been watching me now. How did they know where I was?

"Liano." Trevor was tugging at my sleeve.

"Sorry, what were you saying?"

"Church is boring but Popsy has a heated pool. Mommy bought you swimming trunks. They're blue with little white sharks. I picked them."

Nancy was upstairs and so Trevor's blue lips went unde-tected. I told Trevor to get started on the Life Star, while I looked at the wardrobe Nancy bought for me. I looked around the room and saw the box on the rowing machine's seat. How could I have not seen it before? I used a screwdriver from the tool bench to cut the tape and took out a pair of khaki pants.

They were the right length. The label on the back of the pants, twenty-four, was right. I dug through the box until I got to the black sneakers on the bottom. I took off the boots and smelled them. They weren't *that* bad. I tried the right-foot sneaker. It was a perfect fit. I put on the other one, tied the laces, and walked around the room. How did dense Nancy get all the measurements correct? I looked down at my feet. The sneakers could pass for dress shoes. A light blue long-sleeve shirt, a blue tie with red stripes, and the khaki pants were the remaining parts of the Sunday outfit. Nancy Gropper had gone out and bought me cool clothes. She was dressing me up so I wouldn't be an embarrassment to her at church and with Popsy, but it was still a nice move on her part.

"Emiliano! Come here! I want to show you something extremely awesome."

I sat on the edge of the bed and rested my head on the palm of my hand. What was good about this place? Trevor, definitely. Nancy had possibilities if I could become legal. And Bob Gropper? He was not the man I grew up with, but he was not totally different either. He was like me in many ways. Who is perfect? No one. Not me.

"Emiliano! Are you coming? You said you'd help me build the Life Star."

Death Star or Life Star.

It was up to me to decide.

CHAPTER 19

SARA

The SHU is what the guards call the isolation cell where they've been keeping me. The Special Housing Unit. The only thing special about the cell were the windows near the ceiling, through which I could see the stars sometimes. How many days had I been in that cell before I was taken out for the credible fear interview and my phone call to Emiliano? I didn't know. At the SHU you very quickly begin to lose your hold on reality. At first, I could keep track of time by the type of meals that were brought to me. Oatmeal meant another morning had arrived. But after a while, time became a blur. I didn't know whether I had crossed into the United States ten days ago or the year before. Or maybe it was just a dream.

Was talking to Emiliano also a dream? What was it that he said about the reporter? Every time I thought of that, I laughed. My little brother knew somehow that someone was with me. Either that or he was telling the truth and a reporter was on his way to save me!

I had to repeat to myself what I told him all night long just to make sure that I had given him the right coded message. I had faith that Emiliano would remember what Brother Patricio told him during their Tarahumara trip.

Hope, little brother, hope. Hope is what you got from that trip. Hope is doing the right thing regardless of the outcome. Life's not worth living otherwise. But also, find the right people to help you with your mission.

But did I put Emiliano's life at risk by giving him that message?

I remembered again what I told Juana, my editor at *El Sol*, that I thought the United States system of justice, while not perfect, was the best there was in the world. "Here in Mexico," I remembered telling her, "they can put you in jail and you can't do anything about it. In the United States, there are laws to protect the innocent and the laws are followed."

Could I have been so wrong about this country? I had to believe there were people in this country who would help Emiliano. There must be people who would protect his life and help him save the lives of the women who were in captivity. I was counting on Emiliano to be resourceful enough to find those people.

And as for me? I knew that soon Wes Morgan would break through the barriers that were keeping him away from me. Norma Galindez would call him. I could tell in her voice that there was goodness in her. And then, there was Mario.

Mario brought me my breakfast, lunch, or dinner, depending on his shift. Every time he came, I tried to engage him in conversation. At first, he would answer my questions with a yes or a no, but the evening after my phone calls, he stood by the door and spoke to me like he used to when I did my garbage rounds. I was sitting on the edge of my platform (I refused to call it a bed) with the tray of food on my lap.

"I don't know why you didn't get a desk and a chair," he said. "Every other security room has one."

"Security room?"

"That's what we guards call these rooms."

"Oh. Mario, do you know how long I'll be in this security room?" I asked him.

"Oh, no. They don't tell me that kind of stuff." He glanced at the camera in the corner. "I shouldn't even be talking to you."

"Do people look at what I'm doing?" I looked up at the camera and then at the stainless-steel combination toilet and sink.

"We check up on you but . . . we respect your privacy."

"Privacy. I have lots of that."

"I'm sorry," he said. There was sadness in his eyes. He wanted to say more but he stopped himself. I decided to take a chance and ask him for a favor.

"Mario. It's not right that I am locked up in here. You know that. It's not true that I am here for my own safety."

He looked at his feet, embarrassed. He shook his head apologetically and started to open the door.

"Please!" I pleaded. "Just give me one minute."

He stopped, his back to me.

"Check to see if there are any messages for me. There must be one from my lawyer. His name is Wes Morgan. He calls every other day. He must have tried to see me a few times by now. Call him back and tell him I'm being held here in . . . this security room. You don't have to say who you are when you call him."

Mario did not respond. He kept his back to me while I spoke and then walked out, locking the door behind him. For a moment all hope left me. Then I thought about how he had quietly listened to what I said. I knew that he would help me if he could. Then, about ten minutes later, Mario returned. I was still sitting on the platform, the tray of untouched food next to me. Mario picked up the tray, and with his back blocking the camera, he put a note into my hand and closed my fingers around it.

"Flush it," he whispered to me, and then walked out of the room.

I lay on the platform and after a few minutes I turned on my side and opened the piece of paper that Mario had given me. I read it close to my chest, protecting the note from the camera.

Message from Sandy Morgan.
Dad was killed yesterday. We think someone
was trying to rob his gun collection when Daddy walked in.
I'll come see you as soon as I can. It won't be this week.
It hurts so much.

I rolled the piece of paper into a tiny ball. I sat on the toilet, dropped the paper between my legs, and then I lowered my head and cried in silence. I cried for Sandy's hurt. I cried for Wes Morgan, who took my case and always refused to talk about a fee. *You can pay me when you're a rich journalist,* he said to me. I pictured him driving all the way to El Paso to file a complaint when they told him he couldn't see me. He believed I was worth fighting for. I'm sure he had been asking for me the past few days and was threatening Mello with all kinds of lawsuits if he did not produce me. I cried because I no longer had anyone to defend me.

But most of all I cried because I had as good as killed Wes Morgan. I knew in my heart that he had been killed by the people who wanted the phone. The business card that Mello showed me must have been the one that Father gave Wes Morgan.

Emiliano, please, please, please find a way to open the phone and put these evil men in prison. And dear Lord, let it be a prison just like this one and make it forever.

CHAPTER 20

EMILIANO

"Emiliano, wake up!"

I felt a gentle shaking of the shoulder and for a moment I expected to see the face of Brother Patricio urging me to get ready for the long day's hike that awaited us. But the familiar smell of cologne quickly brought me back to reality.

"What time is it?"

"It's nine, but you need to take a shower and get dressed. We like to get to church by ten forty-five."

I sat up, rubbed my eyes. I couldn't remember a time when I had slept past 7:00 a.m. "I'm not going to church," I said, pulling the white quilt up to my neck. I had won the Sunday church battle a long time ago against more powerful adversaries. Bob was not going to succeed where Mami and Sara had failed.

There was a clanking sound. I half opened my eyes and saw Bob pull a stool from beside the rowing machine and place it in front of my bed. Bob cleared his throat.

I propped the pillow behind my back and placed my phone under the quilt. Now all I had to do was wait. Something was in Bob's mind besides church, that much I could see, even in my foggy state.

Bob bent to look in the box next to the bed. He took out the long-sleeve shirt and examined it. "Nancy told me she had gotten you a few things. They fit okay?"

"She could have asked what I liked."

I regretted the resentment in my voice, but I was not in a good mood. I had stayed up most of the night worried about Sara and trying to decide what I would do with Hinojosa's phone when I was contacted.

Bob placed the shirt on the handlebar of the stationary bike. I noticed the blue tie with red stripes already there. "For church," Bob said.

Bob crossed his legs and placed his two hands on his lap. "Nancy told me about the talk you two had yesterday."

Were we really going to have that kind of conversation? Could it wait until I had two cups of coffee? Or better yet, could it wait forever? Maybe it was better to plunge ahead and get it over with. "She doesn't want me here. She's afraid she's violating the law, harboring an illegal alien."

"She's afraid. It's normal. It's nothing against you. The whole thing that happened to Sara and . . . to you . . . with men trying to kill you. It's scary if you're a mother. When I got the call from your mother to help, I went in spite of Nancy's fears. Abe's too. It was hard for them. But, bottom line, here you are. And Sara could be here too if she hadn't turned herself in."

"She had no choice. Either that or a man died."

"I understand. I understand all that. I'm just trying to let you see that it is not unreasonable for Nancy to be nervous. About you being here and working with people who know us.

Some of those people, like Mrs. Costelo, could turn you in to immigration. She doesn't like Abe."

"Mrs. C is not going to turn me in. *She* likes me."

"If you are trying to tell me that Nancy doesn't like you, you're wrong. Would she trust you with Trevor if she didn't? She sees how much he's grown attached to you in such a short time. Don't you think she's grateful for that? These clothes she bought you . . ."

"To look good in church and at Popsy's."

"Man, Emiliano." Bob shook his head. There was sadness and disbelief in his voice. "Have you really changed that much? What's happened to you? You're a good person. Were." He stood and then sat down again. "We're trying our best here. Nancy . . . she's reserved. Yes, she's afraid. But like I said, you're here. You don't know how much it took for me to get you here . . . and we don't ask much from you. I need you to help me. Help me out here."

"Help you?"

"Come to church and to Abe's house with us. If you don't come it will be harder on me. And . . . on Trevor. He won't understand."

"Why hard on you?"

"Abe wants to meet you. I promised him I'd bring you. He called this morning from Washington, DC. He had an important meeting with one of the heads of the Labor Department. Abe's the head of a committee that advises the government on safety regulations for heating and refrigeration workers. Anyway, he called a little while ago to make sure you were coming over to his house for Sunday lunch."

"To check me over?"

"He wants to get to know you. Can you blame him? You're staying in the house with his daughter and his only grandson."

"Why isn't your word enough?"

"Emiliano, come on."

"And what does it matter who I am or what kind of person I am? I'm illegal. I could be a saint and it wouldn't make a difference."

"You have to understand their thinking. Nancy and Abe are very law abiding. They . . . it's a different mentality. Breaking the law is a big deal for them. It's like a sin. Only there are no venial sins or mortal sins, no small sins or greater sins. Breaking any law is all the same—a sin."

"That's stupid. Going faster than the speed limit is the same as killing someone?"

"To you and to me maybe that sounds stupid. The consequences of breaking different laws are different, sure. They know that. But they have this view of who they are. They see themselves as the kind of people who never break the law. Not ever. So it is hard to be associated with people who do. Do you understand?"

"Yes, I understand."

"I'm only a few months from my citizenship papers coming through. It should have happened by now, but it looks like everything's backed up when it comes to immigration. And as soon as I have a little time, I'll talk to an immigration lawyer; maybe there's something we can do to make you legal even now. It's just been so busy at work. You won't believe it. But I think we won that bid I was telling you about. From Safeway.

That's big. Very big. But it will mean a lot of work too. More people . . ." Bob stopped when he saw me raise the palm of my hand.

"Okay, okay. Let me take a shower and get dressed. We don't want to be late for church."

"Thank you. Thank you, son."

I watched Bob weave his way through the exercise machines and out of the room. I waited until the door was closed and then kicked the quilt from my legs. I don't know what came over me when I was with my father. Away from him, there were moments when I felt a little of what I used to feel before he left us. But in person, there was something in me that wanted to oppose him, push him away, argue with him.

St. Paul's Episcopal Church looked like a small castle. Trevor, sitting next to me, stuck the instructions to the Life Star inside his coat pocket as we pulled into the parking lot. Trevor was wearing gray pants and a red bow tie. He smelled like Bob. I unbuttoned the top of my shirt so I could breathe. Nancy got all of my measurements right except the neck size. With the tie on, I felt as if I were inside a permanent choke hold.

"Is Popsy coming?" Trevor asked.

Nancy turned around to answer. "Popsy is flying in from Washington, DC, this morning, so he's going straight home from the airport. He'll have lunch ready for us at the house after church." Then, looking at me: "My father is usually an usher at this service. He had to fly to Washington for a meeting with the U.S. Department of Labor."

Nancy Gropper waited for me to look impressed. That

must have been the fourth time that morning that either Nancy or Bob mentioned Popsy's important meeting in Washington. I looked out the window instead. After all that hurrying, we were early. There were only a handful of cars in the lot. When I went to church with Mami and Sara, a long, long time ago, we usually got there just as the music started. There were rules on how late we could be for Sunday Mass to count. Sara claimed you had to get there before the gospel reading. I thought if you got there before Communion, you'd be safe. But all that was before I stopped believing in God. Although, out there in the desert when I was dying . . . I prayed to someone.

Bob and Nancy walked in front holding hands. It was the first time I'd seen them hold hands. Bob had a gray suit with a pink tie. Nancy wore a white, flowing dress that made her look young and full of life. She had a necklace of black pearls, and two gold bands around her wrist. Two elderly men with white pants, blue blazers, and red ties gave each of us a booklet the thickness of a supersize comic book. Nancy led us single file to the second pew from the right and waited for me to enter first. Trevor sat next to me.

Bob was kneeling. His hands clasped each other fervently and his eyes were tightly shut. I watched his lips move. Bob seemed to be honestly praying and not just putting on a show. Was he asking God to forgive him for abandoning his Mexican family?

The pews filled with men in jackets and suits, and women with hats that looked elaborate and expensive. I kept thinking that any moment, one of those men was going to tap me on the shoulder and say: "Give me Hinojosa's phone." But how could they contact me in church? Maybe it was good to be inaccessible to anyone, first here and then with Popsy. I needed all the time I could get to think, to decide.

There was a sweet smell that came from perfume or from the dozens of flowers in the altar, I couldn't tell. Then there was a single blast from an organ behind them and joyful music filled the space inside the church with a thickness that could almost be touched. Sound came from the front and from the back of the church but also from the ceiling. It enveloped all of us. For a few minutes, after the service started, I imagined I was in a theater. Dozens of white-robed choir members surrounded the altar, holding thin, black books in front of them and singing with abandon, as if they wished to be heard way up in heaven. Then came a long parade led by a boy not much older than Trevor holding a tall brass cross. The boy's skin was so pale and thin, I could see the veins of his temples. Behind him were acolytes and a dozen men and women dressed like priests.

After a while, the drama became more subdued. People responded to one of the priests from words written in the booklet that was handed to us. There were long readings from various parts of the Bible, and all I could think of was that time was ticking, ticking never to come back and unless I did something with the phone, Sara could get killed. Trevor, next to me, had also lost interest and was reading the instructions for the Life Star. My mind had gone on to imagine by who and how I would be asked to return the phone when we pulled into the driveway of Abe Gropper's house.

"Let Popsy see you with your coat and tie on."

Nancy was talking to Trevor and not to me. Trevor had

unclipped his bow tie and was now taking off his jacket. I followed his lead and loosened the knot of my tie—the same knot Bob had tied for me. I breathed for the first time that morning. Trevor rang the bell by the door and the sound woke me up. In front of me stood an enormous house, the biggest one I had seen in Aurora. We were standing in front of tall oak doors under a porch held up by white pillars. There were four large windows on the front of the house and behind us a circular driveway with a fountain in the middle. At the end of the front yard, there was a brick wall that separated Abe Gropper's property from the street on one side and from a golf course on the other. Above us, hanging from the roof of the porch, was a brass chandelier not unlike the ones I had just seen at the church.

"Buenos días!" I was startled by the sound of Spanish words. A woman not much older than Nancy with skin the same color as mine was holding the door open. She gave Trevor a quick hug before he ran inside. The woman had a black dress with a white apron and her mostly white hair pulled back in a bun.

"Hello, María," Nancy said, walking into the house as if she owned it. "Popsy make it back from the airport?"

"Yes, he's in the back. He got in around ten thirty."

"Hola, María!" It was Bob, speaking Spanish for once. "Te presento a mi hijo, Emiliano."

"Emiliano! Mucho gusto!"

"Igualmente," I said, taking the hand she offered. María held my hand firmly and for longer than customary, as if to let me know that there was kinship between us.

"Pasen, pasen. El Señor Gropper está en el patio."

"Okay, no more Spanish, you two," Bob said, returning to his old self.

María gave him a look that seemed to say: *You can fool everyone else but not me.* Then she leaned closer to me and whispered, "Ven a verme en la cocina si te cansas de hablar Inglés."

If I had had my way, I would have followed María into the kitchen right then. Instead, Bob took my arm and led me through a long hallway lined with large and small antique clocks. Some were on top of dark-looking tables, some stood on the floor, and some hung on the walls. The sound of different kinds of ticking filled the air.

"Abe collects them," Bob explained. "Look at this one." We stopped in front of a wooden clock with two miniature woodsmen sawing a woman on a table in half. Each movement of the saw equal to one second. The woman had her arms straight up and her mouth open in a big O. I wanted to say something to the effect that I knew what the woman was going through, but my brain was working slower than usual, and I couldn't put the thought into words, much less words in English. "Ten thousand dollars," Bob said. "Abe bought it last year on a trip to Austria." Then, as if remembering something, "When you talk to Abe, call him Mr. Gropper unless he tells you to call him Abe."

We kept on walking toward the glass doors at the end of the hall. Nancy was out on the patio pouring herself what looked like tomato juice from a very skinny glass pitcher. The back of Abe's bald head stuck out from a plush chair next to the table with the drinks. I could see an aquamarine pool down the patio steps. Bob ran his hand over his hair and took a deep breath before turning the knob to the door. He seemed nervous. But about what?

"Don't worry, his bark is worse than his bite," Bob said.

"I'm not the one who's worried."

Bob walked to Abe's front and motioned for me. "Abe, I want to introduce you to Emiliano."

I had imagined Abe Gropper as a big, imposing man, but the man I saw sitting on the patio chair was short and chubby, with a face that was a wrinkled, slightly more masculine version of Nancy's. He reminded me of the little man in the Monopoly game. There was a white pillow under him that made him seem taller than he was.

"Emiliano," Abe said, pronouncing my name correctly. He floated a hand out to me like he wanted me to kiss it. I gave the fingertips a small, awkward squeeze. "My apologies for not getting up. Sciatica." Abe grimaced.

Nancy put her glass down and grabbed a gray cushion from one of the other chairs. "Put this behind you. You have to keep your back very straight."

Abe waved her away. "I'm fine. Where's my grandson?"

"He must have gone straight to the playroom. I'll go get him." Bob seemed only too happy to go back into the house.

Nancy was about to sit down when Abe said, "Why don't you go inside and let me and Emiliano have a chat so we can get to know one another?"

I waited until Nancy had left and then sat on the edge of a chair and prepared myself for an unpleasant experience.

We were sitting under a red umbrella that cast its shade on Abe. It was the first truly hot day since I had arrived in Aurora, but Abe was wearing a pink sweater that looked expensive. Below the hem of his white pants, I saw the super-tight, almost transparent socks that old men liked to wear. The light brown leather loafers seemed like the only comfortable piece of clothing on his body.

"Pour yourself a Bloody Mary." Abe pointed with his chin at the skinny pitcher.

"I don't drink alcohol," I said.

"No? Why not?"

I had not thought of the Jipari oath in a very long time, but I remembered it just then.

I will abstain from all intoxicants. I will be honest with myself and others. I will use the knowledge and the strength the desert gives me for the benefit of others.

Was I still a Jipari, then? It must be as Brother Patricio always said—once the Jipari oath is in your blood, it stays there. Then it came to me: Who are the others for whose benefit I'm supposed to use the knowledge and strength the desert gave me? Did those "others" include the Groppers, including Popsy?

I was aware that Abe was examining my silence, as if determining whether my failure to respond was a hostile act. "I don't like it," I finally said. I smiled to let him know that I was not made of the same weak ilk as his son-in-law.

Abe grinned sarcastically. "I never met a Mexican that didn't like to drink."

"There's a few of us," I joked, trying to defuse the hostility

I sensed, both in me and in the old man. There was no need to antagonize Able Abe more than was necessary.

"It's heated," Abe said when he saw me turn my head in the direction of the pool. "I keep it going year-round but mostly I use the hot tub."

It was a stunning pool with a waterfall flowing out of a miniature mountain on the deep end. Abe's backyard reminded me of Perla Rubi's house.

"Right over there I'm going to build a combination tennis and basketball court. Only I'm going to have it built so it becomes a skating rink in the winter. Maybe that'll get Trevor interested in sports."

How many Mexicans did it take to keep the pool and the enormous backyard as pristine as it was? Another memory came to me just then: the two flashes of light I saw just before losing consciousness in the desert. When you almost die, it is very hard for a pool to impress you.

"One day all of this will belong to Nancy and Bob and Trevor." Abe paused to make sure the meaning of his words fully registered. "They could move in now. The house is too big for one person. Two if you count María."

"Why don't they?"

"Nancy wants to pretend she is independent." Abe reached for the glass of Bloody Mary and drank what was in there. He filled his glass from the pitcher. There was a plate with stalks of celery next to the pitcher. Abe stirred the Bloody Mary with a celery stalk. "It's probably better. We're both stubborn, ornery, and moody."

I did not know what *ornery* meant, but it sounded like Nancy.

"Your father has done well for himself, don't you think?"

I wasn't sure what Abe Gropper meant by "done well." As in, not bad for a Mexican? As in, by marrying Nancy Gropper?

"What do you mean?"

Abe shot me a look that said something like *Isn't it obvious?* Then he gasped and leaned forward, tucking the pillow farther down his back. "I mean that I gave him a job replacing filters and now he's practically running the place. When I retire, the business will be his. His and Nancy's." Abe let that sink in. Then, "I got to hand it to him. I didn't think he had it in him. I thought he was just another illegal who will work for three months max before he gets homesick and leaves. He showed me, all right."

"And then he married your daughter."

Abe laughed and reached for his back. "Ouch! When it hurts to laugh, then you know you're getting too old." He shook his head. "'And then he married your daughter.' You got some moxie, don't you?"

"Moxie?"

"Look it up. It's a good English word."

Abe was staring at me with unblinking eyes. I looked away. In the staring contests that Sara and I used to have, Sara was always the first one to blink. But there was something menacing in the way Abe stared at me. I regretted looking away. It showed fear and I did not want Abe Gropper to think I feared him.

"You were painting Irene's house?"

"Irene?"

"Irene Costelo. Let me tell you something," Abe said, leaning forward. "She's a crazy woman. And a liar. Did she tell you her husband sued me?"

I shook my head. I didn't feel obligated to tell Abe Gropper what Mrs. C had said to me.

"Yeah. Crazy bastard. Claimed I didn't install his gas furnace correctly. I went back and fixed it but not because he sued me. Then I hired the best lawyer in town and sued *him*. He ended up paying me for slander."

I watched Abe carefully. I remembered the quiet anger behind Mrs. C's words and knew that she, and not Abe, was telling the truth.

"Ahh, hell! Go on and believe whatever she tells you, what do I care?"

That right there must be what *ornery* means. Ornery is how you get when you drink in the middle of the day. When ornery men start to yell at you, it is time to leave. I stood. "I'll go find Trevor."

"Sit!" Abe commanded. I sat down slowly. I was obeying out of courtesy and not because Abe Gropper had any power over me. "I have something for you." Abe dug in the space between the cushion and the side of the chair and pulled out a thick, white envelope. He waved it in the air momentarily and then threw it on the glass table. "Open it."

I knew by the bulk of the envelope that it contained money. Could it be I had judged Abe Gropper wrong, that underneath the orneriness, there was generosity? I searched the man's face for kindness, but there was none.

"Go on. Open it."

The envelope was not sealed. I opened it and saw the hundred-dollar bills.

"Five thousand dollars. All yours. There'll be another five thousand when you do what I ask."

"Do what?"

Abe grinned, like he knew I would bite and ask that very question. I tried to swallow, but my mouth was dry. My heart beat uncontrollably and there was nothing I could do to slow it down.

"It's very simple," Abe continued. "Bring me the phone."

"The phone?"

"I understand your sister told you that someone was going to contact you and ask for the phone you've been carrying. Well, that would be me. I've contacted you and now I'm asking. Bring me the phone and then get out of town."

For a moment a chill of fear traveled down my spine. And then I chuckled. Able Abe. I did not see it coming.

"Something funny?"

"A little. Do you know what's in that phone?"

"All I was told is that the phone is a matter of national security."

"And you believe that?"

"I believe that the person who is asking me is trustworthy and has no reason to lie to me. If he tells me my government needs that phone, then it must be so."

I shook my head. For some reason, Abe's words and gestures calmed me down. A peace came over me. Big Shot did not want any trouble. He wanted it "to go down easy." Abe was a jerk who had been played and lied to by Big Shot. That was good; it told me that maybe they would be unwilling to hurt Sara . . . unless they had to. They were willing to pay good money to get the phone. Ten thousand dollars was a small fortune. More than one hundred thousand pesos. Enough to open a small business, to take care of my mother for a long time, to help Sara with her asylum case. I looked behind me. Bob and Nancy had not come back. Did they know what Abe was going to propose? The thought that Bob was part of the scheme to get the phone back and get rid of me broke the peace that I had begun to feel. I thought I had stopped thinking of Bob as my father, but at that moment I realized I had not been successful. It was crazy to feel sadness at the thought that Bob wanted me gone, but I did.

"What happens after I give you the phone?"

"Poof. You disappear. Tomorrow morning, after Bob and Nancy go to work and Trevor is in school, you come here, get a taxi or walk, I don't care. Write your father a note. Tell him you didn't like it here and are going back to Mexico. You come here with all your things ready to go. You hand over the phone. Someone will be here to make sure it hasn't been tampered with. I'll have a bus ticket for you to Dallas, Texas. Then you'll be taken to the bus station. It won't be hard to get a bus from Dallas to the border. I'll give you the remaining five thousand tomorrow."

I felt a kind of relief when he suggested that I write my father a note. My father wasn't part of the plan and that was good.

"I don't have a choice, do I?"

"No."

"If I don't come tomorrow morning, then what?"

Abe Gropper looked at me with a mixture of admiration and pity. It reminded me of the way I used to look at opponents on the soccer field when they knew they were going to lose but kept on giving it their best. Then the expression on Abe's face changed to one of controlled fury. He leaned forward and pointed at me.

"Listen. You will find this hard to understand, but I will tell you anyway. I have nothing against you personally. I have nothing against Mexicans or any other foreigner except those that want to do this country harm. Hell, I hired your father when he didn't have papers. I got María to help my wife, and I kept her even after Sally died. But enough is enough. There's a limit to the number of people we can help, and we reached it. If we go beyond a certain point, the country will be destroyed. It will lose the glue that keeps us together as Americans. That's what I believe. You people in Mexico build walls to keep out the Guatemalans. When we do it, all of a sudden we got no compassion. Give me a break! I have a lot to lose here. It took me years to build up a successful business. I bid on government contracts. I just came back from Washington, DC, where I met with the assistant director of the U.S. Department of Labor. I can't afford to have you around."

Abe grabbed his chest. He looked as if he was about to have a heart attack. When he recovered enough, he said, "You don't understand. It was my idea to give you ten thousand dollars. It was my idea to give you a bus ticket. I advocated for you on account of your father! I fought for you! Do you understand? Be here tomorrow morning or go home and get the phone now.

And take that with you!" Abe pushed the envelope with the money closer to my side of the table.

I saw the veins on Abe's neck thicken with blood. If I didn't do as Abe ordered, the man would explode or implode.

"The phone is not at my father's house. It will take me a while to get it," I said, standing up. "I'll be here with it tomorrow morning."

"Don't do anything stupid. This is a no-brainer. It's what's best for you and your sister. This is an opportunity that will not be offered twice."

I felt the veins in my own neck swell. Why bring Sara into the conversation? Was that a not too subtle threat? How hard would it be to smash the empty pitcher on the old man's bald head? It was one thing to want to get rid of me; I didn't want to be here any more than Abe Gropper wanted me here. But why threaten Sara? She wanted to be in the United States, and so far from what I had seen, the country would be lucky to have her. Was there anything in the Jipari code about nonviolence? No. But there were the fútbol matches where I felt like whacking a rude or arrogant opponent, yet I managed to play with control. I did it for my teammates because to play angry was to play stupid. When you are angry, your vision narrows, you stop seeing the whole playing field. I took a deep breath. I opened the glass door and then stepped inside. I stood there breathing hard. Brother Patricio would have been proud of me. I had kept my cool. And that was good. I could not afford to play stupid.

I needed to see the whole playing field.

CHAPTER 21

EMILIANO

That night, when everyone was asleep, I used a broom to dig out the metallic bag with Hinojosa's cell phone and blew the dust away. I placed the bag against my chest and held it there for a few minutes. It was time to decide.

I didn't think that Abe Gropper knew what was in the phone. But Abe Gropper was not only a dishonest jerk, like Mrs. C said, he was also connected to criminals, whether he knew they were criminals or not. The ray of light in all of this was that it did not look as if my father knew what Abe Gropper was doing.

But, Papá, do you know what kind of family you married into?

I had to admit that a part of me agreed with Abe Gropper. Returning Hinojosa's cell phone and getting paid ten thousand dollars *and* a ticket back to Mexico was a no-brainer. Sara was in danger. I could tell by the tone of voice in her phone call. What would happen to her if I didn't turn the phone over to Abe Gropper? What would happen to me? Returning the phone seemed like the easiest, safest way out. But was it the right thing to do? How does one decide? My inner compass was telling me to do what was needed to save Sara. But it was also telling me to do all I could to stop Big Shot, to hurt him, and while I was at it, to stick it to the big jerk Abe Gropper and all the other arrogant bastards who thought that Sara and I were not worthy to be in their country. This Big Shot was involved in human trafficking. He was bringing women from Mexico and selling them as slaves. Wasn't that why he wanted the cell phone so badly, to protect his sorry, criminal, evil ass? And Sara and I were unwanted garbage.

Does the inner compass work if the magnetic force is anger?

Maybe. Sometimes. It helps.

What was Sara trying to tell me when she reminded me of the Tarahumara trip with Brother Patricio? If I could only decipher that, I would know what I had to do.

At some point during one of the long, grueling hikes up in the Tarahumara mountains, I realized that there was no way out other than to keep going and after a while I stopped wishing I was someplace else and that's when the trip taught me its lesson.

You are learning endurance, Brother Patricio told me.

Endurance for what? I asked.

For hope, Brother Patricio answered. *Hardship creates endurance and endurance creates character and character creates hope. And hope is the conviction that what you're doing is worth doing regardless of the outcome.*

When I got home, Sara had asked me if Brother Patricio had said anything about not stealing anymore. And I remember telling her what Brother Patricio said about hope.

Was that what Sara wanted to tell me during that last phone call? It had to be. Hope. That phone was my hope, her hope, and the hope of many.

I had come to Chicago so I could give the phone to Yoya's people and so they could use the information in the phone to save the women who had been enslaved by Big Shot. Wasn't that the thing that required my endurance and my hope? Wasn't that what I was being asked to do? What would my life be like if I ran away from what was being asked?

Then, in a flash as quick and bright as lightning, the last words that Sara spoke came to me.

Do it for Linda.

Linda had been imprisoned and abused for months by Hinojosa and people like him. The women risked their lives by stealing Hinojosa's cell phone and sending it to Sara. *Do it for Linda* meant fight for them. Do not let their sacrifice and the lives of other young women be for nothing.

I had to fight. For what? For the Lindas and the Saras and the Trevors of the world. For those who are hurt and for those who are good. Because life's not worth living as a coward. Because whatever little courage I had should be used for the benefit of others.

That was Sara's message.

I was still a Jipari after all.

I waited another hour until I felt as much peace as I was ever going to find with my decision and then I called my mother, using the international SIM card I bought with the phone. I knew a phone call in the middle of the night would worry her, but I needed to hear her voice. I had to shake off whatever doubts I still had so I could do what needed to be done. My mother's voice would help with that. I also needed to explain to her that I would no longer be staying with my father. It would be better if she found out from me. I had gone over and over what I would say and decided not to tell her about Abe Gropper's offer, or about Hinojosa's cell phone or where I was going. I told myself that telling her the truth would put her at risk. But the real reason was that I could not stand to pile more suffering on her.

I turned on the fluorescent lights and read the instructions on the calling card. On the eighth ring, my mother answered. It seemed about a hundred years since the last time I spoke Spanish.

"Mami, soy yo."

"Emiliano? What happened?"

"Nothing, Mami, nothing. Everything is okay. I needed to talk to you. Did something break? I heard something fall?"

"I bumped into the cage with the dumb parrot."

"I thought Tía Tencha kept him in the bathroom."

"I made her take him out. I didn't like the way he looked at me. But why are you calling so late?"

"Mami, listen. I don't want you to worry but . . ."

"What? What's happened? Is it Sara?"

"No. I'm going to . . . I'm not going to be staying at Papá's house anymore. I'm . . . I'm going back to Texas. I'm going to be working at the ranch of Mr. Larsson. He's the man I stayed with when I was sick, after I crossed into the United States. Remember, I told you about him?"

"But why? Are you not getting along with your father? With his wife?"

"It's more a question of . . . work. I really liked it there and . . . ah . . . Mr. Larsson needed me, Mami."

I stopped and waited for my mother's response. Was she buying it? I had never been able to lie to my mother.

"Son." My mother's voice was full of the kindness I so needed to hear. "What was that oath you took as a Jipari? The part about being honest."

She had seen through me and deep down I was glad she had.

"Be honest with yourself and others."

"Did you think you could not be honest with your mother?"

"No, but . . ."

"You have to make sure not to stutter if you're going to lie."

"I can't tell you the truth, Mami. I just can't right now. But I don't want you to worry. I have money and a phone and a phone card to call you. I'll make sure you know I'm okay."

"Are you going to a safe place?"

"Yes."

"Your father doesn't know where?"

"No. It's better if he doesn't."

"It's all right, son. You do what you need to do to be safe and to keep Sara safe. I had a feeling something was wrong. The danger followed Sara . . . and now you."

"You . . . probably need to be careful too."

"Tencha and me are going to Tomasita's house for a while. You know Tomasita, her daughter. She's married to a doctor?"

"Yes, that's a good place to be."

"Do you have pencil and paper? I'll put Tencha on the phone to give you the number."

"Yes. One second."

"We'll leave tomorrow morning. Emiliano, son. I trust you.

You don't have to lie to me. I know it's hard for you with your father. But it is good you were with him. It is better that you know him and . . . I know he cares for you. The man I married is a good man. Stupid, yes. But not a bad man."

"Yes, Mami."

"I love you very much, son. Here's Tencha with Tomasita's number."

I walked to the tool bench where there was a pen and a pad of paper and wrote down the number. After I disconnected, I tore off the top sheet, folded it into a square, and placed it in my wallet, in the same compartment where I had placed Mrs. Costelo's note. I sat on the bed with the pad and pen and wrote.

Hey Trevor,

    I'm going to go away for a while. I'm going back home to be with my mami. I wanted you to know how much I liked building things with you and going to the park and practicing soccer. You were the best part of my visit to Aurora. The Swiss Army knife was given to me a few years ago by a good friend. The compass on the handle actually points north. It's helped me to find my way in the desert lots of times. I want you to have it. Maybe, if you are ever lost, it will help you find your way. Thank you for letting me build the Life Star with you. I know you didn't really need my help, so it was nice of you. If I can find a way to come see you, I will.

    Be good. Liano.

I placed the note and the knife inside the portion of the Life Star that Trevor had constructed. There was a hooded gray sweatshirt that belonged to my father on top of the dryer. It smelled like him and the smell filled me with a sadness that I had never felt before. I stuck Hinojosa's cell phone in the right pocket of the sweatshirt. From now on, that damn phone was going to stay close to me at all times. If for nothing else, to remind me of the courage I needed. I packed the clothes I had brought with me into my backpack, sat on the edge of the bed, and took a deep breath. I looked in my wallet and read the name of the retired Chicago policeman that Mrs. C had given me.

"Are you sure, Emiliano?" I asked.

"Yes," I answered.

I went upstairs and looked out the living room window. It was raining, but in front of our house there was a gray car with someone smoking inside. Big Shot's man making sure I made it to Abe Gropper's in the morning.

I went back to kitchen, opened the door, and stepped out into the cold night. I went out the backyard and over the fence into the neighbor's yard, away from the front street where the car was parked.

I walked toward the park that Trevor and I visited.

The North Star shone in that direction.

CHAPTER 22

EMILIANO

I woke up with a start when I heard the child's voice.

"Mommy, there's a person sleeping in here!"

I crawled to the opposite end of the plastic tunnel and made my way down the jungle gym. I waved at the astonished mommy and made my way out of the park. The sun was out now. I calculated that it must be around nine. Sleep and exhaustion had overcome me despite the frantic sound of the rain beating on the plastic tunnel. The gray, hooded sweatshirt I was wearing no longer smelled like my father's cologne. It now smelled musty. I felt the two cell phones in its pockets: my burner phone on the left and the bag with Hinojosa's on the right.

I walked in the opposite direction of the park and away from my father's house. When I reached Galena Boulevard, I stopped to orient myself. There were kids my age walking toward the high school that I knew was near the park where I had slept. They were late for school, but they didn't seem to care. A boy looked at me, as if trying to recognize me. I had a backpack not as fancy as theirs but similar enough that I could probably pass as a student if my clothes were not wrinkled and damp and if I were wearing Nancy's black sneakers. Besides that, my skin was brown and theirs was white. Something the students also noticed.

"East Aurora High is that way," the boy said, pointing with a thumb over his shoulder.

The laughter from the others in the group told me the directions were not meant to be helpful.

Nevertheless, I walked to where the thumb had pointed. I kept my head down. What would Abe Gropper do when I didn't show up this morning? Whoever wanted the cell phone would come out looking for me. Abe must have told the criminals he could get the cell phone and now they would be desperate. Perhaps Abe was in trouble now. His scheme to get the cell phone had not worked. I ducked quickly into the doorway of a restaurant when I saw a van that looked like one of Able Abe's. When I saw the van slow down, I opened the door to the restaurant and went in. From the window, I could see that the van was a carpet cleaning company.

"Can I help you?"

I turned quickly. The man talking to me was putting pink, fluffy flowers into a vase. Besides María, the man was the only Mexican I had seen in Aurora. There were sombreros and sarapes on the walls. The tables had purple tablecloths. A menu on one of the tables read: TACOS JALISCO. The man looked at me with suspicion.

"You speak Spanish?" I asked.

"Not too much. You here for the dishwasher job?"

"No." The smell of refried beans and chorizo pulled me momentarily to my house in Juárez, to Sara and Mami laughing as they sliced onions and peppers.

"You want something to eat? We open at eleven, but I can get you something."

I almost said yes. I was hungry, and a hot corn tortilla would feed more than just my body. But I had to move out of Aurora as quickly as possible. The sight of the white van had reminded me of the danger I was in and of what I needed to do. I was on a mission—for Sara.

"No. Thank you. Can you tell me how to get to Chicago?"

"Chicago? Why you want to go there?"

"To see the sights."

The man looked me up and down and then laughed.

"To Chicago? Best way is the train. You can catch a bus across the street to the station."

"And if I walk?"

"To Chicago?"

"To the train station."

"Oh, man. That's far. It'll take you an hour. Take the bus."

An hour's walk was nothing. It was safer than waiting on the street for a bus. "I prefer to walk."

The man shook his head. "Just go down Galena and cross the river. About a block after the bridge, take a left. You'll see the station."

"Thank you."

"Hold on. I'll get you a burrito to go. Don't worry, they're made already. I just have to put them in a bag."

The man came back with a paper bag and I began to take my wallet out. "It's on the house," he said. "When you get to Chicago, go to this neighborhood called Pilsen. People will know where it is. There's lots of Mexican shops and restaurants there. There's a place call El Catrín. It's a shoe repair shop. Chuy, the owner, has gotten some of the guys in the back a Social Security number, an ID. You'll need those if you want to get a job. The ID, you'll need for everything."

"Do I look illegal?"

"You speak good English. But you also look like you don't know your way around. If you don't want to get picked up, you got to look like you know where you're going."

I chuckled. The man sounded like Brother Patricio just then. "Thank you for the burritos."

I sat on a milk crate in an alleyway and ate the two burritos. I chewed slowly, savoring each bite of flour tortilla, beans, egg, chorizo, jalapeños. When I finished, I walked on the street parallel to Galena Boulevard. There was less traffic there and it was a one-way street in the opposite direction I was walking. I was less likely to be seen if I walked on a side street and I could see who was coming toward me.

Forty-five minutes later I was on a bridge behind a round-domed building constructed on an island in the middle of a river. A sign read HOLLYWOOD CASINO - BUS PARKING. The river moved slowly, imperceptibly. The color of the river was the same brown-green of the Rio Grande. I turned left on the first street after the bridge and walked until I reached a stone building with railroad tracks behind it. A few cars were parked in front. I stepped under the station's awning and entered. I was making my way to a stand with schedules and maps, when I saw my father sitting on a bench, looking at me.

I stood there, paralyzed by opposing forces. One force would have me turn around and run back out. The other force seemed to come from the past, from the time when the man sitting there had taught me how to dribble a soccer ball around Coca-Cola bottles. Bob sat there, eyes forming a question: *Which force are you going to choose?*

I removed my backpack and sat next to my father. The station was clean, cheerful-looking. There were ticket-dispensing machines and planters with red geraniums. A barefoot man with a green garbage bag at his feet sat on a bench in front of us. The man was having a hard time keeping his eyes open.

"Trevor didn't want to go to school today," my father said. "He didn't understand why you left." My father's voice was calm and deliberate. He didn't seem to be in any kind of hurry.

I lowered my head and stared at my smelly boots.

"This didn't work out the way I hoped," my father said.

"Why are you here?"

He reached in his back pocket and pulled out an envelope. The same envelope that Abe had offered the day before. "I figured you'd make your way to the train station this morning. There's not that many ways to get out of Aurora."

"You knew?" I asked, my eyes fixed on the envelope.

"No. Abe didn't tell Nancy until this morning. When you didn't show up at Abe's house today he called her and she told me. I went straight to Abe's. I told him I thought I could find you."

"And do what?"

"Talk to you. Convince you to do what's best for you."

"What's best for me is to leave. Is that what you mean?"

My father fixed his eyes on the barefoot man. The answer was yes. But he couldn't say it.

I pressed on. "What if I give you the cell phone? Do you still want me to leave?"

I wanted him to answer the question. I wanted to hear the words, so there would be no more doubts, ever.

"Emiliano, son. Things didn't work out. You coming to Aurora, living with us, it got too complicated. Yes, Nancy and Abe had concerns about you being here and the legal consequences, but I still got you here and could have kept you here. I fought for you. The cell phone pushed their fears over the edge. It took things to another level. I . . . agree with them, son. It is now too dangerous for all, including you. People know where you are. All it would take is a phone call to ICE. I don't know who wants the cell phone or why or how they found Abe. All I know is that Abe and Nancy are scared out of their minds. They've done their best to protect you so far. The ten thousand dollars is the best way they can think of keeping you from getting hurt. Abe came up with the plan."

"Who told Mr. Gropper about the phone?"

"I don't know. Abe said that they would have arrested you if he hadn't talked them out of it. It was probably some government official. Abe came up with the plan to offer you money to leave. I know he comes across as pushy and self-centered, but he really has your best interests at heart. We all do."

"He threatened Sara."

"He said what he needed to say to convince you."

"You know. People want to kill me in Mexico."

My father covered his face with his hands. I got the impression that this was what worried him the most. But not enough, apparently. He shook the envelope with the money.

"This will help you and your mother find a safe place. You can hide in Mexico. If you don't give them the phone . . ."

"Giving you the cell phone and then getting out of the United States. That's the only alternative."

"Emiliano, what do you want me to say?"

"I want you to say it! Say it!" Then, lowering my voice, "It's important."

"All right. Okay. Giving me the cell phone and going back to Mexico is the only alternative. What else can I say? I tried, son."

It was done. I felt a quiet, sad peace. It was like the river I had just crossed or like the rare shade you sometimes find in the desert. I leaned back on the bench. The image of our house in Juárez destroyed by thousands of machine-gun bullets came to me. Evil was a stone thrown on calm waters, its ripples extending in larger and larger concentric circles. Perla Rubi's father, Hinojosa, Abe Gropper, and now my own father were the ripples of evil. It was so easy to become another ripple. All you had to do was let it happen.

"Okay," I said.

"Okay?"

"Yes. Okay," I repeated. "You can have it. Here, take it, I need to go to the bathroom." I tossed the backpack at his feet.

Bob grabbed my arm just as I was standing. "Don't do anything stupid. Please." I know he was trying not to sound menacing, but he didn't succeed.

"The cell phone is in my backpack. I'll get it for you when I get back. I need to go to the bathroom."

Bob loosened his grip on me when he saw that I was leaving the backpack behind.

I opened the door to the men's room and immediately saw what I hoped to see. There was a row of three windows up on one of the walls. I zipped up the sweatshirt and climbed onto a rusty radiator. I reached and pushed the window out. There was just enough space for me to crawl through if I could only pull myself up. With my arms fully extended, I grabbed the windowsill and got my chin up, but the wall was smooth, and I could not use my legs for leverage. I jumped down and saw a bucket with a mop in a corner of the bathroom. I placed the upside-down bucket on top of the radiator and the new height allowed me to push myself up and out. I came down in the back of the station and ran quickly to the side parking lot, where I crouched between two cars. A few minutes later I saw Bob come out the front entrance with the backpack in one of his hands. Bob walked over to a gray Mercedes parked in a handicapped space in front of the station. It looked like the same dark car I had seen outside Bob's house that morning. Bob conferred with the driver. The driver opened the door and got out. He was a tall, well-built, blond man in his thirties with blue pants and a white, long-sleeve shirt. I figured he was the man smoking in the car this morning and the man who was supposed to take me to the bus station from Abe Gropper's house. Either that or kill me.

Bob and the driver walked around the station. When they came to the side facing the parking lot, I crawled under the car. The legs of the driver were so close I could have touched them by extending my arm.

"He's around here," the driver said. "Or he went over to the farmers' market."

"The phone is in the backpack," my father said. "You don't need the boy. The phone is all you need."

The man opened the backpack and searched. "It's not here. Damn it! I told you not to let him out of your sight! He had to go in that direction. To the farmers' market. Come on!"

I saw the man and my father hurry away and get into the gray Mercedes. I crawled out and lifted my head slowly over the hood of the parked car. Bob and the driver pulled away in the Mercedes. I was able to see that the license plate had the picture of Abraham Lincoln on it. But I could make out only two letters and a number.

"AR9," I repeated to myself.

CHAPTER 23

SARA

Mario brought me a sheet of paper and pencil with my lunch. I looked up at the camera when he handed them to me.

"No one is in the monitoring room. I checked."

"Thank you. How did you know?" I had been yearning for paper and pencil.

"You're a reporter so . . . But don't get your hopes up about getting anything you write out of here."

"I won't."

"Do you know how La Treinta Y Cuatro got her name?" Mario said, out of nowhere.

"No. Do I want to know?"

He laughed. "Her real name is Rosaura Martel. No one knows how she got the name of La Treinta Y Cuatro. But a lot of us think it refers to the thirty-four days that she kept a detainee in isolation. A Fort Stockton Detention Center record."

"Wonderful," I said. "That's just what I needed to hear."

"It's good you still have a sense of humor."

"What else do I have left?"

Just as he was leaving, Mario said, "Director Mello is making plans to move you. I saw some paperwork."

"Where?"

Mario shrugged. "Maybe El Paso. Sometimes women are moved there when their hearing's been scheduled so they'll be closer to the IJs." He must have noticed the blank look in my eyes. "Immigration judges."

I thought immediately of Norma Galindez. Maybe she saw the merits of my asylum claim. Maybe she called Wes Morgan and found out he had been killed and decided to help me. And then the negative thoughts came, and these carried the weight of truth. Maybe Emiliano understood my message and did not return the phone, and I was about to suffer the consequences.

"When?" I asked.

"Soon. Two or three days at most. It's good, isn't it? Things have not been good for you here. Someplace else will be better."

"Or worse. Mario . . ."

He raised his hand and asked me to stop. "I can't."

"You can call someone for me. One phone call. Sandy Morgan in Alpine. When you find out where they're taking me. Call her."

Mario looked up at the camera and then shook his head. "That's the woman from the message I gave you. The message about her father getting killed."

"Yes."

He stood in place, shuffling his feet. Then, with sadness in his voice: "I have a family. Two daughters, six and four. My parents live with us. My wife's brother just moved in. They all depend on the sixteen dollars an hour I make here." He turned around and opened the door and stepped halfway out.

"One phone call. When you get home. Who will know? Please, Mario."

He turned to me. There was color in his cheeks. "I don't know what's going on with you or why they got it in for you. But it must be something heavy. Yesterday, one of the other guys told me that La Treinta Y Cuatro had a new freezer delivered to her house. And then, after that, she got two boxes of frozen steaks taken to her house by a delivery truck. He lives across the street from her, so he saw the whole thing. Someone got to her, right? We have a saying here: el que da quita. It means—"

"I know, he who gives can take away."

"I wish I could help you. I really do. But I can't afford to get noticed by the same people who are giving La Treinta Y Cuatro freezers and steaks."

Mario walked out and shut the door with a bang before I could say anything else. I felt sorry for him. I couldn't really blame him. Maybe I asked too much from people. Did I ask too much from Emiliano?

I felt like kneeling down and praying the way I did when I was a child. But the only prayer that came to me was for God to help my little brother put all these animals in jail. And I didn't know if that kind of angry wish counted as a prayer. Instead, I sat down on the floor, and using the breakfast tray for support, I wrote a letter to Emiliano on the piece of paper that Mario had brought me. Emiliano would never receive the actual letter, but I felt that my written words would find an invisible route to his heart.

Dear Emiliano:

I am writing because this is my way of being close to you and I know that the hope and love behind my words will find their way to you and you will feel their strength.

The first thing I want to tell you is to stop thinking that all this is your fault. Knowing you, you are still blaming yourself for our attack in the desert. If it helps any, I can tell you that I have plenty of blame for myself also. I could start with my decision to take that cell phone from Juana Martinez's drawer and go on from there. I made you keep the cell phone and made you promise to contact Yoya.

So, you see, there's plenty of blame to go around. There's plenty of hurt to go around too. For me and maybe for you too. I know that being with Papá's new family could not have been easy. But I want you to think about the fact that maybe Papá is to be commended for all he did for you and me despite the opposition of his wife and father-in-law.

It's good for me to write you this letter so you can see that I'm not the same Sara you used to know. This Sara is struggling to see the good and to seek the light. I don't know if I can even pray anymore, if you can believe that. I miss the faith that I got from being around Mami, and I miss the laughter that came from our joking around with each other. Just now I remembered the time when you coated the toilet seat with Vaseline. Only, you didn't expect Mami to be the first one to sit on it. Remember the shout she gave in the middle of the night? That was the first time I heard her swear and I'm glad she was swearing at you when she did it!

I have been in isolation for I don't know how many days, and things happen to how you see the world when you are all alone. I'm not myself. The only thing that kept me going was the contact that I had with the women here. There are mean women here, don't get me wrong. Why should this group of human beings be any different than any other group? But, Emiliano, these women are carrying so much suffering and their future is so hopeless. I hope that soon I can get out of isolation so that I can spend whatever days I have here with the other women. If I were cut off from the suffering and the hopelessness of the other women, my soul would shrink and die. I will do what I can for them, fill stupid forms and translate and write letters, but these efforts will be pitifully small compared to what is needed. And anyway, it's not so much my efforts to help as it is about my being in contact with that suffering.

The one thing that is becoming clear to me is that I need to believe that my life has meaning regardless of how long it lasts. It has to have a purpose now and not only when I get out of here. I want to share this with you, and please don't think I'm sounding like Mami's telenovelas, because if something happens to me, I want you to continue doing what is right.

No matter what happens to me, you must keep going in the direction I know you have taken. Remember you used to tell me that out in the desert, once you find the right direction, all you need to do is walk. One step at a time. This path that you have chosen is the right path and I say this full of worry and concern for your safety. In a way none of us could have anticipated, I think that you are fulfilling Mami's prophecy: In the United States you will be the Emiliano that God wants you to be. Be careful. Watch your step. I'm walking beside you.

I love you very much, little brother. Be good.

Sara.

CHAPTER 24

EMILIANO

I left the Aurora train station and walked for three hours on Liberty Street—a name I found appropriate under the circumstances. The temperature dropped whenever the sun disappeared behind gray clouds, so I kept the sweatshirt on. Now and then I reached into the right-hand pocket and touched the metallic bag with Hinojosa's cell phone. What inner voice prompted me to put the phone in my pocket rather than in the backpack? How could that not be a sign that I was doing the right thing? Somewhere back in Texas, Sara was praying for me. I had lost everything else in the backpack, but all I needed was in my wallet. I had most of Mrs. C's money in there and her note with the name of the retired policeman and the place where they could tell me where to find him.

Stan Kalusa—St. Hyacinth Basilica

All I knew was that St. Hyacinth Basilica was somewhere in Chicago, and Chicago was east of Aurora. I knew that Chicago was an hour's drive from Aurora. An hour's drive, assuming you drove on a highway, was, say, fifty miles. I had a long way to go. At the pace I was going, I would get to Chicago in . . . thirteen hours. I saw a concrete bench next to a coffee shop and sat down.

It was overcast and the air cool enough for me to keep my sweatshirt on despite the body heat generated by the walking. I saw a police car stop on the opposite end of the street. I stood up and went into the coffee shop. Through the glass window of the shop, I watched the policeman write a ticket. I bought a large bottle of water and waited until the police car drove away. I had this sense of constant weariness, like when you're going down a steep, rocky cliff. One wrong step and you're gone. How can anyone live with that kind of fear?

I went out to the same bench and slowly drank the water. Calculating distances and the speed of walking reminded me of Sara. When we crossed from Mexico into Big Bend National Park, she had urged me to walk faster. I had slowed down to three miles an hour after the sun was up and Sara thought that was too slow. I remembered how she walked behind me, and I could almost hear her thoughts. She was thinking that walking for a paltry six hours a day was such a waste. We could get to Sanderson in half the time if we walked for twelve hours a day. The memory made me smile.

I was repeating to myself the license plate of the Mercedes back in Aurora when an old Lincoln Continental with a sign on the door that read NAPERVILLE TAXI stopped in front of the coffee shop. The taxi driver, a young man whose size and weight made him look older, got out and walked into the coffee shop. He came out with a tall cup of coffee. I watched him struggle to get behind the steering wheel without spilling his drink. I waited until the taxi driver was breathing normally again and then approached him.

"Excuse me. How much do you charge to Chicago?"

The taxi driver looked at me the way you looked at someone who couldn't afford to buy what you were selling.

"Where in Chicago?" The man was taking the plastic top from the cup to let the coffee cool.

I was about to say St. Hyacinth Basilica, but I stopped myself. From now on, I was going to be careful with my trust. "Downtown."

The taxi driver ripped open a packet and poured the sugar in the coffee. After the fourth packet, the taxi driver said, "You have to pay what the meter says, but I'd say a trip to downtown Chicago run you about ninety bucks, not counting tip."

Ninety dollars was a lot of money. If I couldn't find Gustaf's friend, I would need all the money I had to survive. "Thank you," I said to the taxi driver.

"Hey," the taxi driver called after me.

I turned to face him.

"Cheapest way to Chicago is the train. Ticket to Union Station in Chicago run you about eight bucks. You got eight bucks?"

I nodded.

"Hop on. I'm going to the station now to wait for fares. I'll give you a lift."

I hesitated. "What station?"

"Naperville. It's ten blocks if you want to walk."

Naperville was the next station down the line. I didn't think my father and the man in the Mercedes would think to wait for me there. I went around the car, opened the door, and got in. The taxi driver lowered my window.

"You're kind of ripe, man," he said, wrinkling his nose in disgust.

I lifted my forearm to my nose and sniffed. Is that what ripe smelled like?

"I got caught in the rain," I told him.

"Mmm-hmm," the taxi driver said as he made a U-turn. "My dog smells like that when he gets wet. No offense, man."

"No offense."

I noticed the green-and-yellow cardboard pine trees hanging from the rearview mirror. The deodorizers could not hide the lingering smell of cigarette smoke in the car. An air-conditioner vent sent a cool stream of air directly on my face and I felt suddenly sleepy. Maybe ninety dollars for a comfortable ride to Chicago was not too much to pay, especially if I could nap on the way there.

"Now, don't go buying the ticket on board or they'll charge you extra. I never ride the train, but that's what my customers tell me."

We were at a stoplight and I was about to speak, when the police car I had seen by the coffee shop pulled next to us. I slid down a few inches on the seat. When the light turned green, the taxi driver waited a few moments for the police car to pull ahead.

We drove in silence for a block and then the taxi driver spoke. "People around here are all riled up over whether Naperville should be a sanctuary city. You know what that means? Sanctuary city?"

"When the police don't ask if you're illegal." We had

newspapers and televisions in Juárez. We discussed the United States immigration policies in school. We were not ignorant.

"You're smarter than me. I had to read up on it. Naperville's not a sanctuary city like I hear Chicago is, but these cops aren't going to bother you unless you're doing something bad or . . . done something bad." The taxi driver gave me a meaningful look.

"I haven't done anything bad," I answered, maybe too defensively. Being illegal was not the same as bad, was it?

"Then, I wouldn't worry about the cops around here. As long as you're moving, they don't care where you come from. But it would help if you didn't smell."

Every time I spoke to someone, it was like I was carrying a neon sign on my forehead flashing the word *illegal*. What was it? My accent? The brown skin and black hair? The fact that I looked lost? All of those things? What did the burrito man say to me? *You gotta look like you're going someplace and you know how to get there.* Except, how was I going to find out how to get there without asking for directions?

"I'm moving."

"Mind if I give you some advice?"

"No. I don't mind."

"Get rid of that sweatshirt. PU! Man. The hoodie doesn't help either."

I nodded. I lifted the front of the sweatshirt to my nose. The ever-present smell of Bob's cologne was faint, but still there. Sunlight broke through the gray morning, and the taxi driver pulled down the sun visor. When we got to the station, I tried to give the taxi driver one of my five-dollar bills, but he waved it off. "Hell, I was coming down here anyway."

I stopped at the entrance to the station and looked around carefully. But this station, unlike the one in Aurora, had no surprises waiting for me. I bought a one-way ticket to Union Station, Chicago, the last stop on the line. In a newsstand, I picked up a map of the City of Chicago that included train routes and listed the city's greatest attractions, including St. Hyacinth Basilica on Wolfram Street. I continued studying the map after I got on the train. I could take the blue line train from Union Station to a station called Logan Square. From there it was only a few blocks to St. Hyacinth Basilica. I folded the map and stuck it in my back pocket. After the conductor took my ticket, I took off the sweatshirt, folded it, and used it as a pillow. I could feel Hinojosa's cell phone against my cheek. I was asleep a few moments after I closed my eyes.

It was almost 6:00 p.m. when I finally found my way to the Basilica of St. Hyacinth. I made a few wrong turns, but I got there solely by following the map I purchased at the Naperville station. It was like being back in the cathedral of Ciudad Juárez. The smell of candles and lilies, the pictures and statues of saints. There was even a small altar dedicated to the Virgen de Guadalupe.

I sat in one of the pews close to the confessionals and counted fourteen people scattered throughout the church. An old woman in the pew in front of me prayed the Rosary in a language I did not understand. In front of the church, I had seen a sign that listed the times for Masses in English and in Polish. There was a redbrick building next to the church, where the priests probably lived and where I could ask where I could find Stan Kaluza.

Seeing Mrs. C's shaky handwriting brought a lump to my throat. Or maybe it was the old lady saying the Rosary that reminded me of my mother. Or maybe it was the Virgen de Guadalupe—I don't know the reason why, but tears filled my eyes. From past experience, I knew I could say, "No, you're not coming out," and most of the time tears would obey. But right there, in that quiet place, I wanted to open the door to them. What had I done? Did I make things worse for Sara? I did not do what Big Shot wanted and now Sara would pay for it? My sister was in a damn prison and in danger and my father . . .

What about Bob?

What about him?

Don't you want to cry about that?

I wiped my eyes with the sleeve of the PU sweatshirt. I had to get up and find someone who might know Stan Kaluza, but the comfort and familiarity of the church made it hard for me to move. Confessions started at 6:45. I could wait until then and ask the priest about Stan Kaluza. Just then, the burner phone in my right pocket rang and vibrated. The old lady saying the Rosary turned and shushed me with a finger on her lips. I stood and walked out.

"Emiliano, this is Sandy Morgan. Do you know who I am?"

It took me a moment but then I knew. "Sara's friend. The park ranger that found her."

"Yes. My father was Sara's lawyer. He . . . my father . . . passed away last week."

I didn't tell her that I knew. "I'm sorry."

"I got your phone number from your message to my dad."

"Is Sara all right?"

Her voice told me Sandy was worried about something. I wanted her to tell me what it was.

"That's why I'm calling. I just got a message that Sara was going to be moved out of the Fort Stockton Detention Center."

"Move where? When?"

"The man didn't say where. I think it was a guard who called, but he didn't leave his name. He sounded as if this move would not be a good thing. He said the move would be soon. Two or three days at the most. They would move her after it got dark. Why would he say that? And why do they have to move her at night?"

All that I could think was that the move was the result of me not giving Abe Gropper the phone. It meant that Sara had two or three days to live.

"Emiliano?"

"We have to get Sara out of there! Is there anything you can do?"

"I went to see her yesterday, but they wouldn't let me in. I'll go again today. It's not a visiting day, but maybe I'll take one of my father's lawyer friends. These detention centers—the law can't reach into them since the people they hold don't have any rights. It burns me up! I'll keep trying, Emiliano. I better go and see what I can do. I thought you should know."

I don't know how long I sat on those church steps. Two or three days. I counted the hours until Thursday night. Assuming it got dark around 9:00 p.m. in Fort Stockton, I had forty-eight, maybe seventy-two hours to save Sara's life.

I had to find Big Shot and put him out of commission before then.

CHAPTER 25

SARA

La Treinta Y Cuatro took me out of the isolation room and escorted me to a small fenced area outside. It was after supper and everyone was inside but there was still light. La Treinta Y Cuatro walked silently and seemed worried about something. I wondered if she had a family. Maybe one of her kids was sick at home and still she had to come to work. Was she a good mother, a good wife? What was she like deep inside—basically good or basically bad?

I covered my eyes when I stepped outside. The rolls of razor-sharp wire on top of the fence reflected the sun in a thousand shards of light. The sun was still blazing even though it was beginning to set. Unlike the outside yard for the general population, the outside area for detainees in isolation was like a cage. But it was outside, and outside, at least for fifteen minutes, is better than inside.

"What day is it? Do you happen to know?"

"It's gonna be Monday all day." La Treinta Y Cuatro took out a pack of cigarettes from her pocket and offered me one. I declined. She lit one and turned her head to blow the smoke away from me.

Maybe she's good deep down. Just had a tough life, I

thought, assessing La Treinta Y Cuatro's character. She sold out her goodness for a brand-new freezer and a box of frozen steaks.

"You from around here?" I asked, maybe pushing my luck.

"Shut up."

Maybe deep-down nasty.

La Treinta Y Cuatro finished her cigarette and flicked it out of the fenced area. Then she stepped out, locked the door behind me, and left. I went to one end of the fenced area and grabbed on to the chain links. I looked at the white roof of the cafeteria and saw smoke rising from black pipes. I heard a noise behind me and when I turned, I saw Mello. He was wearing the usual white shirt but had loosened the knot on an ugly brown tie. He reminded me of the tired office workers who I used to fight for bus seats on my way to work. Mello never wore a uniform. He was an employee of the private company that was hired to run the detention facility. Someday, I thought, I'm going to write an article about the moneymaking business of detaining immigrants. I smiled. Was it a good sign that I was thinking of articles to write?

He spoke from the other side of the chain-link fence, holding a blue folder in his hand. "Looks like you might be going home, Sara."

I did not understand.

"Back to Ciudad Juárez. The asylum officer did not find that you had a credible fear of persecution."

Mello opened the folder and took out a piece of paper. He placed it against the fence so I could come and read it. I stepped forward. It was two paragraphs long. It had my name, my alien registration number, and the date and time of the interview. It described my fear of "an unnamed Mexican cartel" as not one of the classes of persecution protected by law. Then I read the signature.

"This is signed by a Cynthia Teller. My asylum officer was Norma Galindez. What is this? You invented this piece of paper just like you invented affidavits from Guatemalan women wanting to hurt me. You're making all this up."

"It's an official finding that will not be questioned," Mello responded calmly. "All I have to do now is process this Voluntary Departure form that you signed early this morning." He held the paper and again I stepped up to read.

"I didn't sign that!"

"Sure you did! This is your signature, isn't it? It's easy to understand why you did it. Once you found that your credible fear interview had gone south, you decided you would be better off going back to Mexico." Mello opened the folder and took out another form. "Here's your signature again. This one is on a Request for Administrative Segregation form. You asked us to put you in solitary confinement because you were afraid for your life. As you know, there were two detainees from Guatemala who did not like you. We have signed witness statements for that as well."

"They are all lies—"

"Everything that we have done in here has been pursuant to ICE regulations. If that reporter your brother mentioned ever shows up, we'll be ready."

There was a slight, sarcastic grin on Mello's face. He was making fun of Emiliano.

"You can't do this, Mello."

"Usually, in a voluntary departure situation, the detainee pays his or her own transportation back to Mexico or wherever they come from. But we're going to give you a ride to the border free of charge."

I glared at Mello. "You know that once I get to Mexico, the first thing I will do is write a long article about what you are doing here. I have friends at the *El Paso Times* who will publish it for me, gladly."

I was bluffing. I knew that I would be killed the minute I stepped onto Mexican soil. Or, more likely, on the way there.

"Sara." Mello placed the paper he was holding back in the folder. "You don't get it, do you? You don't count. Right now, you are nothing but a number, a piece of paper that needs to be processed along with thousands of similar pieces of paper. Credible fear findings, appeals, deportation orders—all of them pieces of paper that no one reads. Mountains of paper that go from one person to another until one poor soul finally sticks it in a big blue envelope and seals the envelope."

"I get it, all right. I get that you have been bought."

"Oh, Sara," Mello said mournfully. "I wish your brother had cooperated."

I smiled. My Emiliano had received my message. He did not return the phone, and by the looks of it, they did not know where he was.

"This is a mess. I honestly wish we had just given you that bond you asked for. I don't know what's so important about that phone your brother is carrying, and I don't want to know. All I know is that my job is on the line if I don't do what people are asking me to do, and I worked too hard to get here to lose it all now."

"Just let me go." I shook the chain-link fence. "Open that door and let me out. You can say I escaped."

"I wish I could do that, Sara. I really do."

I took a few steps back and slumped against the fence. Then, I immediately stood up as straight as I could. I felt powerless. What could I do against these people who could create life and death by inventing an official-looking document?

"When? When are you sending me back to Mexico?"

"You'll be with us a couple more days. It takes a while for the paperwork to get the right sign-offs. And who knows, maybe your brother will come to his senses. Why is he doing this? What could be in that phone that is worth bringing all this on him and you?"

I thought of telling Mello about all the lives that the information in that phone would save. Would it make a difference if I did? Was he basically good but just weak? I decided not to tell him. Maybe I was doing him a favor by letting him be a mindless instrument of evil.

Instead, I said, "The only question worth asking is how you can live with yourself and do what you are doing?"

Mello nodded quietly. I had the impression that it was a question he had considered before and somehow found an answer that allowed him to live with himself. Then he looked up and clenched his jaws. He was leaving the human being behind and putting on the official who had to do what he had to do. "Your brother will be sent a message. Let's hope he gets it and considers what is best for you . . . and for him."

"How? How will you send him messages? Do you know where he is?"

"I don't, Sara. I only know what I need to know." He busied himself tying a string around the blue folder. He tucked the folder under his arm and said, "I need to process your Voluntary Departure form." Then, looking at his watch, "Why don't you stay out here another half hour. Enjoy the cool air."

I saw Mello turn around and walk back into the building. I sat on the ground with my back against the fence. I knew what was happening and that made not being able to do anything even worse. They were moving me so I wouldn't be found, so I could not talk. But what worried me the most was the "message" that they planned to send my brother.

Emiliano, I don't know where you are. I hope you are not alone. I hope that you have found at least one friend who will fight with you.

But fight you must.

CHAPTER 26

EMILIANO

"You waiting for someone?" A man with a black robe was speaking to me.

I stood and cleared my throat. "I am looking for Stan Kaluza. They told me someone at the church would know where I could find him."

The priest moved a step closer to me. "Stanislaw Kaluza. And who is looking for him?"

"An old friend of his told me to ask for him here."

The priest was an imposing man, tall and gaunt, dark eyes sunk deep in their sockets. He was studying me as if trying to look into my soul. He must have found something in there he could trust, because he said, pointing with his index finger, "Take that street and then the next right. Walk until you get to the park. Stanislaw lives on the street in front of the park— North Springfield Avenue. Look for the house with the flag. You can't miss it."

"Thank you, Father."

It occurred to me that I was calling a perfect stranger "father."

"Tell Stanislaw that he's overdue for the sacrament of

reconciliation." Something like a smile crossed the priest's stern face. "Oh, and don't call him Stan. He doesn't like Stan."

"Stanislaw," I repeated.

"Right."

It wasn't hard to find the park. The sound of an aluminum bat hitting a baseball and the shouts of people cheering could be heard a block away. A kite in the shape of a butterfly floated above the green field. Groups of people gathered around small, portable grills and the smell of hamburger and sausage reminded me that I hadn't eaten since those two burritos a hundred years ago.

I saw the flagpole with the United States flag as soon I turned onto North Springfield Avenue. Stanislaw Kaluza's house was the smallest on the street. A two-story wooden structure with a concrete porch. In front, there was a small yard behind a waist-high picket fence. The flagpole was in the middle, rising from a circle of white stones and red and white tulips. I took a deep breath and opened the gate. I climbed up the steps of the porch and turned to the snap of the fluttering flag before knocking on the door. I waited a few moments before knocking again.

"Coming, coming. Hold your damn horses." It was a man's voice and he sounded annoyed. When the door opened, I found myself looking into the fiery blue eyes of Stanislaw Kaluza. He looked exactly like the kind of person that Mrs. C would call "rough around the edges." He was tall and solid-looking despite his age, with a crew cut that made him look military and mean.

"What?" Stanislaw Kaluza asked. His grip on the door suggested that he was about to slam it shut.

My mind went suddenly blank. I couldn't find a single word either in English or in Spanish.

"Are you all right, boy? You look like you've just went caca in your pants."

For some reason the word *caca* caused me to break into an uncontrollable fit of laughter. It was as if those tears I held back in the church decided to come out a different route. Stanislaw Kaluza stepped outside, his chest almost bumping into my nose. He was wearing a Hawaiian-looking shirt that most definitely did not go with his rugged, bristled face.

"What's so damn funny?"

I raised my hands in a gesture of surrender. "I'm sorry," I said, gasping, wiping my eyes. I started to laugh again and then forced myself to stop. "It's just . . . I don't know what came over me."

Stanislaw Kaluza's expression had gone from angry to something like curiosity. "What is it? Speak up."

I tried to speak, but the words were still having trouble finding their way from my head to my mouth. I reached for my wallet and took out the sticky note with Mrs. C's handwriting.

Stanislaw Kaluza took out a pair of glasses from his shirt pocket. The glasses were the kind that Gustaf used. Granny glasses, Gustaf called them. Stanislaw grabbed the note from my hand and read. His eyes softened as he handed the note back to me.

"Who wrote that?"

"Mrs. C. Mrs. Costelo."

Now it was Stanislaw Kaluza who turned white as a ghost. "Irene Costelo?"

"Yes, Irene Costelo. She said you could help me."

Stanislaw waited for me to say more. I was tired. I didn't want to play games with this man or anybody else. If he was willing to help, fine. If not, I would move on.

"I'm looking for someone in law enforcement who can help me," I said.

"Help you how?"

"Find the man who is trying to kill me and my sister."

"Irene Costelo said I could help? Tell me exactly what she said."

"I told her I needed to find someone in law enforcement I could trust. She wrote down your name and St. Hyacinth Basilica. She said you were a policeman, probably retired, but you would know how to help me." I didn't think it was necessary to mention the "rough around the edges" part.

"Did she tell you how she knew me?"

"Yes."

The pupils in Stanislaw Kaluza's eyes widened and then I saw the eyelids close. It looked almost as if the man was treasuring the memory of something forgotten long ago. When the eyes opened again, they were not the mean-looking eyes that had come to the door.

Stanislaw spun around and went inside the house. Then, without looking back, he shouted.

"Well, come on in and close the damn door!"

Stanislaw made what he called a Polish dinner. Three kinds of sausage, potatoes, fried eggs, and something he called a "Krakow bagel." He leaned back in his chair and yawned.

"So, here's my take on your situation." He poured coffee into what looked like a beer mug. I had spent the last two hours talking and talking some more. I told Stanislaw everything. Probably more than he needed to know. I started five years ago from when my father first came to the United States and ended with the phone call I received from Sandy Morgan on the steps of St. Hyacinth Basilica. I knew there was a risk that Stanislaw would call ICE. All I knew about him was that Mrs. C said I could trust him. But the more I talked and the more carefully he listened, the more I believed that Mrs. C was probably right. Besides, I had no choice but to trust him.

"Yes?" I said impatiently. Stanislaw's mind had gone someplace else all of a sudden. When he came back, he said, "The guy that's calling the shots, this Big Shot, is the same guy who Abe Gropper saw in Washington. We should be able to find out who he is from what you told me. Some deputy something or other in the Department of Labor. Then, we got that partial license plate number. I'll head over to Michigan Avenue first thing in the morning and get Frank to chase that down."

"Michigan Avenue?"

"That's where Chicago Police headquarters is located. Frank's my old partner. Frank Jaworski. We were together for ten years until he got his detective's shield. They used to call us Arctic and Antarctica. You know, as in the two Poles? He's younger than me, so he stayed on. He's retiring next year. I'm also going to get Frank to check on Gropper's trip to Washington."

"We have to get that guy before he does anything to my sister."

"We're going to move as fast as these old bones can go. But we can't just go in and grab these people. We need to have proper evidence against them so we can arrest them and so that we can put them in jail for a long time."

"All the evidence you need is in this cell phone." I pointed to the metallic bag at the end of the table. "There's stuff in there that people want very badly and are willing to kill for it. Can Chicago Police open the phone first thing tomorrow?"

"They could open it, all right. But without getting a warrant first, they couldn't do anything with the information in it. So let's say they grab this guy in Washington. First thing he'd do is get a big-time lawyer who would say that the arrest violated his rights because it was based on the information on a phone that was opened without a warrant."

His rights? What about my sister's rights?

"Then don't arrest him. Just tell me who and where he is."

Stanislaw laughed. "I like your spirit, boy." He got up and walked to the sink with his plate.

"What if I opened the phone and gave the police the information in it? Couldn't they act on that information? Police act on citizen tips all the time, don't they?"

Stanislaw turned, looked at me like maybe I wasn't as dumb as he thought. "Yeah, that would work."

"There's only one problem," I said, tapping Hinojosa's phone. "I have no idea how to open it. Do you have a computer? I can do some research tonight."

Research of any kind, on a computer or on an old-fashioned book, was not one of my major strengths. But I would do what I could.

"Hold on. Let me make a call." Stanislaw disappeared into the living room, where I heard him use the old landline phone there. He was smiling when he entered the kitchen again. "I got an expert on cell phones coming over tomorrow afternoon."

"Tomorrow afternoon?"

"It's the best I can do. And the timing works well. I need the morning to investigate Gropper's trip and the license plate and work things out with the chief at headquarters and maybe talk to the district attorney. I got to get a whole bunch of people on board, you know. But I got a feeling that they will be interested. It's not often that they get a chance to put a human trafficking ring out of business."

"And rescue the women who are slaves in some form or another."

"Yes."

"And my sister? Can Chicago Police get her out of the detention center?"

"I don't know. That's a tough one, even for CPD. I'll make some inquiries. But . . . let's think." Stanislaw pulled out a chair and sat, his forehead wrinkled in thought. "If we call down there, let's say. If I get Frank to call and identify himself, I'm afraid that might make them hurry up and do whatever bad stuff they were thinking of doing. They're not planning on doing anything until Thursday night. So we got three days. Let's see if we can nail this bastard before then. That's what I would do."

I liked Stanislaw. Good old Mrs. C knew just the right person. "Who's the expert that's coming?" I picked up my plate, walked it to the sink.

"Aniela, my granddaughter. She and her mother live a few blocks from here."

I stopped in my tracks. *His granddaughter? Are you kidding me?* I was barely able to keep my mouth shut. I had to find a way to let Stanislaw know how important it was to find the right person to work on the phone. I would try to do it without hurting the man's pride. But if that didn't work, then let his pride be hurt. My sister's life was at stake. I gulped the last bit of coffee in my cup, then, after clearing my throat, I said, "Opening a cell phone is tricky. Whoever works on it needs to know what they're doing. If you try and fail, it becomes even harder to open."

"It becomes even harder to open, huh? Listen, I wouldn't be telling you Aniela could do it if she couldn't. And you better act like a perfect gentleman around her." He paused. "You know how I knew the note you showed me was written by Irene?"

I shook my head.

"The note said my name was Stan. I never let anyone call me Stan except Irene. I hate the name Stan. You call me Stan and I'm like everybody else. My parents named me Stanislaw so everyone knows where I was from. You can call me Stanislaw or you can call me Kaluza. Period. I had that rule when I was in the army and the same rule held for the thirty-six years I was with the Chicago Police Department. Only exception was Irene. She used to tell me I needed to assimilate and become Stan. You know what I used to say to her?"

"I have no idea."

"I said that to assimilate was to be the same *ass* as everyone else. ASS-i-mi-late, get it?"

"Yes, I think I do."

"Don't be a smart-ass."

I waited for the grin that I knew would eventually come. When it came, I asked, "What time did you say Ariela was coming?"

"Aniela, dummy, Aniela. It means God's messenger. And God is going to be keeping a watchful eye on you, don't you ever forget that. Between His eye and my two, we got you covered. She's coming around two thirty. Walking directly from school. You might want to take a shower. I'm going to give you a pair of my old pants. You're gonna have to shorten the legs considerably. I'll give you scissors, needle, and thread. Make the stitches small so no one sees them. I got some old sneakers that might fit you. Put those things out back and let them breathe for a while."

I looked at his feet and then at mine. His were bigger. I decided I would keep my smelly boots. Who did I need to impress? His granddaughter?

Stanislaw began to clear the rest of the table. "You and Aniela work on the phone, and me and Frank will do the old-fashioned police work."

"I'll wash them." I took the dishes from his hands.

"Thanks. I'm going to get my things ready so I can leave first thing tomorrow morning. Haven't been back at headquarters since I retired." He started to walk out of the kitchen and then stopped. "Listen, I wouldn't make too much out of your father waiting for you at the station. I can see how he thought returning the phone was best for you and your sister."

"And you, what do you think? Do you think he was right?"

"I'm an ex-cop. I like what you're doing. Put the son of a bitch away. It's risky but . . ."

"But . . ."

"At least you and your sister have a chance of making it out alive. If you gave them back the phone, you'd have no chance."

"I could be on a bus to Mexico right now with ten thousand dollars."

"Yeah, right! You would have shown up the next morning at this Able Abe's house and the tall blond in the gray Mercedes would have taken the phone from you and then he would take you to the bus station. Only, you would have never made it to the bus station. There's no way these perps would have let you live. No loose ends. That's the rule. Trust me. This is thirty-six years of chasing bad guys speaking. You are a loose end they need tied."

"What about my sister? Is she a loose end right now?"

"They need your sister alive until they find you. They're hoping that you change your mind and return the phone. They're going to try to send you a message, though. You think this woman who called you this afternoon is on the up-and-up?"

"What do you mean?"

"I mean, what if Big Shot got to her and told her you got until Thursday night or else?"

"No. I don't think so. She sounded worried about Sara. Scared for her."

But what if Stanislaw was right and they had threatened Sandy Morgan? Now they would have my cell phone number. I reached into my pants pocket and turned my burner phone off.

"All right, enough talk. Let's hit the sack." I followed

Stanislaw out of the kitchen. He had climbed up the first two stairs when he turned back to speak to me. "Look. It's your phone. I know you got doubts about Aniela. You don't know her like I do. Listen to what she has to say about how she would go about opening it, and if you don't think you can trust her with the phone, then just tell her. She's a tough cookie. I know her and I know what she's capable of doing, but it's up to you. We'll find someone else if that's what you want."

I nodded. Then Stanislaw bounded up the stairs two steps at a time. He seemed happy to have a task and a mission again. And I was glad he was moving fast.

CHAPTER 27

EMILIANO

I don't know how I made it until 2:45 p.m. When the front door opened and Aniela walked in, I was a desperate mess. All day I could barely keep myself from calling Sandy again. I had finally forced myself to be patient and to trust that Stanislaw knew what he was doing, when I saw the young girl's face and was immediately disappointed. I had expected a female replica of tall and sturdy Stanislaw. But Aniela was . . . delicate. That's the word that came to mind when I saw the brown hair neatly pulled back into a ponytail, the porcelainlike nose and gently curved lips. She was wearing black athletic shorts and a gold shirt with a logo of a bulldog on the upper left side. She jumped back when she saw me in Stanislaw's recliner. I pulled myself out with difficulty, trying not to look disappointed. There was no way this frail-looking schoolgirl could unlock Hinojosa's phone.

"You must be the famous Emiliano!" Aniela dropped a gym bag on the sofa and stretched out her hand. Her voice belied her slight frame. Her eyes and tone were as determined and confident as her grandfather's.

I stood and shook a hand with a powerful grip. I could feel the energy inside her. So at least there was that. I got the immediate sense that it would be easy to talk to her. Now all I had to do was find a way to tell her that she had walked all the way to her grandfather's house for nothing.

"Famous?"

"Excuse me, I have to get some water. We had a small accident at the end of physics lab, and I had to stay and clean up."

The mention of a physics lab made me feel a little better. I knew from personal experience that brains were needed in a physics lab. I turned to watch her run into the kitchen. Her thighs, I now saw, had the firm roundness of an athlete's. Maybe she wasn't as frail as I first thought.

She came back out of the kitchen drinking water out of a plastic cup. She saw me watching her and smiled. "Famous because my mom and I were like stunned when Grandpa told us he had taken you in. It just didn't sound like Grandpa. Plus, he said nice things about you."

"Nice things."

"He said you got gumption. Gumption is big in Grandpa's world." There was shyness in her laugh.

"Gumption? Is that like moxie? I learned that word just recently."

"Kind of." She laughed. "Moxie's not a word Grandpa would use. But it could work."

There was a moment of awkward silence when I could not think of anything to say. Finally, I pointed at the bulldog on her shirt. "You play sports?"

"Soccer," Aniela said, putting the plastic cup on the coffee table next to where I had been sitting. She looked briefly at the *Guns & Ammo* magazine I'd been reading before she sat down and folded her legs. "Or fútbol, as you would say."

An unexpected bubble of warmth burst inside me. I sat down on the sofa in front of her and realized that one of my pants legs was longer than the other. I had massacred Stanislaw's pants and there was no place to hide my legs. And if that wasn't enough, every trace of the English language had vanished from my brain.

Aniela saw that I was having trouble finding words, so she continued. "I play sweeper. I would love to be a forward, of course, but my coach puts me in defense."

"Defense is good." I was finally able to speak. "But, right now, we need to play offense. Did Stanislaw tell you why I'm here . . . in his house?"

"You're right. I'm sorry. We need to get down to business. Where's the cell phone?"

I tried not to sound skeptical. "You know about cell phones?" But I could tell by her smile that she saw my doubts.

Instead of answering my question, Aniela said, "What I thought I'd do was take a look at the phone and then do the research as to how best to open it. I'm not going to try anything until I know what has the best possibility of working." She paused as if to see if her words were giving me confidence. "What do you think?"

"Research is good," I said. I remembered my days at Colegio México. There was nothing I found as boring as research. But research was also what Sara was good at. Finding out the truth about what happened and finding out what procedure would unlock a cell phone—there was similarity between those two, no? I stood to go get the phone, and then sat down again. I ran my hand through my hair and looked for the right place to start. I wanted to convey to her all that Sara had gone through because of that cell phone, but the story seemed too long and complicated and maybe I didn't need to tell it.

"I know a little from Grandpa about how important that cell phone is, but it might be good for you to tell me." Apparently, Aniela could read minds. She leaned back in the chair, ready to listen to me.

"It's a long story," I said. "Maybe I don't need to tell you all of it. At least not right now. What I wanted to say about the cell phone, I think you already know."

"What is that?"

"That people have risked their lives and . . . are still risking them because of that cell phone. That people have died because of it, that my sister's life might depend on what we do. That we should do it fast."

"Okay," Aniela said, her eyes moistening. Then, embarrassed, "Well, let me see the damn thing!"

I grinned.

"What?" Aniela asked.

"Just then, you sounded like your grandfather."

"Keep saying stuff like that and the cell phone will be the least of your worries."

I climbed the stairs, silently laughing. When I came down, Aniela had her laptop open. She spoke to me without lifting her head from the screen. "Why don't you tell me about the phone itself. Tell me everything you know."

I placed the metallic bag with Hinojosa's phone on the coffee table. "A policewoman gave us the bag to prevent the phone from being tracked," I informed her.

"Smart woman," Aniela said, looking at me. "What else?"

"My sister and I think the owner used his fingerprint to open it. No one has touched the phone because we didn't want to smudge whatever prints were there or add new ones."

"That was smart too."

"I was supposed to give the phone to someone who would help me open it and also help me with the information that was in it. But that person can't help me anymore."

"I did some research about how to open the phone last night after Grandpa called. But I think we should look to see if the phone has a memory card. People who depend on their phones for their business, who use them as mini computers, sometimes install large memory cards so they can store their documents and carry everything with them. Maybe the owner did that."

"The man who owned this phone would want to have all his documents with him," I said.

Aniela went into her backpack and dug out a pair of latex gloves like the kind that doctors use. "I don't usually carry these in my backpack," she explained. "I had a feeling we might need them."

I knew she was trying to make a joke, but I was too scared to laugh or even smile.

Aniela opened the metallic bag and carefully pulled out the cell phone with her thumb and middle finger. She looked at the phone's front and back and then she set it down gently on the wooden table. Next, she stood and walked over to a desk in the living room. It was a small maple desk filled with newspapers and magazines and envelopes. It looked very similar to Gustaf's desk back in Texas. Aniela opened the top drawer and came back holding a paper clip in her gloved hand. She sat down, bent the paper clip, and stuck it into the top edge of Hinojosa's phone. A moment later a tiny tray popped out and a big smile covered Aniela's face.

"What is it?" I asked, worried.

"The phone has a regular SIM card and a super-duper SD memory card. The SD card has 256 GBs of memory. That's huge. That kind of memory capacity doesn't come with the phone. The owner must have put it in there for extra filing. So it is very possible that it could have the kind of information you need."

"How do we access it?"

"We need to take this card and put it in another phone."

"Do you have a phone?"

"Yes. But the card will only fit certain phones. Not mine." Aniela clicked on her laptop. After a few moments, she said, "I think I know where I can get a phone that will take this kind of memory card. Can you get me an envelope from Grandpa's desk?"

I found an empty envelope and handed it to Aniela. She dropped the card in the envelope. "Hold on to this."

"Can we get a phone that we can use? I have some money. We can buy one."

"This cell phone is an older model. I mean, this is like version seven or eight, and they are now on version ten. It would be hard to find the right model. Fortunately, my mother has an older cell phone that should work."

"Where is she? Can we go see her?"

"She's on her way home from St. Louis. She'll be home tonight."

"Tonight?"

"I know how urgent this is for you. But look, even if we find the kind of information that is useful, it's not as if the police will be able to rush off and grab the criminals. You need to work with Grandpa and his friends at the Chicago Police Department to come up with a plan. Something that will stick in court. The information in the card will only be the beginning of the investigation. The information will allow the police to get warrants to open the phone, that's what Grandpa said. And what if there is nothing in the memory card that is useful? Then we need to try to get the phone open. Now that I've seen the phone, I will be doing specific research as to how best to do that."

"Can you do it? I mean, if the memory card is no good?"

"It won't be easy. Let's hope the owner used the fingerprint scanner. A fingerprint is the easiest way to open a phone and people who are always on the phone prefer it."

"I have a feeling that the guy who owned this relied on his cell phone for many things. He must have kept things in there that are very important or revealing. That's the only explanation I have for why someone wants the phone so badly. But . . ."

"But what?"

"We need to be prepared in case the memory card does not give us what we need."

"You're not going to find e-mails or texts in the SD card. Those are stored in the phone itself or in the cloud. But you might find pictures and documents."

"But if there's nothing there, we need to be ready to open the phone."

Aniela reached into her gym bag and took out one of her school notebooks and a pen. I watched her write. She was making a list. She lifted her face and narrowed her eyes with concentration after each item. When she finished, she looked at me. "According to the research I did last night, this is what we will need in case we have to open the phone." She moved her chair closer to me and showed me the list.

1. *Find suitable print*
2. *Develop print (get bichromatic fingerprint powder, superglue)*
3. *Lift print (fingerprint tape)*
4. *Enhance and develop print (transparent film, digital microscope, laser printer at school)*
5. *Create mold (gelatin liquid, sheet of free molding plastic) or use print (cellophane-like material?) on human finger (?)*

"It will be tricky," Aniela said when I finished reading. "First, we have to hope that the phone was not turned off when it was taken. If it was off, we may get a prompt for a password before we can use the fingerprint scanner. Then we'll need to charge it. I can get a charger for this phone. But we need to assume that the people who want the phone will have a way of tracking it once it is turned on. We'll need to find a place that doesn't transmit a signal. Once we are there, we will need to find a thumbprint belonging to the owner. If we find a print, we need to lift it carefully. We only get one shot. Once you lift it, the print is gone."

"You've really thought about this." I felt guilty for thinking she would not be able to help me.

"Some of it comes from having a grandfather who was a cop. But I also stayed up most of the night looking into this."

"Sorry."

"No, no. I didn't mind. Once I get intrigued by some problem, it is hard for me to let go. I'm very stubborn that way. Another trait I inherited from Stanislaw. I found an article by a Japanese professor which was very helpful. He called it the 'gummy finger' technique. The best part is that the equipment that he used, like the camera and printer, are things we have at school. Some of the other things, Grandpa can get from his policeman friends."

"Thank you," I said. "For doing the research and . . . thinking about this."

Aniela placed the phone in the bag and closed it. She pushed her chair back so she could look at me next to her. "Can I ask you something?"

"Go ahead."

"Who do you think is after this phone?"

"Yoya, the girl who was going to help me with the phone before she got arrested, called him Big Shot. Someone with a lot of power and big status who found a way to use his position to benefit from the trafficking of young women. He is also someone with dozens of connections everywhere and with the influence to have people . . . do what he asks." I thought of Abe Gropper, of my father, of the tall blond man in the gray Mercedes—all of these people directly or indirectly helping Big Shot.

I saw a pink blotch appear on Aniela's neck and then on her cheeks. "We need to get this pig," she said, fixing her eyes on me. She waited a moment and then added, "And if I wanted to talk like Grandpa, I would have used a different word."

"Pig works," I said. "Let's get the pig."

I didn't tell her about Betsy and Bertha, Gustaf's two pigs, whom I liked.

I offered Aniela a fist and she bumped it. We blushed simultaneously.

"Okay," Aniela said, standing. "Keep the cell phone with you. I'm going to make a note for Grandpa to get me a few things from his police buddies." Aniela opened another drawer and took out an envelope and a tiny pencil. When she finished writing, she looked up and told me, "When Grandpa comes home, tell him he needs to get these."

"He's there now. With the Chicago Police. He went to talk to his old partner—to work out a plan for what to do when we get the information from the phone and to find the owner of a license plate."

Aniela was out of the kitchen before I could finish speaking. She dug her own cell phone out of her gym bag and tapped it. She shook her head a few times when no one answered.

I heard her speak into her phone, a disapproving frown on her face. "Stanislaw, this is your granddaughter. I need you to go to the crime lab and get me fingerprint powder, cyanocylate or superglue, and some fingerprint tape. We need this right away so don't dilly-dally with your buddies." She put her phone back in the bag and said to me, "There really is nothing we can do right now. When my mom comes home, we'll come over and try out the memory card on her phone. If we strike out, I'll do more research tonight so we will be ready to open the phone. We can do that tomorrow." She picked up her gym bag and slung it onto her shoulder. "I have to get to soccer practice. You'll be here?"

"Yes. But . . ."

"I know how you feel. Honest. But there's nothing we can do right now." Aniela stood with her hand on the doorknob, considering. Then she waved nervously at me and stepped out.

I watched the door close and felt the silence of the house envelop me. After a few moments I went to the kitchen and picked up the bag with Hinojosa's cell phone and the envelope with the SD card. I was halfway up the stairs when I heard the front door open. Aniela was standing there brushing a wisp of hair from her forehead.

"I was just thinking . . . why don't you come with me to soccer practice. You'll like Mr. Gómez, our coach. He's also my AP physics teacher. It will be good for him to meet you since we're going to need him to let us use the equipment in the physics lab if we need to open the phone."

"I think I better stay here."

"You can give us some pointers on how to play real fútbol,

the way it's supposed to be played. Mr. Gómez played soccer at Georgia State but, I mean, how much do they know about fútbol in Georgia?"

I took a few steps down. "Thanks, but . . ."

"You don't have to talk to anyone. Just sit on the bleachers and watch. It'll be entertaining . . . you won't believe what we're doing to that poor ball."

"I don't know. I . . . I'm not here . . . legally. If I get caught . . ."

"Oh, please! Half of Chicago is illegal in one way or another."

She grinned.

I looked down at my pants, one leg longer than the other, the smelly hiking boots. I'd tried Stanislaw's sneakers, but they were too big.

"You fit right in, trust me." Aniela tried but could not contain laughter. "Come on. Getting your mind off things for a while is always helpful."

I nodded. She was right. My brain was more like a "no-brainer" and I was going to need to be thinking straight if I was going to help Sara. I walked up the stairs and hid the bag with the cell phone and the envelope with the card under the box spring of my bed.

When I came down, Aniela was by the flagpole, waiting for me.

CHAPTER 28

EMILIANO

I sat on the last row of the aluminum bleachers, watching the girls' varsity soccer team go through their afternoon practice. I thought about how rich this school seemed compared to my Colegio México. The field with soft grass where the girls were practicing was surrounded by a red, bouncy track. In the distance I could see a baseball field and beyond that a labyrinth of brick buildings. I shielded my eyes from the afternoon sun and concentrated on the players. After warming up and a series of drills, the coach divided the team into two groups for a scrimmage. It took me all of one minute to see that Aniela was the best player. The coach was right in making her the last line of defense. There were other players with better dribbling and passing technique but none as fearless as Aniela. She was smaller than most of her teammates and yet players seemed to bounce off her as if they had suddenly encountered a concrete wall. Even then, I saw she was holding herself back out of consideration for her teammates. In a real game, she would be as tough as any player on my team back home.

Back home. If I were forced to stay in the United States for the rest of my life, would there come a time when I would stop saying "back home"? Would I eventually stop thinking of Colegio México as my school or of the Pumas as my team?

I wondered how the Pumas were doing. This was the year when we were going to do what no other team in Chihuahua had ever done: win two consecutive state championships. Right now, the team would be practicing in the dusty field in back of Colegio México. Paco would be drawing plays on the ground with a stick, thinking of ways to circumvent Brother Patricio's instructions to play a disciplined, boring, defensive game. Had I ever been happier than when stripping a ball from a player's feet? The tackle in Chihuahua that led to the winning goal and the state championship was like that. The player went tumbling to the ground, but the referee did not blow his whistle even though the stadium was in an uproar. That was a good ref, a smart ref.

Perla Rubi was at that game watching in the stands with the five hundred or so students and family members who had made the four-hour trip from Juárez to Chihuahua on rented school buses. I could feel how proud of me she was all the way down on the field. And then after the game, there she was, standing by the sideline, beaming, waiting for me to push my way through the crowd of congratulating people.

I shook my head to try to stop the flow of memories. I didn't want to think about Perla Rubi. Sara's life was on the line and here I was fantasizing. It was watching Aniela that stirred memories of Perla Rubi. But why? They were so different. "Why don't you find a nice girl who likes you the way you are. Perla Rubi is a fantasy," Paco would say to me. "A figment of your wishes. She's not real."

Aniela was real. So was Chicago. So was my father paying me to go back home. The detention facility where Sara was a prisoner was real. And the United States that Sara thought had the best system of justice in the world—was that a fantasy or was that real?

I was so lost in my thoughts that I did not see Coach Gómez on the sideline motioning me to come down. I snapped into the present only after I heard him blow the whistle hanging from his neck. Reluctantly, I made my way down the bleachers.

"Gerardo Gómez," the coach said, shaking my hand. He was a short man with skin as brown as mine. He was in his forties but in good shape. A weight lifter, judging by the size of his biceps. "Aniela tells me you play."

The scrimmage had stopped, and players were lining up to shoot penalty kicks.

"A little."

"What part of México are you from?"

"Ciudad Juárez." I was beginning to regret my decision to come watch Aniela. I could see the players looking in my direction, whispering, giggling.

"You here for long?"

How long was I staying in the United States? Until they catch me? Until Big Shot is in jail? I had a job to complete in this country and how long I stayed no longer mattered.

"I don't know," I said.

Coach Gómez nodded as if he understood the reason for my discomfort. "Were you on a team in Júarez?"

"The one at my high school."

"Well"—Coach Gómez turned toward the players—"what do you think?"

I caught Aniela's eyes in the distance. She shrugged as if to apologize for the interrogation I was undergoing. I hesitated, then said, "The ball spends too much time in the air and not enough on the ground."

"Exactly!" Coach Gómez said, excited. "I can't get them to pass to each other. Maybe one pass or two and then they kick it into nowhere and hope it lands close to someone wearing their uniform."

A few of the players were now standing by the sideline, practicing corner kicks. Coach Gómez walked toward them. "You have to elevate the ball, Tracy. Hit under. Under."

We watched the ball roll on the ground toward the goal. Coach Gómez shook his head. "That's one of the most sorry-looking corner kicks I think I've ever seen."

Tracy covered her mouth and laughed.

"Do me a favor. Will you show them how to elevate a ball? Why don't you kick a corner for them? One that actually gets off the ground for a change."

"No, I haven't played in a while."

"Come on! That's not something you forget."

"No. I can't." I searched for the field's exit, but Coach Gómez blew his whistle, shouted.

"Listen up, everybody! Emiliano here plays fútbol in Mexico. He's going to kick a corner for you. Ball, please! I want you to see at least one good corner kick in your lifetime."

One of the players rolled a ball to Coach Gómez and he

picked it up and handed it to me. "Don't let us down." Coach Gómez winked.

Now every member of the team watched and waited. I found Aniela sitting with the rest of the players in front of the goal. She had one of those expressions a person makes when they break a fancy dish in a stranger's house. *I'm so sorry!* I could almost hear her say.

I felt red. I had never realized before that red could actually be felt. In my cheeks, my neck, the top of my head. I stared at Coach Gómez, wondering for a moment whether the man was evil or just stupid. That seemed to be *the* question with regard to many of the people I had met in the United States, including my own father. With respect to the grinning Coach Gómez, it was impossible to conclude one way or another. He was probably a little of both.

So, a corner kick, how hard was that? The sooner I kicked the damn ball, the sooner I could go back home where Stanislaw's rough edges would be a welcome relief. I walked to the spot on the field marked for corner kicks. The players waited. I couldn't decipher the expression on their faces. Were they like those people who go to car races hoping for a crash? My eyes and Aniela's met briefly, and I was filled with something that was strange because it was so solid and strong, something I had not felt since I left Gustaf's ranch.

When I got to the corner of the field, I kneeled down to untie the laces on my right hiking boot. I heard oohs and aahs from the players, but I ignored them. I took both boots off so that my feet would be balanced. Then I took my socks off as well. One of them had a hole and my toe stuck out, but I didn't care. I placed the ball on the corner and looked up to see Aniela's smile. I was her friend, she seemed to be saying to me and to everyone else. She had brought me here to this field on this day.

I placed the ball in the middle of the crescent line, took two steps backward, and kicked with the inner part of my right foot. I kicked the ball down and slightly on the side, so it would lift and spin. The ball floated up fast and hard and then swerved in midair, entering the goal a few inches from the top of the far goalpost.

I heard the explosion of cheers. There was still clapping when I bent down to put my socks and boots back on. When I stood, Coach Gómez was beside me, shaking his head. "I don't think I've ever seen a goal scored from a corner. That was something to see. Thank you."

I looked for Aniela. She was walking to the sideline. Teammates were hugging her and patting her back. I had made her look good.

"You're welcome to come anytime. I could use your help. As you can see."

"Thank you."

Coach Gómez grabbed my arm softly. "Anything I can do. Let me know." Then, "Aniela is our best player, as you saw. She's also the smartest student in my physics class. She could have gone to a private school on a scholarship. The school is lucky to have her. We all are."

There seemed to be a hidden message behind Coach Gómez's words. Was he trying to tell me that I was also lucky to be with Aniela? Did he think that we were boyfriend and girlfriend or that I liked Aniela *that* way? I wanted to tell him that Aniela was someone I had just met, someone who was helping me. But what was so bad that people thought we were a couple? Why did I feel flattered?

We walked side by side out of the school grounds. When we reached Milwaukee Avenue, Aniela said, "I didn't know you were such a show-off."

It took me a few seconds to translate *show-off* into Spanish and then to realize that Aniela was joking. "Your coach made me do it."

"Did you really intend to score a goal or did the ball just happen to go in?"

"I intended. Absolutely. Of course."

"Mmm."

Then Aniela went quiet. Her forehead wrinkled in deep thought. I wondered if I should ask her something, just to make conversation, but Aniela looked comfortable walking in silence. Whatever was occupying her mind, it wasn't me. Aniela, on the other hand, began to occupy mine. I knew I shouldn't think about Aniela *that* way. But when I tried to determine what way was *that* way, I got confused. If I felt comfortable with her and liked talking to her and walking with her and if I thought she was super bright and if I admired her play on the field and if I felt butterflies in my stomach when our eyes met, was that the same as thinking about her *that* way?

That whole line of thought was silly and . . . inappropriate. How could I be thinking about a girl when my sister's life was in danger?

"Stop!" I blurted out.

"What?" Aniela gave me a look like I was crazy, which was the right look to give me at that moment.

"I was . . . telling myself to stop worrying."

"It doesn't work," Aniela said. "You can't order your mind to stop worrying. The only thing you can do is distract your mind. Give it something else to focus on."

"How old are you anyway?"

"I'll be seventeen next month. Why?"

"It's just that you seem older. Wiser."

"Wiser?"

"It's a good thing."

"And you? How old are you?"

"I'll be eighteen next January," I said.

Aniela furrowed her forehead and went back to thinking hard about something. I don't know what it was, but I was still sure she wasn't thinking about me. When we got to Pulaski Road, she said, "I got it."

"What?"

Aniela looked excited. "It might just work. I've been worried about the possibility of the cell phone sending a signal. Big Shot could be out there waiting with tracking equipment. I've been racking my brains thinking about how to prevent that and it just came to me. What we need is the equivalent of a Faraday cage."

"Faraway cage?"

"Faraday," she corrected me, laughing. "It's a principle in physics named after Michael Faraday . . ." She stopped and laughed again. Maybe it was the glassy look in my eyes that she found funny. "Look, that bag where you are keeping the cell phone is sometimes called a Faraday bag. What we need is a room that's like that bag where we can open the cell phone. We wouldn't need the room for very long. Just long enough to transfer whatever is in the cell phone into a laptop. I kept thinking all through practice about where we could find such a room. The first thing that came to mind was the walk-in freezer in my school's cafeteria. I mean, it's perfect in many ways. A stainless-steel box. But how would we get in there? Then just now, I got it."

"You were thinking about all this while you were practicing?" I did a quick inventory of the stuff that I had been thinking about and felt immediately guilty.

"Not all the time." She paused. "I did take time to watch you dazzle my teammates." I was on the verge of figuring out what she meant by that, when Aniela exclaimed, a look of triumph on her face, "The medical examiner's office!"

"What?" Did this girl understand that English was my second language? As in a distant second? "You're going kind of fast. My head is spinning." Or was the head-spinning more the case that I was beginning to think of her *that* way?

Aniela started to walk again. She spoke slower this time. I tried not to feel like a big dummy. "When I was fourteen, Grandpa took me to the medical examiner's office. It's the place where they take dead people who are required by law to have an autopsy performed. You know, when the police suspect foul play. Grandpa took me because he thought it would knock some sense into me. He caught me smoking one day in the backyard. He thought seeing a corpse or two would set me straight. Anyway, the Office of the Medical Examiner of Cook County is this massive concrete structure and the rooms where they do the autopsies are down in the basement and when I was down there, people kept complaining about how the cell phones got no signal. So I'm thinking that when we are ready to open the phone, we get Grandpa to take us down there. He has so many friends everywhere that he won't have any trouble getting us in. We go in, do the transfer, and then get out. Even if a signal manages to eke out of the building, we'll be gone before anyone can get there."

Aniela was smiling to herself. I had the feeling she had once again forgotten I was even there. But then, she turned to me and asked: "I'm wise . . . *and* brilliant, don't you think?"

I rubbed my chin a few times. "I don't know about brilliant, but you're definitely smarter than you look."

She bopped me.

"Ouch!" I rubbed my arm with pretend pain and then turned serious. "When do you think all this will happen? With the cell phone?"

"We'll read the memory card as soon as my mother gets home tonight and we can use her phone. If we don't find anything, we'll stop by my school tomorrow to develop the print we lift from the phone with the stuff Grandpa will bring. We'll use the digital microscope and the laser printer in Mr. Gómez's physics lab and then we'll have Grandpa drive us to the medical examiner's office to open the phone. That's the plan. You like?"

"Yeah."

"But what we hope for is for the memory card to be sufficient."

What we hope for.

I noticed that whenever she said "we," I felt less alone. I felt stronger from having her by my side working with me on the mission I had made my own. But wasn't I putting her at risk? "Looking for Big Shot. It might be dangerous."

"We'll be careful," she said quietly. "Grandpa will be a huge help. He could have made detective, you know. Grandma made him take the test and he passed. But he preferred working the streets as a regular cop. He said detective work was mostly filling out reports. I think he enjoyed the people on his beat. It used to be that policemen worked in a particular neighborhood for long periods of time and everyone knew each other."

"Your grandma . . ."

"She died five years ago. Mom and I moved in with Grandpa a couple of years ago after she died and after my mom and dad's divorce, but Mom and Grandpa fought all the time. They love each other to pieces, but they also disagree about everything, especially politics. Grandpa is a staunch conservative and Mom is about as liberal as they come."

"If Stanislaw is conservative, does that mean he doesn't want people like me in this country?"

"People like you?"

"Illegal."

"Has he said anything to you?"

"No. He's been kind to me. He even gave me his clothes to wear." I looked down at my legs.

Aniela laughed. Then a serious look came over her face. "You're real," she said.

"What does that mean?"

"The people his politics want to keep out are just images in their heads or from a television screen or monsters created to scare people. You are flesh and blood. And . . . you're the kind of person he likes."

"He does?"

"Yes. He thinks you have principles. As in, you are doing what you believe is right even if it's hard."

"What about you—what do you think about illegals—people like me and my sister?"

"Oh, God. Please don't ask me to try to articulate what I feel about immigration."

"Come on! It would be good for you to *articulate*."

"Articulating is not my strongest point."

"I'm waiting."

She stopped walking and sighed. "Okay. I am totally but totally confused about what our immigration policy should be. If it were up to my mom, we would not have borders. Everyone from anywhere that wants to come in could come in. Does that make sense to you?"

"It doesn't seem realistic."

"Right? There would come a point where everyone would suffer. Those who are here and those coming in."

"But that point is a long way away."

"Yes. So, in the meantime, there should be a way for this country, for every country that has resources, to be as helpful, as compassionate, and as kind as they can possibly be to those countries that don't."

"That's good, Aniela."

"No, it's not. Not really. It's easy for me and people like my mom to talk about being compassionate. My mom goes to marches, she sends money to places that care for immigrant children, she blasts the president's policies on her Facebook page, but when I asked her if we could sponsor a Central American refugee family by letting them live with us in our apartment, she hemmed and hawed and said we couldn't do it, as much as she *wanted* to. We have two extra bedrooms. Our apartment is too big for us. But you know what she said when I asked why we couldn't do it?"

"No."

"She said just what you said a few seconds ago. *It's not realistic.* Of course it's realistic. It can be done. What she meant is that our lives would totally change. Our lives as we know them would get inconvenient, more uncomfortable. And she's right. Even if we sponsored one family, there would still be hundreds, thousands who need help. So I don't know. And then, there is all this hatred everywhere. No one listens to each other. Each side has good ideas, but they're just interested in calling each other names. It's just hatred. My mother thinks her hatred is justified because her cause is the right one, but it is still hatred, isn't it? How is liberal hatred different from conservative hatred? I *hate* living with so much hatred." She laughed and then I laughed. She started walking again. "That's my articulation of immigration, such as it is. You asked for it."

"I did. I asked for it."

"Can I ask *you* something?"

"Sure."

"Do you like the United States? If you could stay, would you stay? I mean, assuming that Mexico wasn't dangerous for you, would you go back?"

"Oh. Those are hard questions. Let me see. I think that in Mexico I feel like I belong all the time. I never feel not wanted like I do here sometimes. Here I'm always looking over my shoulder even when no one is there. Even at night." I chuckled. Then, "There are so many problems in Mexico, and it can be very difficult to be . . . who you were meant to be, you know? You could be super smart, but it is hard, and you need a lot of luck, to find a job that uses your smarts. But still, knowing that you belong and are wanted is major. So, would I go back? I have something I need to do here, and after that? I honestly don't know how to answer your question."

"You don't feel wanted here?"

"My father's wife did not want me in her house. She said it was only because I was violating the law. She said that she liked me as a person. Her father, Abe Gropper, wanted me out of the country. He said it was nothing personal. But the truth is that I felt it was personal. Regardless of the reason, the feeling of not being wanted, how can it not be personal? But I have . . . at times felt wanted here in the United States. Not so much because of the places as because of the people. I felt at home with Gustaf Larsson, the man who rescued me in the desert. I felt like I belonged when I was with my father's stepson, Trevor. I felt wanted when I was with him. There was this lady I worked for, Mrs. C, Mrs. Costelo. I felt like she accepted me. I feel that way with your grandfather, believe it or not, even though he is a staunch conservative, as you say."

"You didn't feel wanted when you were with your father?"

A lump instantaneously formed in my throat, and liquid rushed to my eyes. It took me a while before I could speak. "Not always," I finally said.

Aniela's eyes watered as well. There was a long silence between us that did not feel awkward. Then, Aniela said, "After the divorce, after my father moved out. He would tell me that he still loved me. That I shouldn't take the divorce personally. But how could I not take it personally? The divorce was a rejection of me as well. That's the truth. The truth can hurt, but it is always good."

We stood facing each other. I wanted to speak, to say something about Sara and how she had always fought for the truth. The truth is why she had to come and why she wanted to come to the United States. And here in front of me was someone else who felt the same way. I wanted to say so many things but could not think of a single word.

Aniela grabbed my hand and squeezed it quickly. She pointed to her right. "We live that way about three long blocks. It's the street just after the place where they sell flowers. On Kildare Street. 333 Kildare. It's an ugly three-story building. Just in case you get tired of watching Stanislaw's fishing shows."

"I don't mind them. They're . . . relaxing."

"*Relaxing* is a kind word."

"I think I can find my way from here," I said. "Straight until I get to the park and then turn left. Look for the house with the flag."

"Okay. I'll see you tonight. I'll come over with Mom as soon as she gets home."

Before I could say anything, she had taken off at a run. I watched her for a few minutes and waited for her to turn. I knew she would turn. She had to.

When she turned and waved, I stretched out my hand toward her. Then I ran to Stanislaw's house.

CHAPTER 29

EMILIANO

I was out of breath and sweating when I entered Stanislaw's house. Stanislaw and a short, heavy bald man with the face of a pouting baby were sitting at the kitchen table. They had a pot of coffee between them. Both of them had "bad news" written all over their faces.

"This is Frank Jaworski, Detective Jaworski, my ex-partner," Stanislaw said, barely looking at me.

Frank Jaworski pushed his chair back and stretched his hand across the table.

"Sit," Stanislaw said softly.

"What's wrong?" I asked, pulling out a chair.

Detective Jaworski looked at Stanislaw, and Stanislaw nodded. Whatever it was, it would be better if Detective Jaworski told me about it.

"It's Irene Costelo," Detective Jaworski said. "Aurora police found her dead this afternoon. They think it was a burglary gone wrong."

A burglary gone wrong? Where had I heard that before? That's what Yoya's friend said about the killing of Wes Morgan. I lowered my head and rested my chin on my chest. Then a wave of anger filled me. I banged the table with my fist. "It wasn't a burglary," I said. Stanislaw and I looked at each other. "That's the message you said they were going to send me, isn't it?"

Stanislaw shrugged. "It's possible."

"What's the message?" Detective Jaworski said, mystified.

"Give them the phone or people will keep dying. My sister too."

"I see," Detective Jaworski said.

Stanislaw said to me, "I know what's going through your mind. But you're wrong. It's not your fault, boy. Irene is not blaming you for her death, you can be certain of that. She just wants you, us, to find her killers."

I looked away from him. At that moment I wasn't sure whether keeping the phone was worth all the death and suffering. I had received Big Shot's message loud and clear. If he could kill Mrs. C, who had nothing to do with anything, how hard would it be for him to kill Sara?

Stanislaw gripped my forearm. "Listen to me. This is no time for drama and no time to lose your resolve. Your best shot at keeping your sister safe is to bring this criminal down. We made some good progress today."

"What if I'm putting you in danger? What if Aniela is in danger? What if they tortured Mrs. C and she told them where I was?"

"Stop that. That's crazy talk. Irene Costelo wouldn't do that. And she did not die in vain. I'm not going to let her death be for nothing. Now, are you going to be the man Irene sent to my door or not?"

I thought of Sara. She wanted me to fight no matter what. I

knew that. Mrs. C would want me to as well. I nodded to Stanislaw that I was ready to go on.

"Good," he said.

"So," Detective Jaworski said, "like Stanislaw said, we got most of the puzzle put together. We'll talk you through it. Let's start with the license plate of the Mercedes. It's from a rented car. The man who rented it is Al Moss. He works for a big-time lawyer in Washington, DC, named Mathew Rupert. Guess who Abe Gropper talked to when he was in Washington, DC."

"He said he had been with a deputy director of the Labor Department."

"Naah. Gropper was just puffing himself up. He met with Rupert. But . . . Rupert *does* represent the Department of Labor in various legal matters and his contact there is a man named Wilfred Jones, who happens to be a deputy director in the Department of Labor."

"So . . ."

"He could be your ultimate Big Shot. We don't know. But we know that Rupert is the man who runs the operation, and Moss does his dirty work."

"Can we get them? We need to move fast. Rupert or Moss killed Mrs. Costelo. I know it."

"Aurora Police is handling that investigation," Detective Jaworski said. "You're actually their main person of interest."

"Me? They think I did it?"

"You're famous, or infamous. An illegal alien kills the elderly woman who gave him work. It's the kind of news that a lot of people like to hear." Detective Jaworski looked at his watch. "The news is on right now. You're probably the big headline. You want to see?"

"That's all right, Frank. We can do without the TV right now." Stanislaw turned to me and said, "What about the cell phone, did you get it open?"

"Aniela is coming here in a while and we're going to try the phone's memory card first. It's not actually opening the phone, but it might get us something useful. We needed her mother's phone to read the card."

Detective Jaworski raised his hands. "The less I know about you opening the phone, the better. I don't want to mess up any future arrests."

"Why don't you make yourself useful, then, and go get us some pizzas," Stanislaw said.

I went outside to wait for Aniela. I inhaled deeply. I wished I could be certain that what I was doing was the right thing. The resolve that Stanislaw wanted me to have was . . . shaky. I wanted it to be as solid as the Sierra Madre mountains. But that kind of certainty is rare and when it comes, it seems like such a gift. The last time I felt that kind of solidness was when I was dying in the middle of the desert. I was certain that my life had been such a waste and also that if I were allowed to live, I would do my best to make it count. That was the kind of determination I needed now.

I don't know if the sureness I needed ever came. The best I could do was to remind myself that Sara wanted me to fight.

She wants me to fight.

When I believed this with as much confidence as I could

muster, I took out my phone and got Gustaf's number from his note in my wallet.

"Emiliano. Are you all right?"

Gustaf sounded older, tired.

"Yes. And you?"

"As good as can be expected. You heard about Wes Morgan?"

"Yes. Actually, I'm calling about Sara."

"Go on."

"Remember when we were stopped outside of Sanderson and that Border Patrol officer was about to check the back of the trailer."

"Yeah . . ."

"You told him you knew him. He played football with your son."

"One of Antonio Lopez's sons. Used to come over with Jimmy. I don't remember his name, but he was afraid of horses, I remember that."

"Raúl. He said his name was Raúl Lopez. Is he a good person? You think he'd do what is right?"

"Well . . . if he's anything like his father, he would. Why?"

"I need him to check up on Sara. It has to be someone from the inside. Her life is in danger. Ask Raúl Lopez to look in on her. They might be moving her to another facility any day now. It's urgent, Mr. Larsson."

"Say no more. I'll drive over to Antonio's place as soon as we hang up."

"Thank you."

"Emiliano. Well, you already know. You're always welcome. Your buddy Amigo misses you."

"I know. Good-bye, Gustaf."

I sat on the steps and looked up when I heard the flag flutter above me. Inside, I heard my name come out of Stanislaw's television set. I was on the news. An illegal alien suspected of killing Irene Costelo. A neighbor was asked his opinion. That kind of killing was the reason why walls should be built. The Aurora Police were searching for me. All of Chicago was after me.

The United States finally wanted me.

CHAPTER 30

EMILIANO

Aniela and I sat side by side on Stanislaw's living room sofa, a beat-up purple thing as ugly as it was comfortable. Aniela's eyes were focused on the metallic bag with Hinojosa's cell phone. Laughter, a woman's, came from the kitchen, and Aniela and I turned our heads in that direction.

"This must be some kind of record," Aniela said. "Mom and Granddad have been together almost ten minutes and they haven't fought."

"It's the pizza. It's hard to fight when you're eating pizza." Pizza was always a happy time at our house in Juárez. I smiled.

"I'm so sorry about Mrs. Costelo. I'm praying for her. And for your sister, Sara."

"You pray?"

"I'm part Polish," Aniela said, by way of explanation. "You?"

"I don't know. Does prayer count if you don't believe in God?"

"It's probably the kind of prayer God likes best."

I stopped talking as Aniela opened the SIM card tray in her mother's phone and inserted Hinojosa's SD card into it. Stanislaw, Aniela's mother, Sofia, and Detective Jaworski all came out of the kitchen and stood in a semicircle watching Aniela.

There was total silence in the room as Aniela turned her mother's phone on. Total silence except the sound of my heart doing somersaults inside my chest. I felt like when I was at St. Hyacinth's and the tears started to come out. Something wanted to break inside of me or explode or gush out in some kind of burning liquid. I wanted Sara to be next to me. I wanted her to punch me in the arm and tell me to stop being a baby— like when we watched scary movies late at night.

Aniela handed me her mother's phone. The screen seemed to be moving, but then I realized that it was my hand trembling. I placed the phone on the coffee table, where it would be more stable. On the screen, I saw the icons for two files in the shape of green folders. I tapped on one entitled BENEFICIARIOS and saw the picture of a young woman about Sara's age. She was standing in front of a white wall, with an expression I recognized as hopelessness. These women had given up, surrendered. They knew there was no escape. In the corner of the picture, I read a letter *A* and a number. I touched the picture with the tip of my finger and the image of another young woman appeared before the same background, but with a different number following the letter *A*. I kept tapping and watching different young women appear before me. All the women were young, attractive, and were undoubtedly Mexican or Latinas. I stopped after a dozen pictures and handed the phone back to Aniela. She looked at a few pictures and then gave the phone to Stanislaw. Detective Jaworski and Sofia peered over Stanislaw's shoulder.

"You recognize them?" Stanislaw asked.

"No," I responded. "But I think I know who they are. We

call them Desaparecidas. Girls kidnapped from the streets of Juárez and then killed . . . or used."

Aniela grabbed the phone from Stanislaw's hand and pressed on the folder entitled WORK ORDERS.

"What are these?" Sofia sat next to Aniela and looked over her shoulder.

"Some kind of immigration forms." Aniela read: "Petition for Nonimmigrant Worker, Department of Homeland Security, U.S. Citizenship and Immigration Services, USCIS, Form I-129." She handed the phone to me.

The first page of the form contained information about the petitioner: Odessa Agricultural Cooperative, located in Odessa, Texas. I scrolled down until I got to Part 3 where the form called for the name of the "beneficiary." Below that were the names of three women. I gave the phone back to Aniela, waited for her to read, and then said, "Beneficiary is beneficiario in Spanish."

I remembered that the e-mails sent to Mello were from the head of the Odessa Agricultural Cooperative. At the bottom of the form was his name: Marko Lisica.

"What does that mean? What did you find?" Detective Jaworski asked impatiently.

No one answered. I sat there dazed, trying to understand what I'd just seen. Aniela took a laptop out of her gym bag and Googled "USCIS Form I-129." After a few minutes of reading, she answered Detective Jaworski's question. "Form I-129 is a form used in a program to bring temporary agricultural workers into the U.S."

"Our Big Shot is using the program to bring the kidnapped women from Mexico into the United States."

The nervousness and fear that churned in me suddenly became a hot, acid-like anger. I stood and clenched my fists. Big Shot became real just then. A living, evil, flesh-and-blood creep. I wanted to run or scream or hit someone.

Stanislaw sat, more like fell, on the recliner in front of the sofa.

"Human trafficking?" Sofia asked.

Stanislaw and Detective Jaworski answered her with a stony nod.

"Oh, my God!" Sofia said.

Aniela grabbed my hand and pulled me down next to her. She was scrolling through the documents in the WORK ORDERS file. "There must be fifty separate forms in here. There's other types of forms. This one is called ETA 9142 A and another is ETA 790. These are from the United States Department of Labor." Again, Aniela searched in her laptop. After a few minutes she said, "That makes sense. The Department of Labor has to certify that agricultural workers are needed before Immigration Services grants the temporary worker visas."

It took me a few moments to understand how the Department of Labor was involved.

"You're telling me that two government agencies are in cahoots to bring women into this country for . . . to make slaves out of them?" Sofia asked. Then, glaring at Stanislaw, "Why doesn't that surprise me in this administration?"

Stanislaw stared at Sofia. "We're talking about human beings, criminals, rats, not agencies. If these people have this much power, you can be sure that they've been at it for longer than this president has been in office."

"Yeah, well, with this president, the rats feel more empowered to come out!"

"Grandpa, Mom. Please. Not now." Aniela took a white cord out of her gym bag and connected one end to Sofia's phone and the other to her laptop.

"Do you see the name Wilfred Jones or Mathew Rupert anywhere?" Stanislaw asked.

"The forms were prepared by the law firm of Rupert and Brodie," Aniela said.

"We got the sons of bitches!" Stanislaw said.

"We don't have Wilfred Jones," Detective Jaworski said.

"Come on, Frank. You have enough to go to a judge and get a warrant to open the phone. Jones will be in there. Anyway, you got enough to get Rupert, and you know as well as I do that if you squeeze Rupert, he'll give up Jones or whoever is calling the shots."

"I don't know. I don't see enough probable cause that a crime has been committed. I see pictures and I see immigration forms."

"What if I could show you that the women listed as beneficiaries in this phone are women who have gone missing in Mexico?"

And there it was: the certainty that had eluded me before.

"How about that for probable cause?" Stanislaw asked Detective Jaworski.

"That would work," Detective Jaworski said, looking at me. "The only question would be if CPD has jurisdiction. Has a crime been committed in Chicago?"

"I can give you the information you need to bring out the

people responsible for this human trafficking and for Mrs. Costelo's murder."

"That's Aurora, but it's close enough. If I get Aurora Police involved. I could see us getting a warrant. Go ahead, I'm listening."

"I have a plan. But how do I know you won't deport me afterward?"

"He's not stupid," Stanislaw said.

"I can't stop ICE from deporting you, but I can make you a confidential informant of the Chicago Police Department. That will give you some protection. How's that sound?"

I nodded.

"I'll get the paperwork started. What's your plan?"

"Let me work on getting you the information on the women and then we can put the plan together."

Stanislaw and Sofia went back to the kitchen. Aniela finished copying the files from Hinojosa's memory card. She placed the card back in the phone and closed the metallic bag. She closed the laptop and placed it on the table next to the cell phones. "I was kind of looking forward to opening the cell phone," Aniela said, pretending disappointment. "I was going to take the day off from school tomorrow."

"You can still take the day off. We need to get Big Shot."

"Do you really have a plan?"

"Yes."

"Does Grandpa know what it is?"

"I'll tell him after everyone leaves. But I need your help before then. The Chihuahua State Police and the Mexican Federal Police have websites with pictures of missing women.

We need to go through the pictures on those websites and find links to the women in the phone files we just saw."

"Got you. Let's do it." Then, after a while, she said, "I hope it's long-term."

"What?"

"Your plan," she said, and briefly looked into my eyes.

"Maybe."

What is *long-term*? A week, a month, a lifetime?

All I knew was that it included tomorrow.

CHAPTER 31

EMILIANO

I sat at the head of Stanislaw's kitchen table. The metallic bag with Hinojosa's cell phone was in front of me. To my right sat Detective Jaworski and to his right was Ann Rogers, a detective from the Aurora Police Department. Stanislaw was at the opposite end of the table. Detective Jaworski stopped speaking when Aniela entered the room. I was glad to see that she had decided to skip school. She pulled the chair next to Stanislaw and smiled at me.

"Sorry to interrupt," she said.

The detective went on. "I was just going over what we've pieced together with the information that you guys gave us last night. We've put a lot of the pieces together in the past twelve sleepless hours. So, as I was saying, we're looking at a human trafficking scheme that depends on a number of key players. The scheme was facilitated by three, possibly four criminals working in various governmental agencies. Hinojosa and his associates in Mexico 'procured' the young women. The names of the young women were sent to the Odessa Agricultural Cooperative, which submitted an application for temporary workers to the Department of Labor. The approved labor certification was then sent to the Customs and Immigration

Service. The U.S. consulate in Juárez then granted H-2A visas to the women listed in the I-129 forms. The young women were then brought, probably flown, into the United States. Their entry was 'legal,' in the sense that they had visas. What we don't know yet is where those women ended up. We suspect that some went to prostitution rings, others were placed with individual men, others may have been placed in homes as domestic workers."

During the silence that filled the room, I thought of María, the woman who worked for Abe Gropper. Then I thought of Sara—she too could have been one of those young women taken.

Detective Jaworski continued. "The key for this scheme to work is the labor certifications. We found out that it was Deputy Director Jones who gave the order to approve all requests from the Odessa Agricultural Cooperative."

"And Rupert?" Stanislaw asked.

"Rupert gives the whole business the cover of legality. His firm fills out the labor and immigration forms. And Rupert, with his powerful connections and influence, smooths the process with bribes and threats. We think that he and Jones are then involved in selling the women to the highest bidders."

"It's sickening," Stanislaw said.

"You got that right," Detective Jaworski responded. "We're going to have to get the feds to help us in order to make all the arrests, but the important thing now is to find the women who have been enslaved."

"And the perps who killed Irene Costelo," Ann Rogers said.

"Yes. And this is where Emiliano comes in. Tell us your plan."

"The plan is for me to return Hinojosa's cell phone to my father," I said softly.

"What?" Aniela asked.

"It really is the only way . . ." Aniela's worried expression stopped me. "I called my father this morning on my burner phone. I said I wanted to go back to Mexico and that I would give him the bad guy's phone in return for a bus ticket to the border and some money. I told him I'd meet him at the bus station today at one. Then I hung up."

Aniela shook her head. "Who's to say Rupert's men won't be there to grab Emiliano and then kill him? Why leave a loose end?"

Detective Jaworski spoke up. "We'll have undercover officers throughout the station. If they make a move against Emiliano, we'll be there."

"Will they be fast enough to stop a bullet?" Aniela asked. Her tone was only slightly sarcastic. Then, "I don't understand what returning the phone to Emiliano's father will accomplish."

Detective Jaworski took a deep breath. "Here's what we have. Emiliano is now a registered confidential informant with the Chicago Police Department. Thanks to the files you gave us, we were authorized by an Illinois Superior Court judge to place a listening and tracking device inside Hinojosa's phone. All we did was open the back of the phone to place the device. We did not touch any of the data in the phone. We didn't even charge the phone. You copied the contents of the phone's memory card but left it intact. They're not going to know the phone has been tampered with. Emiliano called his father, like he told you, and will meet him in a couple of hours. Then we just follow the cell phone wherever it takes us. We investigate whoever touches it and we listen to the conversations that take place around it. But we are pretty sure the phone will lead us to Rupert. When that happens, we will have Rupert connected to the missing women who Emiliano and Aniela have linked to the files in the phone. It's a solid case. Once we have Rupert, we will go after Jones and will get them to reveal the location of the women."

Aniela interrupted. "That phone will be checked to see if it's been opened and then it will be trashed."

"It's true," I said. "The phone will probably be destroyed but not right away. We may catch some conversations before then that could be useful."

"And that's a good start," Detective Jaworski said. "The idea here is to have enough jail time hanging on Rupert and Jones that they will tell us where we can find the women."

"When I talk to my father . . . when I give him the phone, I will try to get him to tell me about Mrs. Costelo. He will know something about it . . . We think it was Rupert's bodyguard who killed her. If so, Rupert will be charged with the murder as well. We can use that against Rupert to tell us how to find the women."

There was a moment of silence. It was a lot of information to take in at once. Finally, Aniela asked what everyone was thinking.

"What if your father was involved in Mrs. Costelo's murder?"

I took a deep breath. It was a question I could not stop asking, but not the most important one. The one that weighed the most was: Did Raúl Lopez get to Sara in time? But there was no more time for questions. "The only thing that matters now is finding the women."

"How exactly do you expect it to go down at the station? You all thought of that?" Stanislaw asked, concerned.

It was Detective Rogers who responded. "We think Emiliano's father will be accompanied by someone who can inspect the phone to see if it has been turned on or unlocked and they will quickly see that it hasn't. Emiliano will also be wearing a wire so we can record whatever his father says about Mrs. Costelo. We can move in quickly if something is going wrong."

"No way!" Detective Jaworski and Stanislaw objected.

"We need to record any information about Irene Costelo," Ann Rogers said firmly. "Aurora has some good tech too, you know. I can put something on Emiliano that no one will ever detect."

"Unless they search him," Stanislaw pointed out.

Ann Rogers continued. "Look, no one knows that we exist. By 'we' I mean Chicago Police, Aurora Police. Emiliano is returning the phone to his father because he has seen the news reports about the murder of Irene Costelo, the same news reports that name him as a primary suspect and that have the whole city in an uproar about yet another crime committed by an undocumented immigrant. He's had it. They killed Irene Costelo to send him a message. Okay. Message received. Here's your damn phone, I'm out of here. Besides, as Frank just said, if anyone makes to search him, our undercover agents will be there." Then Ann Rogers asked me, "What do you think, Emiliano? Are you okay with a listening device on your person?"

I lowered my head in thought. "What will happen to my father . . . if he's involved?"

Ann Rogers spoke softly. "As far as Aurora Police is concerned, it depends on what he says. If he acts like he knew about the murder of Irene Costelo, we'll have to bring him in."

I hoped he didn't know. What did my mother say? *Your father is not a bad man, stupid maybe, but not bad.* There was more hope than certainty in her words.

"My take on your father," Detective Jaworski said, "is that he hasn't done anything big enough for any state or federal prosecutor to waste their time with. They'll be too busy going after some very bad people, like the ones who have the women. Your father's connection to the criminal world is very weak, but, unfortunately, there is a connection. He is connected to Abe Gropper, who is somehow connected to Mathew Rupert and Wilfred Jones. Your father doesn't have to be a criminal in order to be connected to criminals. When he agreed to get the phone from you instead of letting you go your way, he became part of the criminal web."

"He wanted the phone to protect me." Why was I so desperate to defend my father?

"If that's the case, it will become clearer to us all if you wear a wire," Ann Rogers said.

I looked at Aniela, hoping to see an answer in her eyes.

"The truth is good," she said to me.

"Okay," I said to Detective Rogers.

"Then we're all set," Detective Rogers said. "Let's get Emiliano ready."

"I have a final question."

Everyone looked at me.

"What's going to happen to me after all this?"

"Yeah," Aniela said, understanding why I was asking. "Is he risking his life for you so that you can then deport him?"

"We can't make any deals or promises with a confidential informant regarding his immigrant status. Only Immigration Services is authorized to do that. But"—Detective Jaworski grinned—"we know they've given visas based on phony labor certifications, visas that resulted in human trafficking, so I have a feeling that we may be able to *persuade* Immigration to agree to some kind of visa."

I liked the confidence of Detective Jaworski.

"You should get him to put all that in a document signed by a U.S. attorney," Stanislaw whispered to me. "Don't trust anything he tells you." Stanislaw winked at his old partner.

"I trust you," I said to Detective Jaworski.

I walked out and sat on the front steps of Stanislaw's house while Detective Rogers went inside to get the listening device activated. A few moments later, Aniela sat next to me. The flag snapped with a sudden gust of wind. Bees buzzed over the red and white tulips that surrounded the base of the flagpole.

"They bloomed the day you came," Aniela said.

"What do you call that red color?" I pointed with my chin at the tulips.

"Vermillion," Aniela answered. "It's one of the two colors in the Polish flag. The other one is white."

"In Mexico we call that red rojo sangre."

We watched a bee dip into the petals of a white tulip. "Are you afraid?"

"Not so much of what will happen to me. Of seeing my father."

"Of what he tells you?"

"Just of seeing him. It will probably be the last time I see him."

"You think so?"

"Do you see your father?" I asked without looking at Aniela.

"Yes. It's hard. His new wife looks like she's about twenty. She's actually twenty-nine."

"But you go see your father anyway. You've forgiven him?"

"He's just stupid."

"That's what I hope my father is—just stupid." Then, after a long pause, "When I was crossing over from Mexico, I got lost in the desert. I had a foot infection and was dehydrated. I almost died. I knew I was dying. Just before I lost consciousness, I . . . this is hard to put into words . . . I entered a different place. It was a place of . . . forgiveness. I guess that's the best description I can come up with. I forgave my father. I forgave myself for all the stupid, selfish things I had done in Mexico. It was easy. It was easy to forgive in that place. Not like in this world where it's so hard."

"It is hard," Aniela said, speaking as if from personal experience.

"Then when I met my father, I couldn't keep any of the . . . forgiveness I found in that . . . place."

"But now you know that place exists. You were there."

"Yes."

"You're thinking about that place now because . . ."

"I don't know if I can forgive my father. And forgiving the people who killed Mrs. Costelo is impossible. It's just not possible."

There was a long silence and then Aniela said, "I know my father is a self-centered jerk. The woman he married is like him, only worse. She pretends to like me, but I can feel her hostility. I hated both of them for a long time."

"You found a way to forgive them."

"I just know that hatred is poison. Hate was poisoning me. It hurts to hate. Hate turns you into something you're not meant to be. Then I kept seeing how much we were all alike. All the ugliness that I found in my father and his wife, I saw in me. I think that was what I was hating—the arrogance and the superiority and the way they used people, all that was, is, in me. What I said inside about the truth being good—I wasn't talking about what I knew about my father. I was talking about what I knew about me."

I looked at her. "That's hard to believe. That you are all those things you said about yourself. Arrogant, using people."

"Believe them."

Just then, I saw my father consumed by his work, by the desire to advance, by the need to prove to Abe Gropper and everyone that he was a success. Then I remembered how I convinced Javier to help me put heroin in the piñatas. All that I did to get Perla Rubi and her father to accept me. There were similarities, weren't there? Maybe if I were in my father's place, I would have done as he did.

"The big difference," Aniela continued, "is that I don't like those things about myself. My father and his wife take pride in them. I know what's in me and I try not to act accordingly."

"Emiliano," Detective Jaworski called from inside, "we're ready."

"Your granddad was right," I said. "You are special."

"Me? I'm not the one saving God knows how many women."

I stood, then sat down again when she touched my arm.

"I have to tell you something. But please don't laugh or make me feel silly."

"I promise."

"I . . . I've never kissed anyone. I mean, maybe when I was a little kid. But not really. I've had opportunities. I don't want you to think I haven't. But I told myself that I would never kiss anyone I . . . okay, promise not to laugh . . . that I would never kiss anyone I couldn't see spending the rest of my life with. Not that I would *actually* need to spend the rest of my life with that person . . . but that the person I kissed would be the *kind* of *person* I could see myself spending the rest of my life with. Oh, God, I screwed this up royally. Forget everything I just said, okay?"

"Has anyone ever told you that you're *too* smart?"

"No . . ."

But Aniela could not speak because I moved closer to her with my eyes closed and kissed her lips softly.

"Don't worry," I said to Aniela, my forehead resting on hers. "I understand what you were trying to say about the person you kiss. I'm just grateful you thought of me that way."

"Okay," she whispered. "Emiliano?"

"Yes?"

"What will you do after this? Where will you go?"

"You mean assuming I'm still alive?"

Aniela grabbed my hand and squeezed it. "Be serious!"

"I don't know. I was thinking I'd go back to Texas. Help Mr. Larsson with his ranch. I'd be close to Sara. I'm hoping she'll be okay."

"She will be. I've prayed for it." There was a pause, then, "If that's what you want, I think I can get Grandpa to drive you there. It would be good for the two of you to travel together. Maybe you can get Grandpa to articulate his views on immigration."

"Would you like that?"

"Yes," she answered softly. After a while she looked at me and said, "Then he would know the way and he could take me next summer. Would *you* like that?"

"Yes."

We looked into each other's eyes, saw the future, and we were there.

CHAPTER 32

EMILIANO

Detective Jaworski stopped the car four blocks away from the bus station in downtown Chicago. Just before I got out, he said, "It could be that they'll want to see you get on the bus. If that happens, just go ahead and get on. Let them see you on your way to Mexico. Then get off at the next station and call Detective Rogers and we'll come get you."

"Okay."

"Just so you know, there's three other undercover officers in the station. Outside in a van, you got Detective Rogers and two Aurora police officers. If anybody tries to grab you, we'll be on them before they take three steps."

"I'm not worried."

Detective Jaworski pushed the button on a walkie-talkie. "Ann, you there?"

"I'm here."

"I'm going to do a test run on your gadget. See if it's as good as you say it is."

"Go ahead."

Detective Jaworski got out of the car and indicated for me to do the same. When we were outside, he said to me, "Say something. Speak normally."

"Hello. Testing. One, two three, testing."

"That's a go." Ann Rogers's voice came over the walkie-talkie in Detective Jaworski's hand. Then he leaned close to me. "Looks like this piece of crap works after all."

"I heard that!" Ann Rogers responded on the walkie-talkie.

My father was sitting on a bench facing the main entrance to the bus station. Next to him sat the same blond man I saw at the Aurora train station, the driver of the gray Mercedes.

"Hello, son," my father said, standing. He kept both hands by his sides. The blond man rose from his chair slowly, his eyes on the paper bag in my right hand.

"Is that the cell phone?" the blond man asked.

"Yes," I said, offering the bag.

The blond man took out Hinojosa's cell phone and said, "I need to check it. Stay here." He walked to a counter where people sat working on their laptops and charging their phones. He sat on an empty stool facing us and plugged the phone into his laptop.

"Let's sit," Bob said.

I sat next to him and reminded myself to not look around the station for Detective Rogers and the others.

Bob took an envelope out of the inside pocket of his coat. It was the first time I had seen him wear a sport coat. "I got you a ticket all the way to Laredo. You'll need to transfer to another bus in St. Louis and again in Dallas. I wrote down the times when each bus departs. But you'll only need one ticket. There's also two thousand dollars in there. I wish it could be more."

"Abe Gropper offered me ten thousand," I tried to joke.

"That was Abe. This money is from me."

"Thanks."

"Why did you run like that? Last time?"

"I promised Sara I would give the phone to someone who could open it and who would use the information to make sure Hinojosa went to jail. Sara went through a lot to save Linda and the other women from Hinojosa. I owed it to her to try to do something with the cell phone."

"And now? Why did you change your mind? Why did you call me this morning?"

"The person I was supposed to give the phone never responded. Then things started happening. I saw on TV that Mrs. Costelo was murdered, and they were saying I did it."

"Emiliano, you have to believe me. I had nothing to do with that."

I hesitated for a moment before asking the questions I needed to ask. My father's answers could send him to jail. Did I really want to do that? No. No, I didn't want to hurt him. It felt good to know that. But I *needed* the truth, regardless of the cost. "Who's that guy?" I pointed with my chin at the blond man. "Who killed Mrs. Costelo?" I held my breath, waiting for my father's answer.

"It wasn't me. You know I would never do something like that." He looked to where the blond man was sitting. "His name is Moss. I don't know his first name. After we didn't find the phone in your backpack, Abe told Moss's boss, a Mr. Rupert in Washington, that you worked at Mrs. Costelo's house for a few days and that maybe you had hidden the cell phone there. We knew it wasn't in my house because Nancy first and then Moss and me, we turned the place over. Every inch inside and outside. There was also a possibility that you had gone to Mrs. Costelo's house, that she was hiding you. Where else would you go? You don't know anyone else in Chicago. Mr. Rupert told Moss to go to Mrs. Costelo's house to see if you were there and to look for the phone."

"This Mr. Rupert told Moss to kill her?"

"No, it wasn't like that!" He sighed. "Look, I don't know what Mr. Rupert told Moss. Moss says it was an accident. Mrs. Costelo came out of nowhere while he was looking for you and for the phone and hit him on the side of the head with an iron skillet. Moss turned instinctively and punched her. That's all it took. She must have had a heart condition. You can still see the bandage on the back of Moss's head . . . What? Why are you smiling?"

"Nothing. I was just imagining Mrs. Costelo hitting him with an iron skillet."

But I was also smiling because I believed my father. He didn't know Mrs. Costelo would be killed. And now we had enough information to arrest Rupert.

"Son, you can't think I had anything to do with her death. Do you?"

"I think that at the very least you're connected to some very bad people. Starting with your father-in-law."

"That's not true. Somehow the people who want the cell phone found out that you were with me and they found out I worked with Abe. They got to Abe through contacts that Abe has in Washington. He thought getting the phone from you was his best way of protecting you, Sara, Nancy, Trevor, all of us. That's the honest truth."

"Well, whoever wants the phone won. Getting people killed, putting me in jail for something I didn't do, it's not worth it."

"Are you going to be all right? They're calling you a person of interest in Mrs. Costelo's death."

"Why don't you go to the police and tell them the truth? Tell them Moss over there did it."

Bob turned suddenly silent.

"I didn't think so," I said.

"I wouldn't be able to keep Abe out of it. I have Nancy and Trevor to think about."

"Able Abe Heating and Cooling will be your company in a few years."

"Put yourself in my place, Emiliano, please."

"I have. I think . . . when all is said and done, I would have acted differently. I would have fought for my son and my daughter more."

Bob's eyes turned red. "I deserve that. I'm sorry, son. I'm sorry."

"Me too," I said. Moss was walking toward us.

"It's clean," Moss said to Bob. "I powered it up and checked when it was last used. It hasn't been opened since almost a month ago. Everything's there in the memory card. No one's messed with it."

We stood.

"That's your bus." Moss pointed to a line of people waiting at an exit.

I walked to the end of the line before Bob had a chance to say anything. When my turn came, I showed the driver my ticket and then entered the bus. I took a window seat. Bob and

Moss stood next to each other in silence. They were waiting for the bus to pull out of the station. Bob looked small and weak next to Moss. I recognized the cologne in the envelope I was still holding.

I stretched out my hand in the direction of my father when the bus started to move.

CHAPTER 33

SARA

Sometime in what seemed the middle of the night, La Treinta Y Cuatro and a male guard I'd never seen before took me out a side entrance to the detention facility and into a blue van. All the lights inside the pods were off and all the detainees were asleep. La Treinta Y Cuatro carried a paper bag. The bag was closed, but it looked heavy. I thought maybe it had the clothes I had on when I first came to the facility God only knows how long ago. The male guard carried under his arm the same blue folder that Mello had the last time I saw him. I assumed that inside were all the "official" documents Mello had shown me, including the Voluntary Departure form with my fake signature.

It was an unmarked van with four rows of seats. La Treinta Y Cuatro led me into the second row, and she sat way back in the fourth. There were no seat belts and I wasn't handcuffed, but I noticed that the doors of the van were locked and could be unlocked only by the driver or from outside. The inside of the van still retained the heat from being out in the sun all day, but when the guard started it, a stream of cold hit my face and I thought what a luxury that was, to have an air-conditioned ride to my death.

I wondered if Emiliano had felt as numb as I felt just then. I knew that he had nearly died out there and that a horse saved him by standing over him until Mr. Larsson came looking and found both Emiliano and the horse. It's funny that what I regretted the most about dying was the loss and sorrow that Mami would feel. I was so familiar with a mother's sorrow, especially the kind of open, ongoing sorrow of the mothers of missing daughters. Would my body ever be found so that Mami could at least properly mourn?

We were on a small paved road. No one passed us and we passed no one. Now and then a truck would go by in the opposite direction.

"Where are you taking me? Rosaura?" I remembered her name. "Don't do this. You don't have to do this."

"Shut up. Don't talk." La Treinta Y Cuatro said, then she shouted, "Miguel, turn down the air. I'm freezing in here. And turn down the damn radio."

Miguel, I said to myself. *Please be a good man.*

I leaned my head against the window and pretended to go to sleep. I thought about the article I would write when I was free. No, it would be a book. It would include my experiences at the detention facility and tell the story of women like Lucila. But who would believe such a book? Who would believe a story of detention officers faking documents and vans delivering women to their death? Could such things happen in the United States? The United States. This isn't Mexico. The rule of law rules here.

I would include Emiliano's story, of course. How he fared in Chicago with Papá and with Papá's new family. And what he decided to do with Hinojosa's phone. How he fought back against evil. It would have to be a novel so I could write about Emiliano's thoughts and feelings and decisions, but it would be a truthful novel. Truthful. As truthful as I could make it.

I think I was halfway through the plot of my future novel when I finally heard the heavy breathing that told me La Treinta Y Cuatro was asleep. I turned my head slowly and saw the closed eyes and open mouth of La Treinta Y Cuatro. I rose slowly and moved to the first-row seat. When I looked back, I saw that there was a grapefruit in La Treinta Y Cuatro's lap.

"Miguel," I whispered. "You don't want to commit this crime. You don't want to be a part of this evil."

Miguel searched in the rearview mirror. La Treinta Y Cuatro was still sleeping.

"Get back," he said. But he spoke softly so as not to wake up La Treinta Y Cuatro. That was a good sign, I thought.

"Miguel, you're in love. I can tell by the kind of music you've been listening to. Love songs. Romantic Mexican ballads. What is happening to me could happen to the woman you love. If it happened to me, it could happen to her. The only thing keeping evil from taking over the world are good people like you and me."

"Shh," he said, worried. "Get back or it will be worse."

"Worse? Worse how? How can it get worse than this? Are you talking torture? Torture, Miguel? All you . . ."

What I was going to say is that all he had to do was slow down a little and unlock the door. I would jump out. He could keep on going. But I couldn't finish the sentence because something exploded against the back of my head, in the small area where my head and neck connect, to be precise. When I opened my eyes, I saw a grapefruit roll next to my feet.

"Keep driving! Keep your eyes on the road!" La Treinta Y Cuatro shouted.

I picked up the grapefruit and looked at it. How could something soft and pink cause so much pain? I felt a weight next to me on my seat and when I turned, La Treinta Y Cuatro was there. I offered her the grapefruit with a *Did you lose this?* look and then I tried to hit her with it, but she was too fast and had much more experience fighting. Her closed fist landed on my mouth and I immediately tasted blood. I felt the van swerve and I started to slide off the seat, but La Treinta Y Cuatro's left hand gripped my throat and held me in place.

"Don't slow down. Keep driving!" she yelled as she used her free hand to grab my ear and pull my head forward with all her strength. Then, half standing in the seat, she swung my head back against the window. I heard the crack of glass. Or maybe it was my skull. There was a flash of white. And white was also the color of the pain that filled all of me.

The last words I heard before the white turned to black were Miguel's. "I have to pull over. There's a Border Patrol cruiser behind me flashing its lights at us."

That could have been what he said. Or maybe that was just the sound of hope.

EPILOGUE

Sandy brought me this notebook so I could start working on my novel. Well, first an article for the *El Paso Times*. I have to write with my left hand, only a few words a day until I get better at it. Who would have thought that a grapefruit could do so much damage? The grapefruit that La Treinta Y Cuatro threw against my neck caused more injury than getting my head cracked against the window of the van. The window smash resulted only in a cut and a concussion. The grapefruit caused nerve damage. The doctors here at the hospital in Alpine cannot say when I will be able to move the fingers of my right hand.

An immigration judge allowed my release on a bond of five thousand dollars, which my father paid. In a day or two, I will go live with Sandy. A hearing for my asylum petition is scheduled for next month.

The article for the *El Paso Times* will start with my experiences in finding Linda in Juárez and then go into all that happened to Emiliano and me in the United States. The part I can't wait to write about is the corruption that Emiliano discovered in Hinojosa's cell phone. How agricultural work visas were used for human trafficking. Emiliano tells me that, so far, fourteen women have been freed.

It was a couple of powerful men who wanted the phone back: a high-ranking official in the Department of Labor and his high-priced lawyer. They were protecting not only their identities but the identities of wealthy businessmen, criminals in charge of prostitution rings, lonely, sick men who wanted their own personal slave. In the end, there was a web of responsibility that ranged from intentional evil to greed to ignorance. The evil of two men rippled down to detention facility guards and even ordinary but weak law-abiding citizens, like my father. The article I write will be about all of them. It will uncover evil, blatant and subtle, deliberate and masked by good intentions. I will tell the truth.

Sandy told me this morning that the women back at the facility thought I was a hero for getting La Treinta Y Cuatro and Mello kicked out of the facility. Only, I don't feel like a hero. All I did was survive. The heroes are people like Mario, the guard who risked his job by calling Sandy Morgan. Then there is my own personal hero—Raúl Lopez, the Border Patrol officer who rescued me after Gustaf Larsson contacted his father. My situation is much different from that of women like my friend Lucila. How does not moving a few fingers compare with the suffering of a mother being separated from her child? I am going to be all right. I have people fighting for me. But who does Lucila have back in El Salvador? No one.

I just read what I wrote above, and it sounds as if I am ungrateful. It's as if the blow from the grapefruit took away my ability to feel the joy that comes with gratitude, the simple joy of being alive. Even Mami's voice, when I talked to her yesterday, sounded so distant. It was as if I were talking to her from the other side of life. And when Emiliano told me that he was coming to live with Mr. Larsson, that he would be near me, that the Chicago Police Department was helping him get a student visa for next year and that he's met someone he really likes, instead of rejoicing, all I could feel was relief.

Happiness seems like a gift that is arbitrarily given. Why me? That's the question people ask when something terrible happens to them. Why me? But shouldn't we ask that same question when something good happens? Why am I allowed to enjoy the bounty and the freedom of this country, and others aren't? It seems as if the only way to be happy is by deliberately ignoring the unhappiness of so many.

Sandy says that I have the beginning of PTSD or maybe I'm already in the throes of it. She says it wasn't just the grapefruit but all that has happened before: the threats by Hinojosa, people machine-gunning our house, almost getting raped and killed in the desert, the loss of home and family, the constant fear that I might lose my Emiliano.

"It will go away, and you will be Sara again," she said.

And I believe her. I will see light everywhere again along with the darkness that I have now experienced. I will. And I will find a way to work for that light. To add the flame of my small candle to it. But I don't know if I will ever be the same Sara again. It is not possible to have seen the sorrow and hopelessness in the eyes of those women in that detention center and ever be the same again.

I will stop here for now. This writing seems so poor. I don't know what other word to use for it. So poor. But what can I do? All I can do is try to tell the truth. It is all I have. I will try again tomorrow and the day after. I will try to tell the truth.

Because trying is all.

ACKNOWLEDGMENTS

This book is fortunate to have received the love and wisdom of two editors. Thank you, Arthur A. Levine, for bringing me on board some twelve years ago, for journeying with me through six wonderful books, and for encouraging and shaping the birth of this book. Thank you, Emily Seife, for helping *Illegal* become the book it was meant to be. Thank you, Faye Bender, my friend and tireless advocate of my work. I especially want to thank Charlotte Weiss and Jaqueline Llanas of the South Texas Pro Bono Asylum Representation Project (ProBar) for their patience and help in answering all my questions and for their work and sacrifice on behalf of our immigrants. Finally, thank you, Jill Syverson-Stork. Without you there would be no book.

ABOUT THE AUTHOR

Francisco X. Stork emigrated from Mexico at the age of nine with his mother and stepfather. He is the author of seven novels, including *Disappeared*, which received four starred reviews and was a Walter Dean Myers Award Honor Book; *Marcelo in the Real World*, which received five starred reviews and the Schneider Family Book Award; *The Last Summer of the Death Warriors*, winner of the Amelia Elizabeth Walden Award from ALAN; *The Memory of Light*, which received four starred reviews; and *Irises*. He lives near Boston with his family. You can find him on the web at franciscostork.com and on Twitter at @StorkFrancisco.